LAW ENF
HALL C

MW01137029

1818 – 2010

Revised Edition

BY WILLARD J. LANGDON

To contact author:
Willard J. Langdon
wjmklangdon@charter.net
770 - 536 - 1813
cell 770-634-5736

ISBN: 1439268193
ISBN-13: 9781439268193

www.createspace.com/900000518

CONTENTS

WHY DO THIS
REVISED EDITION?

There are many reasons but the main one is:

There is not any one person who can remember it all, or who did it all. The word of mouth, along with research, passed on from one generation to another generation of law enforcement officers needs to be captured.

*Dedicated to all Law Enforcement Officers in Hall County, GA,
past and present, for without you, there would be no history.*

*A special dedication goes to all officers who were wounded or
died in the line of duty in Hall County, GA.*

FOREWORD

Willard J. Langdon, a retired U S Army Ranger, former Hall County Deputy, and retired Georgia State Probation Officer, wrote *Law Enforcement in Hall County 1818 – 1980* while a Deputy and criminal justice student in the late 1970's. He attended Gainesville College and later earned a BA degree in criminal justice at Brenau University.

His interest in the history of Hall County law enforcement was peaked when he selected that subject as a topic for a college paper. Doing more research on the topic as a special assignment at Brenau, he was encouraged by his instructor, Alex Taylor, and former Hall County Library Historian, Mrs. Sybil McRay, to put his work into book form. That was the beginning of a project that took several years to complete. Using early tax records, deed books, old newspaper articles, and archives in Atlanta, he was able to uncover the year by year history of law enforcement leaders and their problems and accomplishments in the county.

Tornadoes did not make his work any easier. The Gainesville, GA tornadoes in 1903 and 1936 destroyed many of the county's records. Getting the facts was a time consuming task. Among the surprising facts that turned up was that Hall County once had a female Sheriff, and that no Republican had ever been elected Sheriff before Dick Mecum in 1980.

The first edition of the book, *Law Enforcement in Hall County 1818 - 1980* was published in 1981.

Years later Willard discovered that the company which originally published his book had dissolved. Many people were asking for the book but he could not accommodate them.

For the first edition, Willard did most of the work himself. He attributes the completion of the book to Mrs. McRay, as well as others including former Sheriff Ed England, who encouraged him to complete the project. I met Willard in the late 1970's while he was involved in the research for his first book, and I was happy to be of assistance.

Now, after thirty years, people are still requesting copies of Willard's book. He is now in full retirement, with the time to do more research for a revision. This new book has captured the past thirty years and makes the previous years more complete with more research, new photos and interviews to share the history of *Law Enforcement in Hall County, GA 1818 – 2010.*

Willard has tried to be as original as possible in recording this history. In this revised edition, he has attempted to give a much better view of our officers and the criminal justice system, and how they both have changed throughout the decades.

Betty Wilson Allen,
daughter of former Sheriff C. W. (Cal) Wilson, and retired from the City of Gainesville, GA, with thirty years service

PREFACE

"May I see the history of the Sheriff's Department?" This is the question I asked at the Hall County Sheriff's office in the late 1970's as I was attempting to get information for a paper while a student at Gainesville College. I was astonished to find that there wasn't anything available about the department or the previous Sheriffs. I walked in with a blank pad, and departed with the same.

I contacted Mrs. Sybil McRay, Hall County Library Historian, and asked to see the history of law enforcement in Hall County. I did not like what I heard. Mrs. McRay replied, "There is not any history. Oh, there are bits and pieces of history and bits and pieces of information, but nothing has ever been compiled." She suggested that I write a book – she had thousands of books in the library, she said, but none on this subject. Mrs. McRay said, "Willard, you have got to do this book, for you will be the first to write a book on the law enforcement of our county."

Later, while completing my degree at Brenau University, my Criminal Justice instructor, Alex Taylor, also encouraged me to do the same. My life at that time was at maximum capacity. I was a fulltime deputy sheriff, attending college at night, and working as a flight instructor during any spare time. I had to refer back to my training as a U. S. Army Ranger – quitting is not an option. I completed the first edition of *Law Enforcement in Hall County 1818 – 1980* in 1981.

Many have requested copies of the book through the years, but it has long been out of print. Further, thirty years have passed, and much more history has been made, which, if not recorded, will be lost.

Hall County law enforcement officers deserve to have this revised edition published.

ACKNOWLEDGEMENTS

Thanks to all who offered photographs and gave their experiences and memories to this project. Many deserve to be acknowledged, but only a few are mentioned here.

Special thanks to the former and current members of the Hall County Sheriff's Department and the Gainesville Police Department for the extension of brotherhood to a former deputy – State Probation officer retiree.

Very special thanks go to Betty Wilson Allen for her many contributions, and thanks go to Milton Martin Toyota, The Times, Bob McMahan, Ina and David Griffin, Judy Free, Kiley Sargent, Jeff Shoemaker, Harold Black, Hoyt Henry, Jr. (Buddy), Terry White, Judy Mecum, Gene Earls, Chad White, GPD Chief Brian P. Kelly, Jeff Strickland, Sheriff Steve Cronic, Alex Taylor, Sheriff Bob Vass, Sheriff Dick Mecum and Chief Frank Hooper, Jr. So many helped that I can't name everyone.

Many thanks go to my wife, Margaret Kelley Langdon, for typing, editing and composition.

It has been fun!

INTRODUCTION

Have you ever thought about why one would become a law enforcement officer, with less than adequate pay for such a hazardous job, while putting their life in jeopardy every day? Someone who writes a blank check made payable to their community for amounts of up to and including their life? When, on the other hand, one could probably secure a position with regular hours and all the perks and benefits available in the public sector. *I don't know. . . .*

I don't know the answer to these questions! Based on the officers I interviewed for this project, there is something special inside these ordinary people that make them want to serve mankind – duty first – disregarding comfort and benefits.

This book is about our brave officers who, for many decades, have taken an oath to consider their own safety second to their commitment to upholding the laws of Hall County and the State of Georgia.

It goes without saying that without our dedicated officers, it would be a far different world for us all.

I hope that you get as much enjoyment from this project as I did in capturing it. I have done my best in sharing the memories and changes in law enforcement during the history of Hall County, GA, 1818 – 2010.

PART I

LAW ENFORCEMENT IN HALL COUNTY, GA 1818 – 2010

Willard J. Langdon

OFFICERS WOUNDED / DIED IN THE LINE OF DUTY

HALL COUNTY, GEORGIA

HALL COUNTY SHERIFF'S DEPARTMENT

1. Deputy Ode Kiser – Shot in the head with bird shot from shotgun in 1944 in Flowery Branch by suspect Walter Finn. The blast blew his hat off. Sheriff Crowe took him to Downey Hospital to have birdshot removed.
2. Melvin Clark – Former acting Sheriff (Revenue Agent). Killed on June 17, 1947, while working as a Revenue Agent and raiding a whiskey still in Banks County.
3. Deputy Lee Grissom – Shot in the abdomen by suspect with a .22 caliber rifle at Greenway Trailer Park in Rabbittown on the night of February 27, 1974. Survived and returned to work in six weeks.
4. Lt. Gib Cronic – Shot by suspect with a .22 caliber rifle on the night of November 8, 1982. He was shot in the abdomen, but was protected by bullet proof vest. He was treated for a blunt trauma wound.
5. Deputy Joseph Allen Groover – K – 9 and SWAT team member. Severely wounded in the right arm on August 11, 2008, with a .44 caliber pistol. After a number of surgeries, he is back on duty. He was injured during SWAT team operation in north Hall County.
6. Lt. James Timothy White – Died in the line of duty after an auto accident in Hall County on October 3, 2005. He was well respected by all his fellow officers – thirty-eight years old. Tim was the first Hall County Deputy to die in the line of duty. His badge #419 was retired.

GAINESVILLE POLICE DEPARTMENT

1. Chief of Police James Kittrell – Shot and killed with a handgun on December 25, 1890, while assisting another officer arrest a woman during a domestic dispute at the Gainesville Train Depot. The suspect was shot and killed by another officer.
2. Officer Henry Davis – Died September 29, 1972, in the line of duty as the result of an auto accident on Dawsonville Highway. He was a four year veteran – twenty-eight years old. His badge #7 was retired.

THE OFFICE OF SHERIFF

The foundations of the office of Sheriff were created over a thousand years ago in England. The sheriff was created because laws needed to be enforced. The word *sheriff* comes from old England. Each *shire*, or county, had a head-man known as a *reeve*. The title *shire reeve* gradually came to be run together in the single word *sheriff*. The term is noted in the King James Version of the Bible in the Book of Daniel Chapter 3, verse 2 -

Then Nebuchadnezzar the king sent to gather together the princes, the governors, and the captains, the judges, the treasurers, the counsellors, the **sheriffs***, and all the rulers of the provinces, to come to the dedication of the image which Nebuchadnezzar the king had set up.*

The English began to call their shires counties about 1400, and the English colonists brought the county system with them to America. The King is the only English institution older than sheriff, and the office of Sheriff is the oldest law enforcement position in the United States.

Sheriff, in the United States, is one of the chief administrative officers of a county. In most states voters elect the Sheriff, and within the last 1200 years, the legal power of the Sheriff has remained almost fully resistant to change. The Sheriff can respond faster to any citizens' complaint than any police department. His fast and efficient abilities for handling such concerns are derived from his constitutional foundation. It is his duty to take charge of prisoners, to oversee juries and to prevent breaches of the peace. He also carries out the judgments of the county. For example, if the court gives a judgment against a debtor, the sheriff seizes his property and sells it to satisfy the claims of creditors. The sheriff may perform these duties himself, or he may give other persons the power to act in his name. These persons are called deputy sheriffs.

CONSTITUTIONAL AND LEGAL PROVISIONS OF THE SHERIFF'S OFFICE

(AS OF 1980)

The office of sheriff in Georgia is considered to be both a constitutional and a county office. The constitutionality of the office stems from the common law and from the constitutional provisions extended to certain offices in existence when the first Georgia Constitution was ratified.

While most of the legal provisions concerning the office of Sheriff in Georgia are contained in the state's statutory and case law, some general provisions of the state constitution do apply to the sheriff. For example, article II, section 2, paragraph I (Ga. Code Ann. 2 – 79 – I), which establishes rules for the election and removal of county officers, applies to sheriffs because of their status as officers.

SHERIFF AS A COUNTY OFFICER

The Georgia Constitution defines a county officer as one who is elected by the qualified voters of the county to a four-year term of office, subject to removal from office upon conviction for malpractice. In addition, a county officer must have resided in the county for at least two years and be a qualified voter. The sheriff is a county officer by this definition.

OTHER QUALIFICATIONS FOR SHERIFF

Besides satisfying the general requirements for a county officer as stated above, a prospective Georgia sheriff must meet the following qualifications:

1. Must be a citizen of the State.
2. Must have been a resident of the County for two years prior to election or appointment.
3. Must be a qualified voter entitled to vote.
4. Elected by qualified voters of the county.
5. Term of office is four years.
6. Must be 21 years of age; however, upon passage of appropriate local ordinances, citizens who are 18 years of age shall be eligible.
7. No person shall be eligible to hold the office of sheriff who does not have all the following qualifications:
    a. Be a citizen of the United States.
    b. Have attained the age of at least 25 years prior to the date of his qualification for the election to the office.
    c. Have obtained a high school diploma or its recognized equivalent in educational training as established by the Georgia Peace Officer Standards and Training Council.
    d. Have not been convicted of a felony offense or any offense involving moral turpitude contrary to the laws of this State, or any other State, or the United States.
    e. Be fingerprinted and a search made of local, state and national fingerprint files to disclose any criminal record; said fingerprints to be taken under the direction of the judge of the probate court, and must be taken on or before, but no later than, one hour following the close of qualification for election to the office of Sheriff.
    f. Give a complete history of his places of residence for a period of six years immediately preceding the qualification giving house number, street, city, county and state.
    g. Give a complete history of his places of employment for a period of six years immediately preceding the qualification date, giving period of time employed, name and address of employer.

The requirements of b, c and f shall be deemed to have been met by any person who shall have served as a duly qualified and elected sheriff of one of the several counties of this state for a period of two years. Each person offering his candidacy for the office of sheriff shall swear or affirm before the judge of the Probate Court, at the time for qualifying, that he has, or meets, all the qualifications required pursuant to the provisions of this subsection.

8. From and after January 1, 1980, no person shall be eligible to hold the office of sheriff unless such person shall meet ONE of the following:
   a. Be a certified police officer as defined in the Georgia Peace Officer Standard and Training Act within six months after taking office.
   b. Possess a two-year degree or its equivalent from a college or university.
   c. Have two years of college or two years experience in the law enforcement field.
   d. Have two years of educational training in police enforcement field.

   These requirements shall be deemed to have been met by any person who shall have served as a duly qualified and elected sheriff of one of the several counties of this state for a period of two years.

9. From and after January 1, 1980, every newly elected sheriff in his first term shall be required to complete a training session of no less than six weeks to be conducted by the Georgia Peace Officers Standards and Training Council as may be selected by the Georgia Sheriff's Association. The training shall be completed during the first calendar year of the first term of the newly elected sheriff's term of office. Any newly elected sheriff who is unable to attend this training course when offered because of medical disability or providential cause, shall within one year from the date such disability or cause terminates, complete the Standard Basic Course of Instruction required of police officers. Any newly elected sheriff who does not fulfill the obligations of this provision shall lose his power of arrest. These requirements shall be deemed to have been met by any person who shall have served as a duly qualified and elected sheriff of one of the several counties of this state for a period of two years.

10. From and after January 1, 1980, no person shall be eligible to hold the office of sheriff unless he attends a minimum of 20 hours training annually as may be selected by the Georgia Sheriff's Association. Any person who does not fulfill this obligation shall lose his power of arrest.

11. As a candidate for public office such person must pay a qualifying fee.

12. Before entering into the duties of office, besides the oath of all civil officers, the following oath must be taken before the Judge of the Superior Court or Probate Court:

   I do swear that I will faithfully execute all writs, warrants, precepts, and processes directed to me as sheriff of this county, or which are directed to all sheriffs of this state, or to any sheriff specially, I can lawfully execute, and true returns make, and in all things well and truly, without malice or partiality, perform the duties of the office of Sheriff of Hall County, during my continuance therein, and take only my lawful fees. So help me God.

NOTE: Sheriffs now receive no compensation except that which is in the nature of an annual salary fixed by law.

13. Such person must take oath of office to the effect that he will support the U. S. Constitution and the Georgia Constitution; that he is not the holder of any public money due this state, unaccounted for; that he is not the holder of any office of trust under the Government of the United States nor any state or foreign state, and that he is qualified to hold the office according to the Constitution and laws of Georgia, and that he has been a resident of the county for the required time.

14. A loyalty oath is also required stating that such person is not a member of the Communist Party.

15. A sheriff is required to give bond with at least two sureties, in the of $25,000 which amount may be increased in any county by local act, conditioned for faithful performance of his duties, by himself, his deputies and jailers.

Excerpted from the Georgia State Code

DUTIES OF THE SHERIFF AS A LAW ENFORCEMENT OFFICER

Historically, the sheriff and his deputies were responsible for all law enforcement activities within the county. As towns and cities developed, the sheriff gradually relinquished to the municipal governments the responsibility for law enforcement activities within the corporate limits, but retained primary responsibility for policing unincorporated areas of the county. This is the situation in most Georgia counties today. The sheriff does retain the authority to intervene if necessary, however, in matters relating to law enforcement activities within the county even when such activities occur within the city limits.

LOCAL LAW ENFORCEMENT FUNCTIONS

As with most local law enforcement agencies in Georgia, the sheriff's department has evolved into an organization of wide responsibility. The duties of today's sheriff include, for example:

1. the protection of life and property
2. the preservation of the public peace
3. the prevention, detection, and investigation of criminal activity
4. the apprehension and confinement of offenders and the recovery of property
5. the expeditious movement and control of vehicular traffic and the investigation of traffic accidents
6. the control of crowds at public events and the regulation of other non-criminal conduct
7. the rendering of services and the protection of property during civil emergencies or natural disasters

8. the responsibility for providing numerous noncrime – related services to the community

When combined, these functions provide the foundation for the overall mission of the modern sheriff's department. This is, namely, to maintain the peace, to protect life and property, and to provide service to the community.

GEORGIA SHERIFFS

The Georgia Sheriff's Association was created in 1957, and since then Georgia has worked hard to bring the Office of Sheriff up to national expectations.

To this end, Georgia was among the first states to mandate qualifications for those seeking the Office of Sheriff. Georgia was the first state to mandate in-service training, and the first state to conduct specialized training for its new sheriffs. The Association also has a vested interest in upholding the sheriff's oath of office, and to that end, has supported and introduced legislation requiring the investigation and removal of sheriffs who violate their oath or who fail to perform the duties and responsibilities of their office. The Association has pushed for stronger sentencing of criminals, and has supported the add-on fines and forfeiture law whereby criminals pay for the training and education of our law enforcement officers.

The qualifications for those seeking to run for the Office of Sheriff are outlined in Georgia Code 15-16-1.

HALL COUNTY DEPUTY – 1980

1980 Pay scale and leave policy for a Hall County Deputy

Starting salary was $400.72 bi-weekly. After the seventh month of employment, the patrolman was advanced to $420.72 bi-weekly. Then the employee was advanced accordingly to the regular step raises outlined in the Civil Service regulations. The employee received one week of vacation for the first year of employment, then two weeks after the first year. The deputy had six paid holidays each year. All personnel worked a minimum of forty hours a week or five days.

The county furnished a complete uniform for the employee except for gun, gun belt and holster. Uniforms were issued on a regular basis thereafter as needed by the personnel due to unserviceability. A high school education or GED equivalency is required. Employee must pass the Civil Service test and have a medical examination report. The deputy was placed on probation for the first six months of employment at which time an evaluation was made by the supervisor.

This is not the entire list of qualifications – just the basics to give a general idea of what it was like back then. Compare this with the qualifications and benefits of today's deputy.

DUTIES AND QUALIFICATIONS OF A HALL COUNTY DEPUTY

(AS OF 2010)

A deputy sheriff performs various duties in law enforcement including patrolling, investigating crimes and securing courtrooms during proceedings assuring all laws of the county and state are carried out in an efficient and effective manner in many situations that are highly dangerous, stressful, and unpredictable requiring quick judgment. A deputy patrols assigned districts to assure all laws are enforced by checking homes and business for any signs of criminal activity such as broken windows and unlocked doors; arrests any suspects found in the commission of crimes; fills out arrest reports and transports the suspect to the Detention Center or to mental hospitals on court order.

He answers any calls from the public requesting assistance in burglaries, domestic violence, or any other situation needing the response from law enforcement authorities; writes reports on all calls answered indicating the nature of call and any findings at the scene; attends public meetings to maintain order; serves warrants and subpoenas upon court order. A deputy sheriff assists the district attorney with case preparation by gathering evidence, assuring the chain of evidence is kept, and testifying in court as necessary. He responds to motor vehicle accidents in designated areas or assists in other areas as needed; assists EMT's, firefighters, and other emergency personnel; performs first aid/CPR when necessary; completes wreck reports by asking questions of involved parties and any witnesses, gathering all pertinent information and calling wreckers as necessary; provides emotional support to victims at the scene; directs traffic as necessary to prevent further accidents and clean up accident scene; reopens the road when clear.

A deputy maintains traffic safety by stopping unsafe motorists, drunk drivers and speeding vehicles by the use of radar and other detection devices; issues citations or arrests drivers and impounds vehicles as needed; reports any malfunctioning signals or damaged and missing signs. He helps motorists with mechanical problems or calling wreckers when necessary; gives directions to motorists; removes debris from the roadways; escorts funeral processions, parades, and provides direction during sports events as necessary; directs traffic at school crossings.

When assigned to Administrative/Court Services Division, a deputy sheriff acts as bailiff in State, Magistrate, Superior, or Juvenile Court providing security and order during all proceedings; guards prisoners and evidence during proceedings; may transport prisoners to and from court during proceedings. He completes all paperwork necessary to have prisoners transported to and from other states; assures all prisoners arrive safely at their destination. A deputy sheriff receives, sorts, distributes, and serves various legal papers pertaining to court orders including divorce papers, lawsuits, fieri-facias, appearance subpoenas, and subpoena duces tecum, eviction orders, termination of parental custody, contempt orders and citations; services bond forfeitures and foreclosures, and performs other related duties as required.

Requirements:

Applicants must have a High School Diploma or G.E.D. No experience is required, but must have Mandated Peace Officer Certification to apply. Valid Driver's License and a satisfactory Motor Vehicle Record (MVR) are also necessary. Salary is $31, 928 to $39,910 as of 2009.

ROLE OF THE LAW ENFORCEMENT OFFICER

Because a law enforcement officer is an important member of society, he/she should exercise all care possible in the performance of his/her duties. The officer must remember that in many cases a citizen's only direct contact with city, county and state government is when he meets the officer. Law enforcement officers shoulder a great deal of responsibility. The police officer's part of the criminal process is the emergency or immediate detention of offenders (arrest) until the rest of the process of the administration of criminal justice can be brought into play. In order to fulfill his responsibility, the officer is given wide, sweeping powers – authority possessed by no other member of society. This authority includes:

1. Immediate power of detention without a warrant *under certain circumstances.*
2. Power of search and seizure without a warrant *under certain circumstances.*
3. Power to take human life without benefit of trial *under certain circumstances.*
4. This authority is a heavy responsibility and abuses of it must be zealously guarded against by the officers themselves.

EXPECTATIONS OF LAW ENFORCEMENT OFFICERS

The fundamental duty of a law enforcement officer is to serve mankind and safeguard lives and property. He is to protect the innocent against deception and the weak against oppression or intimidation and peaceful against violence or disorder. In carrying out this duty, the officer is to respect the Constitutional rights of all men to liberty, equality and justice.

POLICE OFFICER

"The duties which a police officer owes to the State are of the most exacting nature. No one is compelled to choose the profession of a police officer, but having chosen it, everyone is obliged to perform its duties and live up to the high standards of its requirements. To join in that high enterprise means the surrender of much individual freedom. The police officer has chosen a profession that he must hold to at all peril. He is the outpost of civilization. He cannot depart from it until he is relieved."

"It is a great and honorable duty, to be greatly and honorably filled, but there is toward the officer a corresponding duty of the state. It owes him a generous compensation for the perils he endures for the protection of society. It owes him the knowledge of security from want that is to be his in his declining years. It owes him the measure which is due to the great importance of the duties he discharges."

President Calvin Coolidge

A POLICEMAN'S TEN COMMANDMENTS

1. Ask God to give me the strength to do my duty as it should be done.
2. To improve myself morally, mentally, physically and spiritually.
3. To be obedient and carry out all orders from my supervisor.
4. To protect life and property.
5. To report for duty punctually and to be presentable at all times.
6. To be firm and still be courteous.
7. To be willing, cheerful and respectful at all times.
8. To treat my brother officers as I would like them to treat me.
9. To live my life so as to be a credit to my profession.
10. To remember always that I am a public servant and am obligated to give the best that I have in me.

WHAT ARE POLICEMEN?
YOU NAME IT – HE'S IT

BY PAUL HARVEY

Don't credit me with this mongrel prose: it has many parents - at least 420,000 *(now at 870,000)* of them: Policemen.

A Policeman is a composite of what all men are, mingling of a saint and sinner, dust and deity.

Culled statistics wave the fan over the stinkers, underscore instances of dishonesty and brutality because they are "news". What they really mean is that they are exceptional, unusual, not commonplace.

Buried under the froth is the fact: Less than .5 percent of policemen misfit the uniform. That's a better average than you'd find among clergymen.

What is a policeman made of? He, of all men, is at once the most needed and the most unwanted. He's a strangely nameless creature who is "sir" to his face and "fuzz" to his back.

He must be such a diplomat that he can settle differences between individuals so that each will think he won.

But...If the policeman is neat, he's conceited; if he's careless, he's a bum. If he's pleasant, he's flirting; if not, he's a grouch.

He must make an instant decision which would require months for a lawyer to make.

But...If he hurries, he's careless; if he's deliberate, he's lazy. He must be first to an accident and infallible with a diagnosis. He must be able to start breathing, stop bleeding, tie splints and, above all, be sure the victim goes home without a limp. Or expect to be sued.

The police officer must know every gun, draw on the run, and hit where it doesn't hurt. He must be able to whip two men twice his size and half his age without damaging his uniform and without being "brutal". If you hit him, he's a coward. If he hits you, he's a bully.

A policeman must know everything - and not tell. He must know where all the sin is - and not partake.

A policeman must, from a single human hair, be able to describe the crime, the weapon and the criminal - and tell you where the criminal is hiding.

But...If he catches the criminal, he's lucky; if he doesn't, he's a dunce. If he gets promoted, he has political pull; if he doesn't, he's a dullard. The policeman must chase a bum lead to a dead-end, stake out ten nights to tag one witness who saw it happen - but refused to remember.

He runs files and writes reports until his eyes ache to build a case against some felon who'll get dealed out be a shameless shamus or an 'honorable' who isn't.

The policeman must be a minister, a social worker, a diplomat, a tough guy and a gentleman.

And, of course, he'll have to be a genius, for he will have to feed a family on a policeman's salary.

OFFICERS – WHAT THEY DO

They deal in only one specialty – service, and they do not sell it, they give it.

They freeze in winter and roast in summer.

They do it uncomplainingly because it is their job.

They work around the clock providing protection for us while we sleep.

They are on duty constantly, even on their days off, and are subject to call even while on vacation.

They lay their life on the line each time they report for duty.

They perform a thousand tasteless and thankless tasks in the line of duty.

They hold the broken body of a child in their arms and seek the hit and run driver responsible.

They rush into burning buildings and dive into icy water to rescue the helpless.

They deliver babies and they deliver death messages.

They face a maniac killer or armed thug.

They enforce the law – all the laws – yet they do not punish; for that is not their function.

They suffer when their fellow officers are injured or killed.

They suffer even more when one of their members turn black sheep and bring shame to all the others.

They would rather complete their day's work without seeing pain and misery, but someone must do this joyless job.

LAW ENFORCEMENT CODE OF ETHICS

As a law enforcement officer, my fundamental duty is to serve mankind; to safeguard lives and property; to protect the innocent against deception, the weak against oppression or intimidation, and the peaceful against violence and disorder; and to respect the Constitutional rights of all men to liberty, equality, and justice.

I will keep my private life unsullied as an example to all; maintain courageous calm in the face of danger, scorn, or ridicule; develop self-restraint; and be constantly mindful of the welfare of others; honest in thought and deed in both my personal and official life. I will be exemplary in obeying the laws of the land and the regulations of my department. Whatever I see or hear of a confidential nature or that is confided in me in my official capacity will be kept ever secret unless revelation is necessary in the performance of my duty.

I will never act officiously or permit personal feelings, prejudices, animosities, or friendships to influence my decision. With no compromise for crime and with relentless prosecution of criminals, I will enforce the law courageously and appropriately without fear or favor, malice, or ill will, never employing unnecessary force or violence, and never accepting gratuities.

I recognize the badge of my office as a symbol of public faith, and I accept it as a public trust to be held so long as I am true to the ethics of the police service. I will constantly strive to achieve those objectives and ideals, dedicating myself before God to my profession-law enforcement.

"This book is one of a kind with a wealth of information about the history of our law enforcement officers in Hall County, GA."

Harold G. Black, Ret. Cmdr., GPD

PART II

LAW ENFORCEMENT IN HALL COUNTY, GA 1818 – 2010

BIOGRAPHICAL SKETCHES

MICHAEL DICKSON
(First Sheriff of Hall County)

Michael Dickson, the first Sheriff of Hall County, was a Justice of the Peace in Jackson County, GA, in 1811 in Georgia Militia District 268. The son of David Dickson, he was born in 1788 in Green County, GA. From Hall County, Michael Dickson moved to Coweta County and then to Troup County, GA.

ABRAHAM CHASTAIN, JR.
(Sheriff of Hall County 1832 – 1834)

Abraham Chastain, Jr. was born April 28, 1793, in Greenville, SC. He was married on December 28, 1817, to Martha Swafford, who was born March 12, 1800, and divorced in Hall County in 1838. Chastain was Sheriff of Hall County from 1832 to 1834. He married a second time on July 3, 1853, to Harriett D. Wood, and died in Hall County on October 23, 1863.

RICHARD H. WATERS

Richard H. Waters was born October 5, 1808. He served several terms as Sheriff of Hall County from 1846 to 1866, and died March 28, 1877.

COLONEL HOPSON *BOYD*
(Hall County Sheriff 1854 – 1856)

Hopson Boyd was born in Virginia in 1812, and came to North Georgia sometime around 1820. He was Sheriff of Hall County from 1854 to 1856.

ALEXANDER M. EVANS
(Hall County Sheriff 1856)

Alexander M. Evans was born in 1820 in Virginia. His wife was Sophronia (Sophie) Buffington of Hall County. He served as Sheriff of Hall County from January, 1856, to September of that year when he was succeeded by Claiborn Revel.

J. S. LATHEM

Mr. J. S. Lathem, our energetic and efficient Sheriff, has become a resident of the city.

Gainesville Eagle, March 1, 1872

JOHN L. GAINES

(September 16, 1842 – February 21, 1926)
(Hall County Sheriff 1877 – 1886)

Mr. John L. Gaines, aged 83, died at his home in this city Sunday morning from an attack of flu and the effects of a fall a week ago in his room. The funeral was held on Monday at the home, 61 West Washington Street, Rev. E. F. Campbell, pastor of First Baptist Church, officiating. The burial was at Alta Vista Cemetery.

Mr. Gaines is survived by 12 children, John L. and Ernest Gaines of Atlanta; Ira P., Homer, Herbert and Joseph Gaines of Flowery Branch, GA; Mrs. Charles Tumlin, of Fort Gaines, Alabama; Mrs. D. H. Lipscomb of Akron, Ohio; Mrs. E. A. Spencer, Grover, Edward and Miss Genie Gaines of this city.

Mr. Gaines served a term in the Georgia legislature in 1890 and 1892. He was elected Sheriff of Hall County in 1877 and served 10 years.

A TALK WITH J. T. GAINES

"John Gaines was such a well-known and highly respected man; he had quite a number of children. Surely someone has a photo of him," I mused one afternoon. My wife suggested I call some of the Gaines listed in the phone book in Flowery Branch. The very first one I tried, Mr. J. T. Gaines on Church Street in Flowery Branch, told me, "Yes, John L. Gaines was my grandfather. I have an old family photo in the dresser drawer. I don't remember how I got it, but I've never needed it."

J. T. Gaines told me many interesting things about the Gaines family. Sheriff Gaines, he said, owned a lot of property and lived at the end of Gaines Ferry Road (which was named for him). He operated a ferry that would carry one horse and buggy. J. T. Gaines now has the bell that Sheriff Gaines used at the ferry site prominently displayed in his yard. It was used to signal him when someone wanted to use the ferry.

Sheriff Gaines' wife died while they lived on Gaines Ferry Road, and he later sold out and moved to town on West Washington Street below the church. He lived with his daughter, Genie, a school teacher who never married. According to J. T. Gaines, while Gaines was Sheriff, he lived downstairs in the jail and the prisoners lived upstairs.

Another of Sheriff Gaines' daughters, Marie, married E. A. Spencer, who later became Sheriff of Hall County. Mr. J. T. Gaines said that he and Sheriff Spencer used to visit each other, since Marie Spencer was his aunt.

Mr. Gaines said that Sheriff Gaines never had to hang anyone while he was in office; however, Sheriff Spencer had to hang two men. According to Mr. Gaines, "Back in those days, if someone were sentenced to die, the Sheriff had to do the hanging." "There was no electric chair", he continued. He said Sheriff Spencer showed him the two men he had in jail to hang (there was also a woman in the jail connected with the case), and even let him talk to them. It seems the woman, a Mrs. Hawkins, convinced the two men, the Cantrell brothers, to kill her husband. Mrs. Hawkins was sentenced to life in prison and the Sheriff was ordered to hang the Cantrell brothers.

The jail, a two story structure, was located on South Maple Street. The men were hanged at the jail, Mr. Gaines told me. Thank goodness I called the correct number!

Sheriff John L. Gaines (front center) and his family (Mrs. Gaines is seated on his left). He served as Sheriff of Hall County ten consecutive years and served two terms in Georgia Legislature. Gaines died at the age of 83 from an attack of flu.

One of Hall County's best farmers and a leading citizen is John Lilburn Gaines of Flowery Branch. He was born September 16, 1842, in Hall County, and here he has spent all his life. His father was Ira Gaines and his mother Nancy Hawkins, and they were the parents of eight children, four boys and four girls. Francis H., the oldest boy, was in Company D, Twenty-seventh Georgia Infantry, and was killed at the second battle of Cold Harbor. William D. was in Company D, Twenty-seventh Georgia Regiment, and was wounded at Sharpsburg and died at home from its effects. Henry W. T. was the third soldier of the family and is now a farmer in Hall County and runs a big set of mills. The father of these children died April 4, 1891, at the age of seventy-eight. His wife was born in 1815, and is still living, and is remarkably strong in health, as she is in mind. She is a member of the Baptist Church, as was her husband during his lifetime. The subject of this memoir after the war and on reaching manhood began farming. He was elected justice of the peace for a number of years and in 1877 was elected Sheriff of Hall County, and continuously elected for five terms. He then declined to be a candidate again, telling his friends that he had had more than his share. He was elected to the legislature for the terms 1892-93 and 1894-95, and served on the committees of prisons, agriculture, temperance and blind asylum of Macon. On October 18, 1866, Mr. Gaines was married to Mary C., daughter of Pinckney D. Major of Hall County. She was born in Georgia. Their marriage has been blessed with thirteen children, viz: Nancy E., Marietta, Eugenia, Ira P., Robert L.,

Maggie M., John L., Joseph W., Grover C., Homer W., Ernest N. and Hubert H. Mr. and Mrs. Gaines are members of the Baptist Church and Mr. Gaines is a member of the F & AM. Mrs. Gaines owns a magnificent farm of 400 acres in a high state of cultivation, and is a man enjoying the esteem of all who are fortunate enough to have his acquaintance. Mr. Gaines had the same blood in his veins that led his three brothers to volunteer for the country's cause, and he too served through the war with distinguished bravery. He was in all the battles with ex-Senator Colquitt, his superior officer. He was wounded four times at Seven Pines and was in the battles of Fort Fisher, when he was again wounded, and around Richmond and the siege of Petersburg. He was in the first engagement of the war, outside of Fort Sumter, and was in the last battle, fought after Lee had surrendered.

Excerpted from MEMOIRS OF GEORGIA, The Southern History Assn., Atlanta, Georgia, Volume I 1895

JOHN L. GAINES CALLED TO REST

Honorable John L. Gaines, in his 83rd year, passed away Sunday morning at his home at 61 West Washington Street, after a few days of illness from influenza, his death being hastened by a fall in his room in which his hip was badly injured.

The funeral services were held at the First Baptist Church Tuesday morning followed by the burial at Alta Vista Cemetery. Rev. E. F. Campbell officiated at the services. The pallbearers were: J. D. Hardie, John M. Hulsey, B. P. Gaillard, R. E. Smith, J. F. Chamblee, and E. B. Dunlap.

John Lilburn Gaines was born September 16, 1842, a son of Ira P. Gaines and Nancy Hawkins Gaines. He was married to Mary Major in 1866, and to this union were born 13 children, 12 of whom are now living. John L. and Ernest Gaines of Atlanta, Ira P., Homer, Hubert and Joseph Gaines of Flowery Branch, Georgia; Mrs. Charles Tumlin, Ft. Gaines, Alabama; Mrs. D. H. Lipscomb, Akron, Ohio; Mrs. E. A. Spencer, Grover, Edward, and Miss Genie Gaines of this city. He is also survived by one brother, H. W. T. Gaines and one sister, Mrs. John West, both of Tadmore district, this county.

Mr. Gaines was a brave and loyal soldier of the Confederacy, serving in Co. D., 27th Ga. Regiment. He enlisted at the first call to arms and was in the last battle fought after the surrender of General Lee. He was wounded four times in the battle of Ft. Fisher. But being a man of unusual strength and determination, wounds were mere incidents in a day's work, and he lost very little time in consequence.

The family was of good fighting stock and furnished four splendid soldiers to the Lost Cause, two of whom lost their lives. Francis H. was killed in the second battle of Cold Harbor. William D. was wounded at the battle of Sharpsburg and died after being brought home. Two of them – John L. and H. W. T. Gaines – were spared to return to their homes.

Mr. Gaines not only served his country nobly in time of war, but in time of peace as well. After his return home he engaged in farming, but was soon called on to serve as Sheriff of the county, to which place he was elected in 1877, serving five consecutive terms. In 1892, he was elected to the legislature, in which body he served two terms.

He was possessed of an exalted sense of honor and rectitude and was very loyal to his country and its institutions. He was as gentle and unaffected as a child and possessed a most kindly nature. Few persons ever saw him lose his temper, and if he ever did, it must have been through a tremendous provocation.

But there never was time, in fair weather or foul, when he did not do his duty according to the lights before him. When duty called, he followed without questioning. As Will Hay's heroic poem says of Jim Bludue, "He seen his duty a dead-sure thing, and went for it thar and then."

Well does the writer remember when the new Sheriff of Hall put his first man in jail – a little jail across Broad Street from the courthouse. He had just been sworn in, when Ike Cements, a man of tremendous brawn and fighting qualities, got on a tear. The new Sheriff went to him and spoke gently and told him to come on to jail. The man laughed in his face and said, "Well, I guess not." "Yes, you will, Ike – come on," said the new Sheriff, taking him by both arms. Ike began to see things. He saw in a moment that someone was hold of him, and proceeded to go, struggling all the way.

The Sheriff never lost his temper for a moment, but argued with the man all the way, telling him how much better it would be to come on without making any fuss. But he put him in jail. That is the main thing.

The old man lived a long time, and the world is much better off for his having lived. And we guess he was ready and willing, for he had done about all there was to do and was willing to swap off old age . . . for eternal youth.

(Co. D, 27th Regt. Ga. Vol. Inf. – Private. Pension Roll shows he died February 21, 1926.

- Civil War, Gainesville News, February 24, 1926

ANDREW J. MUNDY 1888 - 1900

Andrew J. Mundy was born at Jonesboro, Clayton County, GA on March 8, 1849. This was during the California gold fever. He was married on January 14, 1869, and he and his wife had two sons, J. B. Mundy and H. E. Mundy. He moved to Hall County in 1871, and settled down in Wilson District, farming for a livelihood.

Andrew J. Mundy served as Sheriff twelve consecutive years (1889 – 1900). He and Ed England share the honor of holding office the second longest term.

Mundy served as a Justice of the Peace for his district for a term of six years. In 1888, he was elected Sheriff of Hall County, which position he filled to the satisfaction of the people for twelve consecutive years. This is the second longest term of Sheriff in Hall County.

Sheriff Mundy was frugal and wise and accumulated an estate that was very valuable. He was active in the affairs of his city and county for forty years, the time of his residence here, and had hundreds of friends throughout this area. Mr. Mundy was in failing health for two or three years before he passed away in July, 1916, at the home of Mrs. J. B. Mundy on West Broad Street. Interment took place in the family lot at Alta Vista Cemetery. In his death, Hall County lost one of its best known citizens and one of its finest sheriffs.

Atlanta Journal, February 22, 1926

E.A. SPENCER

1912 - 1916

Sheriff and Mrs. E. A. Spencer

W.A. CROW, SR.

1904 – 1912, 1916 – 1924, 1928 – 1929
LONGEST SERVICE (16 YEARS) OF
ANY SHERIFF

Sheriff W. A. Crow, Sr. served the longest term of any Sheriff – 16 years. He was first commissioned in 1904 and died in office in 1929. Upon moving to Gainesville, Crow lived in what was known as Crow House (later Strickland's Funeral Home). During this era, the streets in Gainesville were dirt and transportation in the city of mostly by trolley.

SHERIFF CROW DIES SUDDENLY
Stricken with Heart Trouble as He Returns Home from Office

Sheriff William A. Crow, one of the most beloved of Gainesville's citizens, a man of splendid character, a conscientious and able public official, died suddenly from heart trouble in the swing at his residence on Monday evening about 5:30. News of his death spread rapidly and regret was general and profound over the passing of this man, whose friends were legion.

Sheriff Crow had just returned from his office and had seated himself in the swing on his veranda, when he slumped forward. Friends rushed to his assistance, but he was beyond aid and did not regain consciousness. During Monday he seemed to be in good health, and his spirits were fine, though he did complain of a pain in his chest in the morning.

The Sheriff's death was due, no doubt, to an attack of influenza, from which he suffered during the winter. Friends say that he had a hard time shaking it off and that a very great change was noticeable in him since he had it.

The funeral service on Tuesday morning at the First Baptist church was largely attended, with many of the city's most prominent business men forgetting business to pay their last respects to this man, whose kindly and Christian nature had endeared him to everyone. It was a beautiful and touching service and was conducted by Dr. Roland Leavell and Rev. C. T. Brown, a lifelong friend and former pastor of Sheriff Crow. Floral tributes, which were very numerous, were banked in front of the pulpit. Interment was in Woodlawn Cemetery.

Mr. Crow was born in Franklin County, but moved to Hall County at an early age, settling in Gillsville. He was a merchant there for eighteen years, serving as the depot agent and later as Mayor of the town.

Moving to Gainesville in 1905, Mr. Crow was elected Sheriff of Hall County. He retired after 16 years service and moved to Florida, but later he returned to Gainesville and took charge of extensive farming lands of the Chicopee Manufacturing Company.

Sheriff Crow was re-elected to his office in November of 1928, after a brief retirement from public service. Except for two terms, he had served as Sheriff of Hall County for 15 years and had acquired a reputation as one of the most fearless and efficient law officers in the state.

Many times during his vigorous campaigns against lawbreakers, Sheriff Crow's life had been jeopardized and he had from time to time suffered numerous gunshot wounds.

In the death of Sheriff Crow, Hall County and the State of Georgia lost one of their most efficient law enforcement officers.

Sheriff Crow was a member of the First Baptist Church and had attended church Sunday morning and evening. He was a member of the Odd Fellow's fraternity.

Besides his wife, Mr. Crow is survived by four sons, Henry, Frank, William A., Jr., and Howard Crow, and two daughters, Mrs. Alden Snow of Tuscaloosa, Alabama and Miss Margaret Crow of this city.

* * *

Sheriff (W. A. Crow, Sr.) while standing at the Palmour Bros. corner yesterday morning dropped his pistol, which fell on the pavement and was discharged. Fortunately, the ball missed the crowd on the streets and spent its force against the brick wall on the opposite side of the street.

- The Eagle, February, 1906

Photo courtesy Jerry Walls
Old Hall County Correctional Institute on Stringer Avenue – 1929

IRVIN L. LAWSON

APRIL 22, 1929 -1936

Sheriff Irvin L. Lawson was elected to fill the unexpired term of W. A. Crow, Sr. who died in office after serving only three months of his four year term (he had served 16 years previously). Sheriff Lawson was in office when the disastrous tornado struck Gainesville in 1936.

Irvin L. Lawson, 80, of Highland Road, Gainesville, who served as Hall County Sheriff from 1929 until 1937, died today at a private convalescent home following an extended illness.

Funeral services will be held tomorrow at 2 p.m. at Dewberry Baptist Church No.2. The Rev. Cornell Stowers, the Rev. Claud Hood and the Rev. Clyde Coleman will officiate and interment will be in Memorial Park. The body is at the residence.

Mr. Lawson, a lifelong resident of Hall County, was in the lumber and timber business for many years and was also a livestock dealer and a farmer. He was a member of the Murrayville Masonic Lodge. A member of Dewberry Baptist Church No. 2, he served as a deacon and taught Sunday School for twenty years.

Survivors include his wife, Mrs. Lottie Lawson, three daughters, Mrs. Grady (Louise) White, Mrs. Edna White, Mrs. Lee (Marie) Cain, three sons, John L. Lawson, the Rev. G. A. Lawson, the Rev. Billy Lawson, one sister, Mrs. Eston Whitmire, and one daughter in law, Mrs. Juanita Lawson Ewing, all of Gainesville; twenty-five grandchildren and eighteen great grandchildren.

Mr. Lawson's grandsons will serve as pallbearers, and Ed England, Hall County Sheriff, and Hall County deputies will serve as honorary pallbearers.

From The Times, Thursday, November 13, 1975

INTERVIEW WITH TERRY WHITE - 1980

It was quite by accident I discovered that Terry White, a former Sergeant with the Gainesville Police Department, is the grandson of one of Hall County's former Sheriffs - Irvin L. Lawson. Terry, like his grandfather, is a devoted law enforcement officer. I learned that it was because of his grandfather's influence Terry decided to become a policeman.

Terry White, grandson of Sheriff Irvin L. Lawson and a former Sergeant with the Gainesville Police Department, holds the pistol willed to him by his grandfather.

One of his most prized possessions is a Smith & Wesson .38 caliber pistol willed to him at the death of his grandfather. The gun has a 5 inch barrel and is an old Model 10 with fixed sights. Terry said he had long admired the weapon, and Mr. Lawson left it to him because he was the only grandson to enter law enforcement. The pistol bears a 1918 patent date stamp.

In recounting some of the things he remembers about his grandpa's administration, Terry showed me the photo of Sheriff Lawson and his two brothers surrounded by the *Black Hats of Chicopee.* Homer Lawson, from what Terry understands, was formerly a Gainesville city policeman back in the 1920's, and he and Marvin Lawson, another brother, became deputies for Irvin Lawson when he became Sheriff.

Terry told how the sheriffs were paid on the fee system (probably furnishing their own cars), and feels they made most of their money by providing meals for the prisoners and in turn charging the county for the meals (depending on what it cost to produce the food). Mr. Lawson had cattle and pigs which he butchered. By producing his own bacon and beef, as well as other farm products, he was able to keep his cost down to a minimum. Terry's grandmother would cook enough biscuits every morning (about 250!) for three groups – their own big family, the hands who helped out on the farm, and the prisoners.

Irvin Lawson had a farm out at Bell's Mill, and before Lake Lanier was formed, it was sandy bottom land. Little River (which was really just a creek) flowed through the land. Mr. Lawson had a bunkhouse out back where the men who worked for him stayed; it was like a small ranch. The men would break the horses in those sandy bottoms.

This is the first homeplace Terry remembers as a child. When Lake Lanier backed up, Lawson had to sell much of the land to the government, but he also kept a good bit that became lakefront property.

Terry's mother, Mrs. Edna White, talks about when she was a small child, her dad would go out to Wyoming and buy boxcars full of horses. He and his sons and farm hands would then drive those horses from the train depot up Green Street (a dirt street back then), and on out Cleveland Highway to the farm. Terry thinks this was during the time Lawson served as Sheriff.

One of the most memorable events Sheriff Lawson related to his grandson was the day the tornado hit Gainesville, April 6, 1936. Lawson had gone to Atlanta to the Capitol on official business. He had stopped down around Duluth for gas when several fire trucks went by, traveling in the direction of Gainesville. After five or six had gone by, he asked the station attendant what was going on – and learned that Gainesville had been wiped out by a tornado!

Terry's grandpa told him of a man who lived in a boarding house on Bradford Street (where a portion of Townview Plaza now stands). He had finished work at one of the mills, come home and gone to sleep. When he awoke he was in a field out at New Holland – still in his bed! Sheriff Lawson, along with all of Gainesville, had a big job on their hands trying to restore some order to the city.

Terry and his grandpa used to sit and talk about law enforcement in Sheriff Lawson's day, and compared it to what it was like in Terry's day. Mr. Lawson didn't envy his grandson's job in law enforcement for several reasons – the main one being a growing lack of respect for the law. In Sheriff Lawson's day, when a law officer appeared, people immediately straightened up. There was no back talk, no acting up because the BIG LAW was there! The Sheriff and deputies didn't have uniforms; they were recognized by their badges and Stetson hats. According to Terry, the BIG LAW, (the Sheriff and his deputies) wore white hats with a cap badge on them, and the special deputies wore black hats with badges. That was how rank was denoted. They also wore a breast badge on their coat.

The Sheriffs of years gone by didn't need search warrants, and there were no Miranda Warnings or affidavits (these came along after 1936) and they had more freedom to enforce the law. If they heard of a still, they would go raid it. If Sheriff Lawson took a man into court for having a liquor still on his property, he wasn't asked his reason for being on the property, how his information was obtained, or if his informant was reliable. The case was cut and dried; the man would be sent up for a few years and they would go on to the next case. Terry laughingly said they knew how to expedite matters back then!

In relating another exciting incident, Terry said, "My grandpa was known as an honest man, and wouldn't lie if his life depended on it. He was a lay preacher, and very much a Christian man. In the early 1930's somewhere during his tenure, Bonnie and Clyde were on the loose, and a rumor spread that they were headed toward Gainesville. My grandpa and a couple of his deputies waited on Athens Highway (129 South) all night and didn't see anything of them. The next day they were reportedly seen in Atlanta, evidently taking another route from Athens. But my grandpa had reason to believe they were in the area and lay ambush for them."

The sheriffs of Lawson's day were "working sheriffs" with illegal booze being the primary problem. Sometimes they would catch a liquor car coming through town, heavy in the back end. They would stop the car, confiscate the booze, sell it at auction and the county received the proceeds. However, the Sheriff would get a percentage through the fee system.

On days when Terry feels discouraged and frustrated in his job, he receives encouragement and inspiration from the photo of his grandpa, his deputies and 'Black Hats' which hangs in his office. He is proud to be known as Irvin Lawson's grandson, and to be a part of the law enforcement profession.

The *Black Hats* were formed by Sheriff Lawson when the officials at Chicopee Manufacturing Company requested that the Sheriff have some deputized men ready in case of any disturbance from a union dispute (which never did materialize). The second time the Sheriff used the *Black Hats* was when President Franklin D. Roosevelt came to Gainesville to dedicate the new court house after the tornado. I gathered most of this information from Mr. Roy Guest, the only known living member of the *Black Hats* at that time.

Sheriff Irvin L. Lawson & the Black Hats of Chicopee – 1934

Ft Row – Jack Fuller, Lou Hawkins, Marvin E. Lawson, Sheriff Irvin L. Lawson,
Homer Lawson, Clayton Smallwood, Herbert Autry and John Carter;
2ⁿᵈ Row – Young Worley, Mr. Johnson, L. T. Deaton, Baxter Oliver, Bill Crow,

Roy Guest, L. T. Loggins, Nesbitt Lee; 3rd Row — Ferd Bryan, Claude Whelchel, Lyman Truelove, Harv Riley, Paul Eberhardt, W. Lee Land, Mr. Gravitt, Clyde T. Cantrell; 4th Row — Coley Cape, K. C. Johnson, Virgil Ladd, Marion Rider, R. E. 'Sparkie' Spence, Jack Holland, Jewell Bennett, A. C. (Coy) Mays, P. H. Chapman; Back row — Melvin Duckett

A.W. BELL

1937 – 1943

Sheriff Arthur W. Bell was serving as city Commissioner when he was elected Sheriff in 1936. Having served one four year term, he was in his second term when he suffered a fatal heart attack. Bell's reputation shows him to be not only an outstanding law enforcement officer, but also an influential businessman.

SHERIFF BELL DIES SUNDAY AT HOSPITAL

Arthur W. Bell, 52, Hall County Sheriff and former Gainesville City Commissioner, died Sunday at Downey Hospital here following an illness of ten days. He was stricken with a heart attack at his home and his condition grew steadily worse until the end.

Funeral services were held Monday afternoon from the residence, 423 Brenau Avenue, with the Rev. H. G. Jarrard, the Rev. W. J. Jones, the Rev.

George Collins, and the Rev. Homer Morris officiating. Burial was in Woodlawn Cemetery here.

Mr. Bell was a native of Hall County, a son of the late Mr. Joseph M. Bell and Mrs. Judie O'Dell Bell. He was a lifelong resident, and had long been active in business and civic affairs of the community. He owned large business interests in addition to his work as a peace officer. He formerly operated a large wagon yard, was a dealer in livestock, wagons and fertilizer, and had also engaged in construction work and handling real estate.

Mr. Bell served one term as City Commissioner of Gainesville from the First Ward before being elected Sheriff in 1936, which position he had held since that time. He was re-elected for a four year term in 1940. His work as a peace officer had been outstanding, and he held the post of Vice President of the Peace Officers' Association of Georgia representing the Ninth District.

He was also a member of the Baptist Church and of the UCT. Members of the local council of the latter organization acted as honorary pallbearers at the funeral services.

Surviving are a son, Corporal A. W. Bell, Jr. of Fort McPherson, a former Hall County Deputy Sheriff; his wife Mrs. Susan Jones Bell of this city; two brothers, Grover Bell of Columbus and Henry Grady Bell of Bainbridge; two sisters, Mrs. Mollie Thompson, Gainesville Route 1 and Mrs. Minnie Dyer of Meridian, Mississippi, and a granddaughter, Carol Sue Bell of Gainesville.

The Eagle, August, 1943

GAINESVILLE REVENUE AGENT SHOT IN RAID ON MOONSHINE STILL

Photo courtesy Dan Clark & Betty Allen
*Pictured above in the late 1930s are (l to r) Sheriffs Melvin Clark, Ferd Bryan,
and William 'Bill' Crow. Melvin J. 'Mel' Clark was Acting Sheriff in
1943 after A. W. Bell died in office. He was later killed in the line
of duty while in his role as a Revenue Agent.*

Growing in size and determination, an armed posse, collecting new members at every farmhouse and crossroads store, combed east and south of Homer this morning chasing moonshining slayers of a Gainesville native Revenue Agent.

The trail of three unidentified moonshiners was still hot this morning going into the 13th hour of the chase with more than a thousand officers and citizens pursuing the accused killers of Mel Clark, United States Internal Revenue Agent.

The band of searchers fanned out in all directions, picking up new help as they went along, started the hunt last night about 7 o'clock and have traveled about 15 miles. Starting three miles south of Homer in Banks County, the manhunters have now gone into Jackson County, approximately three miles south of Commerce.

Farmers have dropped their plows and small town merchants left their stores to join in today, most of them picking up pistols or shotguns before leaving.

The fully armed posse, led by Sheriffs of two counties and Federal Agents, seemed determined to run down the men who killed their companion last night.

An encircling movement had not been attempted at the last report, but members of the posse were trudging across fields and streams right behind the moonshiners. More conservative members of the group were riding the highways in autos, crisscrossing highways and country lanes, but a majority of the group struck out across country.

Men who have returned from the scene after an all night chase seemed confident that the hunt would end soon, as the Negroes cannot last much longer at the pace they must travel to stay ahead of the crowd.

The killing which gave rise to the chase occurred late yesterday evening when Clark and five other Federal Agents were going into the woods near Homer to investigate a reported liquor still.

Approaching the spot, the men separated and were closing in from all angles. Clark was walking down a path while David Ayers, a State Agent, was trailing him. Ayers said he heard pistol shots suddenly. He rushed down the path and found Clark lying on the ground with a bullet wound in his left breast. His pistol had been fired five times, the officer said.

The bullet, fired at point blank range from either a pistol or rifle, entered the left side of Clark's chest, destroying the circulatory system completely, and passing out the back. Authorities said that death was practically instantaneous.

Three black men were seen fleeing through the woods and on into a swamp near Grove River. DeKalb County bloodhounds were rushed to the scene. . .

Clark is survived by his wife, Winnie, of Cornelia, and his mother, Mrs. Lula Clark of Clermont. Also surviving are two sons, Bobbie and Dan Clark, both of Cornelia; six brothers, Gordon and Guy Clark of Clermont, Lest and Britt Clark of Gainesville, Cloud Clark of Flowery Branch, and Rudolph Clark of Murrayville; one sister, Mrs. Joe Kanaday of Clermont, Route I.

- Daily Times, June 18, 1947

WILLIAM A. (BILL) CROW, JR.

(9/22/1943 – 1948)

Bill Crow filled the unexpired term of Sheriff A. W. Bell, and then was elected to a four year term. He followed in the footsteps of his father, Sheriff W. A. Crow, Sr., and left his mark on Hall County by carrying out his duties as Sheriff in an excellent manner.

BUSINESSMAN W. A. CROW DIES

William A. 'Bill' Crow of 2516 Club Drive, NW, Gainesville, director of Home Federal Savings and Loan Association of Gainesville, died yesterday at the Northeast Georgia Medical Center following an extended illness.

Funeral services will be held tomorrow at 11 a.m. at the chapel of Ward's Funeral Home of Gainesville with Dr. Malcolm O. Tolbert officiating. Interment will be in Alta Vista Cemetery. The body is at the funeral home where the family will receive friends tonight from 7 until 9.

Mr. Crow, a lifelong resident of Gainesville, also served as director of the Founders Life Insurance Company of Tampa, Florida. He was one of the founding directors of both Home Federal Savings and Loan and Founders Life Insurance Company. Prior to his present employment, Mr. Crow served two terms as Sheriff of Hall County.

He was a member of the Gainesville Masonic Lodge No. 219, the Yaarab Temple and the Gainesville Elks Lodge No. 1126. He was a Shriner and a member of the Chattahoochee Country Club. He had been a member of the First Baptist Church of Gainesville since childhood.

Survivors include his wife, Mrs. Isabel Neese Crow, Gainesville; one sister, Mrs. S. H. (Margaret) Mills, Gadsden, Alabama; one nephew, William H. Mills, Gadsden, Alabama.

- The Daily Times, Friday, March 24, 1978

＊ ＊ ＊

Sheriff Bill Crow and Ode Kiser answered a shooting call in Flowery Branch at the residence of Walter Finn (behind the old Flowery Branch school house). Finn had lost his temper when his brother poured out his liquor and shot him in the rear with a shotgun loaded with birdshot. After being shot, Walter Finn's brother jumped off a bank and broke his leg.

When the officers arrived at the scene, the victim had already been taken to the hospital, and Walter was inside the house with his shotgun. Sheriff Crow approached the house from the front and Kiser covered the rear door. Kiser could hear Sheriff Crow telling Walter to put his gun down and come out. Finn told Crow to come inside, and, of course, the Sheriff said 'no'. They went on like this for a while, then Walter told the Sheriff to put his head inside the door, and of course, Crow was not about to do.

Kiser decided to circle the house and try to get a fix on Walter while they were talking. However, Walter happened to see Kiser when he passed a window, shot out the window (glass and all), blowing Kiser's hat off his head and filling his head full of those birdshots. Kiser stated it blew his hat almost up to the school house where Joe Edge (who later retired as a Gainesville Police Captain) was sitting on the steps observing the scene.

Ode Kiser tells of incident when his hat was shot off.

When Sheriff Crow learned that Kiser was hit, he backed off until reinforcement came. They surrounded the area with state troopers and county officers. While the reinforcements were enroute, however, Walter Finn slipped out the back of the house with his shotgun and hid in a ditch covered with kudzu. A neighbor had seen him run out the back and told the Sheriff where he was hiding. Sheriff Crow shot a teargas shell directly where Walter was and it landed between his arm and body. Walter Finn came out with his hands in the air.

Sheriff Crow transported Kiser to Downey Hospital where Dr. Whelchel picked birdshot out of his head.

HORACE 'HOSS' CONNER

I learned of this strong-bodied former deputy named Horace (Hoss) Conner from Mrs. Bill Crow, the widow of William A. (Bill) Crow, Jr. According to Conner, when we talked in 1980, he was the only person living from Bill Crow's tenure, deputies and all. The deputies were Ferd Bryan (Chief Deputy), Cal Wilson and Hoss Conner. The jailers were Fred Vandiver and Mr. Gilreath.

Pictured here is 'Hoss' Conner (on far right) along with Troopers Hubert Crowe, Horace Ragsdale, and Eugene Hollis in the summer of 1945

Hoss Conner, a former State Trooper, came to work with the Hall County Sheriff's Department when Bill Crow was Sheriff in 1943 - 1948. They had two cars and three deputies. I asked him if they had marked cars back then, and he acted like I had slapped him.

"We didn't want to advertise who we were; we were on commission," he said. (They did have a red light and siren, but it was built into the grill of the car.) The Sheriff fed the prisoners, bought cars, paid salaries, etc from the commissions received. The deputies as well as the Sheriff just wore their plain clothes and usually didn't display their weapons. They would either carry one inside a jacket or in a shoulder holster.

Conner doesn't recall any drug problems back in the 1940's — but bootlegging and theft was common. He called off a long list of characters that really gave them problems out on Athens Highway in an area called "Wildcat Holler" (it was a white area then, but now mostly blacks live there). He and Cal Wilson had ridden out there one moonlit night, pulled over and cut the lights. Soon someone came by rolling a wheelbarrow. When they stopped the person, it was one of their famous female bootleggers rolling three cases of liquor.

She said, "I'll be damned, Hoss, you're always in the way!" Then she said, "Hoss, you're not going to take my wheelbarrow are you?" He told her, "I'm taking you, the liquor and the wheelbarrow to jail!"

This same *lady* kept her whiskey out in the chicken lot and for a long time got by with it. She had the whiskey in jars turned upside down on the chicken drinkers, but the chickens wouldn't touch her booze! If someone wanted whiskey, she would just walk over, turn the jar over and sell it to them.

Back in the 40's, Sheriff Crow and his deputies worked "til till cain't". On the weekend, Conner remembers he would get up and dress on Saturday morning, and usually wouldn't undress until Monday morning. He emphasized they were on call all the time. They had to serve all subpoenas and would sometimes finish serving them about midnight or 1 a.m., and then have to be in court the next morning. They were required to have a search warrant to look for evidence in a home, but not to search a car.

Conner feels they had more freedom to enforce the law, and he probably wouldn't make it as an officer with the stricter regulations of today. Hoss never carried a blackjack, but when he told a prisoner to get in the patrol car, they either got in or got *put in!* People used to say, "Old Hoss will smile you to jail – just don't ever cross him!"

Most roads were dirt; about the only paved ones were Cleveland Road (Hwy 129 N), a portion of Athens Highway (Hwy 129 S), and the Atlanta Highway (Hwy 13 S). Hoss recalls how Thompson Bridge Road (Hwy 60 N) used to be ankle deep in mud – as so were the streets in the city! The Sheriff's Department had one car especially equipped with chains and high wheels to go on back roads in the winter.

Hoss told me, "One time a trooper and I went down to Davis Bridge where we'd heard there was a load (of illegal liquor) coming through at 1 a.m. We pulled up on the bridge to wait. We soon heard someone coming. The roads were so muddy the only people traveling were those with a special purpose – to go to the doctor or something like that. While we were waiting on that car, we caught three others." Hoss seemed to think it was nothing to catch four cars with illegal liquor in one night.

The patrol cars didn't have radios, and when they finally did get them, they were just trooper receivers. The Sheriff's Department's calls came from the State Patrol. The signal was different from the troopers. Instead of a beep-beep, there was a continuous beep so they would recognize their calls.

Hoss said of Sheriff Crow, "As long as I worked for Bill Crow, he never once told me to go do something. He always said, 'Let's go do it.'" The Sheriff would get extremely upset if his deputies answered a call without notifying him.

Hoss told of the jailer, Fred Vandiver, calling him one night about a drunk out in New Holland causing a disturbance. Conner didn't feel there was any need to call Sheriff Crow and just went on out. He later learned he was dealing with one of the meanest men in Hall County. Conner walked up to the house about 5:30a.m., and the people around the house told him he had better go back and get more officers.

The intoxicated man was sitting at the table, drinkin' and cussin'. He was a big man – about 6'5" – and he just kept telling Conner that *no one man* ever took him to jail. Conner had handcuffed him and led him out onto the porch by holding onto those handcuffs (which kept tightening as he re-sisted). The drunk sat down on the porch, telling Conner *no one man* ever put him in a patrol car. Conner just kept walking down the steps and the drunk followed – bump, bump, bump down the steps. He assured Conner again that *no one man* ever put him in a patrol car, so Conner just opened the car door and stuffed him in enough (still hanging onto those handcuffs!) so that only his feet and legs were outside the car. He told the drunk he'd better get in, and he cranked the car and started off. Needless to say, the drunk got in!

When they arrived at the jail, the jailer had notified Sheriff Crow and he was waiting on them. The Sheriff started to assist Hoss, but Conner asked him to let him finish the job. The drunk was still protesting that *no one man* ever put him in jail – and he proceeded to tell Conner what he had in store for him when he got those handcuffs off. So Conner put him in the cell, still handcuffed! It wasn't long, however, before he was calling Hoss to come remove them because he had resisted so much they had begun to cut into his flesh. From that time on, that drunk respected Hoss Conner and did what Hoss told him to do. Sheriff Crow, on the other hand, was on Hoss' case for going on the call without him.

Conner said of Sheriff Crow, "I worked with a lot of them (officers) and he was one of the best I ever sat in the seat with." Conner continued, "I never saw him lose his head but one time. There was one girl who used to get drunk and when she did, she was *mean*. One time Bill and I were trying to arrest her and she was kicking and hitting and screaming. She hauled off and kicked Bill on the shin, and when she did, he slapped her so hard she turned two flips! He later regretted losing his temper, but he made a believer out of her!"

"The only time in the history of law enforcement in this area that there was perfect harmony between the City Police Department, the Georgia State Patrol and the Sheriff's Department was during Bill Crow's term", Conner continued. Bill Crow would have a meal for all the officers on occasion.

Before becoming the Sheriff of Hall County, Bill was a deputy for his dad, Sheriff William A. Crow, Sr. Prior to that, he was a Federal Revenue Agent for a number of years, and before that he had been employed with Grinnell Company of Charlotte, NC, a major company in the south. Even thought the Grinnell Company mainly installed heating and air conditioning systems for many of the largest buildings in the south, as a private joke between Hoss and Crow, Hoss would kid the Sheriff and tell him he had better go back to plumbing.

Hoss Conner remembers the old jail on Maple Street in the vicinity of Reed's Auto Parts. There was a hanging noose on that old jail, he said. He also recalls there was a prison camp where the old hospital used to be — off Atlanta Highway on Stringer Avenue. The prisoners had a farm and kept stud bulls for breeding cattle in the area. "They had to wear a ball and chain as they worked", Conner said. When the prisoners went to bed, they had to ask permission to turn over. If the warden heard chains rattling and no one had permission to move, there was trouble! The prison camp was in operation there until about 1933 – 34. After it was phased out, Hall County was without a prison camp for a while.

Conner enjoys telling about the special engines in their patrol cars, "hopped up", he called them. He was in a high speed (over 120 mph) chase with a liquor car in one of them on December 18, 1948, just before Sheriff Crow went out of office. He remembers just enjoying himself, listening to Spike Jones on the radio playing *Here Comes Santa Claus.* He decided to give the car he was chasing a little bump; however, his brakes (Bendix air brakes) picked that moment to act up. Instead of 'bumping', it was more like 'ramming'! Their bumpers locked, they went into a ditch and Conner overturned several times. He remembers the incident every time he hears that song.

The only employee at the jail, Conner commented, was the jailer. He had sleeping quarters across from the jail, but took most of his meals and slept there. Conner related one amusing incident about the prisoners at the jail. One night, the Sheriff and his deputies had caught a load of liquor (a big International truck full of it), and they got some of the prisoners and trusties to help pour it out at the jail. Unknown to Sheriff Crow and his deputies, the prisoners had rounded up some # 10 washtubs and placed them in the basement so they could just remove the lids and pour the booze down the coal chute and into those tubs! After they had finished, they put all the prisoners back in jail and went home. Later that evening the jailer called to say that everybody in the jail was drunk!

Conner jumped into his car and went back to the jail. He found every man in the cell drunk; the federal block was drunk, the trusties were drunk! He was sure they wouldn't get breakfast in the morning, because all the cooks were drunk and locked up! They looked all over for that liquor and finally sobered up one prisoner enough to learn how they got the liquor into the tubs and then put it into big commercial washing machines in the basement. They were using dippers to fill up jugs to pass around. No wonder everybody was drunk!

Sheriff Crow, Hoss Conner, Chief Deputy Ferd Bryan and Cal Wilson were law enforcement officers in an era much different from what it is today. Hard working, strong and sometimes obstinate describes them well. But one thing is certain — they were respected then as they are now, and all are remembered as outstanding law enforcement officers.

FERD BRYAN

(JANUARY, 1949 – MAY 6, 1950)

Sheriff Bryan suffered a massive heart attack while in office. While he was Sheriff, there were three patrol cars and five deputies. The major crime was bootlegging.

SHERIFF BRYAN IN HOSPITAL AFTER 'TUSSLE'

Hall County Sheriff Ferd Bryan was in Downey Hospital Friday morning after becoming "exhausted" while making an arrest Thursday night.

Dr. Burns, Sr. said that Bryan came to the hospital in an "exhausted state" and complaining of a pain in the chest. Burns said that his examination will not be completed and that he would know nothing definite about Bryan's condition until x-rays are checked.

Bryan, who was in the hospital recently for a three day checkup, suffered the "attack" while tussling with a mentally unbalanced man at Flowery Branch late Thursday night, Sheriff's office officials said.

- The Daily Times, May 5, 1950

Hall County Sheriff Ferd Bryan died at Downey Hospital in Gainesville about 8:30pm Saturday after suffering a heart attack Thursday night during a strenuous arrest.

Sheriff Bryan, 49, had been under an oxygen tent and in the care of a private nurse with almost constant medical supervision up to the time of his death. He suffered the attack late Thursday night after a short struggle while attempting to arrest a "mentally unbalanced man" at Flowery Branch. Two weeks previously, he had been in the hospital for three days for a physical checkup. Earlier Saturday night Dr. John Burns reported that Sheriff Bryan was a "very sick man" and in "quite serious condition."

In office since January 1, 1949, Sheriff Bryan defeated former Sheriff Bill Crow in the Hall County Democratic Primary of March, 1948. He had formerly served as a deputy sheriff under Crow for three years.

A veteran of WWI, Sheriff Bryan was born near Gillsville in Jackson County. He lived most of his life in Hall County. For two years, during the early 1940's, he held a government position in Washington, D. C. where he met his wife. At the time of his election he lived in Gillsville; he later moved to 117 East Washington Street in Gainesville. Sheriff and Mrs. Bryan had no children.

Sheriff Bryan is the first Hall County official to die in office since former Sheriff A. W. Bell died in the early 1940's.

- The Daily Times, Sunday morning, May 7, 1950

Georgia State and Hall County officers discover a large whiskey still in 1949 (Sheriff Ferd Bryan on left)

Some equipment used to make whiskey at the still discovered in 1949 by Hall County and Georgia State officers. Sheriff Ferd Bryan is second from right and Deputy Jimmy Quillian is on the far left.

MRS. CONSTANCE (CONNIE) BRYAN

1950

On July 29, 1980, I visited with Mrs. Constance (Connie) Bryan, who was the only female to ever serve as Sheriff of Hall County. She filled the office until a special election could be held after her husband, Sheriff Ferd Bryan, died suddenly while in office.

Mrs. Bryan was living in the Atlanta area, and was in good health at 75 years of age. She spoke at length of the conditions while her husband was Sheriff.

CONSTANCE "CONNIE" BRYAN
(1950)

Documents have been filed in the office
of Secretary of State certifying that

MRS. FERD BRYAN

Gainesville, Georgia

is Sheriff of Hall County

for the term 5/9/50 Until successor is electe
and qualified.

Constance (Connie) Bryan

Constance Bryan, widow of the late Ferd Bryan, served as Sheriff of Hall County for 45 days. The only female to ever hold this office, she was a native of Washington, D. C., and was formerly employed in the Senate Office Building in the Communications Department.

Ferd Bryan ran against the incumbent, W. A. (Bill) Crow and one more candidate (whose name Mrs. Bryan couldn't recall). She said it was a "red hot election and the other candidate withdrew – it was too much for him."

When Ferd Bryan was Sheriff, he was paid on the basis of work done, or 'fee basis'. If they broke up a liquor still, caught a liquor car, etc., each offense had a set fee he was to be paid. The Sheriff was also paid for any civil papers served. However, out of these fees, the Sheriff had to buy the patrol cars, pay his deputies and buy food for the jail (for which he was re-imbursed). A report had to be prepared once a month of fees received and disbursements made.

There were no specific qualifications for deputies, nor did they have any predetermined shifts. They worked out their schedule among themselves. At the time Ferd Bryan was in office, there were five deputies, one of whom lived at the jail. They had no uniforms, and there was no hired cook at the jail; the prisoners did all the cooking.

There were only three patrol cars at the time, two Pontiacs and one Oldsmobile. The cars had no markings on them to identify them, no lights on top – only sirens. According to Mrs. Bryan, "it wasn't a custom in those days, but everybody knew the law cars."

Bootlegging was the big crime during Sheriff Bryan's term of office. There wasn't much theft – doors could be left open without fear of be-ing burglarized. There weren't many shootings either. Mrs. Bryan feels the building of Lake Lanier and the subsequent growth in population has made a big difference in crime in Hall County. She said that a Sheriff now has to be more of an administrator due to the population and number of employ-ees, but in Ferd Bryan's day they were "working sheriffs" receiving calls many times all during the night. If they ran into problems and needed assistance, they would call an off-duty officer at home. They worked long hours and expected to be called at all times.

Sheriff Bryan suffered a heart attack while on duty on Thursday, May 4, 1950, having been in office for one year and five months. He was attempt-ing to place a mental patient into a State Patrol car to take him back to Milledgeville. The patient went berserk and in the struggle, Bryan suffered a massive heart attack. He was taken to Downey Hospital (then in the location of the county parking deck), and was treated by their family physician, Dr. Burns.

Mrs. Bryan arrived at the hospital approximately two hours later and found her husband conscious, joking, receiving oxygen and able to recognize the family. She had gone home for some much needed rest when they called her to return on Saturday, May 6, but her husband had passed away before she returned. Sheriff Bryan's funeral and burial were held in Gillsville.

Governor Herman Talmadge appointed Mrs. Bryan Sheriff until a special election could be held (approximately 45 days later). Several people encouraged Constance Bryan to run in the election, making her one of sixteen candidates. She lost the election to Cal Wilson, but she came in second. She said, "I beat as many men as Cal Wilson did." She feels that being a native of Washington, D.C. and not a native Georgian hurt her chances to win. She carried the city of Gainesville in the election, but didn't carry enough districts in the county.

Mrs. Bryan was very proud of having served as a first lady of the county as wife of the "BIG LAW". She was especially honored to have served as Sheriff herself for a short time, and was very proud of her certificate signed by Governor Talmadge. She was a very bright, intelligent lady and held an interest in the happenings in Hall County up until her death.

Constance Bryan has gone down in Hall County's history as its first and only woman Sheriff. Her strength and determination at this critical time in her life should be a challenge to all of us. Mrs. Bryan passed away on December 16, 1980, less than five months after our first interview, and while I was still writing the original edition of this book. Her burial took place in Gillsville. I had learned to admire and respect Mrs. Bryan, and had visited with her several times. I miss her friendship.

CALVIN WILLIAM "CAL" WILSON

(6/14/1950 – 1960)

Calvin William "Cal" Wilson was born in Jackson County in the Dry Pond Community on July 28, 1901. After going through Dry Pond School, he helped his father on their farm until 1925.

While tilling the soil with a team of mules, Wilson fell in love with Ile Mae Ivey, also of Jackson County, and they were married on January 14, 1918.

Cal began his law enforcement career with the Baldwin, GA Police Department where he served for six months before coming to New Holland Mill as a special deputy. He later served five and one-half years in the State Revenue Service until he resigned to run for Sheriff of Hall County.

Calvin W. 'Cal' Wilson

Cal Wilson was one of the Sheriffs of Hall County who was noted for working long hours, sometimes day and night – a "working sheriff". He is noted for bringing to justice those who broke the law, regardless of who they were.

There were sixteen candidates in that Sheriff's race, one of whom was a woman, Mrs. Constance Bryan. Mrs. Bryan's husband, Sheriff Ferd Bryan, had died while in office and she had been commissioned by the Governor to fill the position until a special election could be held. Mrs. Bryan came in second with 1,423 votes to Wilson's 1,890 votes.

Sheriff Cal Wilson was Sheriff of Hall County for ten and one-half years, making his the third longest term. He assumed the duty as Sheriff with only two deputies on June 14, 1950, and left office on January 1, 1961, with thirteen deputies and one secretary. One of his sons, Clarence "Bo Bo" Wilson served as his Chief Deputy and Detective, and his youngest daughter, Betty, served as secretary.

Sheriff Wilson was on the job night and day, enforcing the law in the near and far distant sections of Hall County - 430.9 square miles of Georgia soil. With a staff of deputies, the Sheriff roamed the side roads as well as the main highways, particularly at night when offenders of the law were on the loose. Moonshine was the big activity during this period and the Sheriff and his deputies were involved in numerous high speed chases with liquor cars. Highway 53 W (Dawsonville Highway) is reputed to be one of the main routes for high speed chases.

Many changes occurred while Sheriff Wilson was in office. He was the first Sheriff of Hall County to go to the salary system, to have marked patrol cars, and to have uniformed deputies. Hall County got its first short wave radio base station for the Sheriff's office and jail in 1957. Prior to this, the cars had to communicate through the Georgia State Patrol, who relayed the messages by phone to the Sheriff's office and jail. Sheriff Wilson also had two plain clothes detectives.

Cal Wilson lived in Hall County for 36 years and was a member of the New Holland Baptist Church. He and his wife had four children, J. T. Wilson, Clarence "Bo Bo" Wilson, Sacele Helen Wilson Guthrie, and Betty Wilson Allen.

Sheriff Cal Wilson died of a heart attack at his home on Friday, January 23, 1970, at the age of 68. In his death, Hall County lost a very dedicated citizen and peace officer.

* * *

COLLECTION FOR SUSPENDERS
Sheriff, Whisky-Runner Run Hot Race; Sheriff Loses Pants, Law-breaker Wins

Hall County Sheriff Cal Wilson and State Patrolman H. H. Malone captured 102 gallons of non-tax paid whisky on the old Flowery Branch road Wednesday, but a faulty belt buckle foiled a feast footwork attempt to arrest the whisky runner.

The Sheriff and patrolman were riding on the dirt highway a few miles south of Gainesville when they spotted the car and pulled alongside to investigate.

Sheriff Wilson said he figured the driver would jump and run, so he bailed out of the patrol car as it slowed down to about 20 miles per hour. The driver of the whisky car immediately leaped and headed for the tall timber with Sheriff Wilson in hot pursuit.

The whisky runner scaled a steep red bank. Wilson almost had him at the top when it happened. A belt buckle slipped and down came the Sheriff's pants, and away the driver ran.

"I'd of had him if I could have shaken my pants off," Wilson sheepishly said on Thursday as fellow officers and others gathered around to take up a collection for a pair of suspenders.

The officers don't know the identity of the Negro man who got away. The whisky car's license plate is registered in the name of S. D. Cooper, Hancock Avenue, Athens, the Sheriff said.

(Variations of this incident appeared in *The Times, The Greenville News,* Greenville, S. C., and *The St. Louis Post-Dispatch*)

* * *

WATCH "DRUNK" ON WHITE LIGHTNING

Gainesville — Sheriff Call Wilson's "drunk" watch had to undergo a sobering up process before getting the time straight again. It happened as the result of a fracas on the courthouse steps as the Sheriff was arresting a man on a drunk and fighting charge. The man in custody suddenly started choking the other man involved in the fight. In order to force his prisoner to release the grip, Sheriff Wilson struck him on the head with a pint bottle of white lightning which he had earlier taken from the man. Soon after, Sheriff Wilson's watch stopped running, and he took it to a local watchmaker with the explanation that the timepiece was "drunk".

- Sheriff's Association Magazine

Sheriff Wilson and captured 50 gallon still. Summer 1953

Sheriff Wilson and his deputies were busy cutting stills and arresting moonshiners for several days in the summer of 1953.

Liquor, its use and abuse, caused Sheriff Cal Wilson's deputies to open one weekend with a number of arrests and raids on two big stills.

The deputies came across a 30 gallon copper still with miscellaneous equipment five miles off the Gillsville Highway. The still was in full operation when the officers arrived, but had recently been abandoned. Three hundred gallons of mash were destroyed in the raid.

Deputies also found a 50-gallon copper still in the Peckerwood district with four boxes of mash, or about 500 gallons. The elaborate setup included lanterns and jugs as well as the distilling equipment. All of this was confiscated or destroyed by the Hall County officers.

The still, equipment and mash, deputies estimated, amounted to an investment of more than $500 for the moonshiners. Deputies said that no arrest was made in either of the raids, but an arrest was pending in connection with the 50 gallon still.

In addition, two men were arrested after deputies found 10 gallons of white lightning in a house in the Belton district. The men were charged with possessing non-tax paid liquor.

CAL WILSON'S ADMINISTRATION

... FROM FEW TO MANY

*Cal Wilson being sworn in as Sheriff of Hall County in
June, 1951, by Frank Wood, Ordinary.
L-R: Harry Morris, Jailer, Cecil House, Deputy and Sheriff Cal Wilson*

*December, 1960 – Sheriff Wilson's staff has grown considerably since 1951.
They are shown here at the jail. L-R: (Front) Buddy Martin, James McNeal,
Jimmy Forrester, Pete Doster, Betty Allen, Judge G. Fred Kelley, Sheriff Cal Wilson,
Hall County District Attorney Jeff Wayne, Preston Tribble, Phil Moore and
Lonzo Forrester. (Back) Bo Bo Wilson, Pratt Reece, Q. B. Shelnut, J. R. Maness,
Lenward Cantrell and Theodore Woody.*

HALL COUNTY SHERIFF'S DEPARTMENT AND
JAIL ON JANUARY 1, 1957

Shown here are the 1957 Ford patrol cars and uniformed officers:
L-R — Buddy Martin, Q. B. Shelnut, C. W. "Bo Bo" Wilson, Harry Morris,
Dorsey Peek and S. E. Doster. In front are Sheriff Cal Wilson and
Bob Barton, a radio announcer for WGGA.

NO MORE ELECTION BETS!

*May 5, 1956 Fellow workers at New Holland Mill gather with recently
re-elected Sheriff Cal Wilson to grin broadly at another election bet payoff.
Jep Ledford, pushing the wheel barrow, wagered with Marvin Wood, riding, that Cal
would not win by more votes than the combined strength of his two opponents.
The outcome was obvious. Both second hands at the mill, Ledford and Wood are, in
this photo, taking care of their election wager, a wheelbarrow ride around the
extensive grounds of the mill. Said pusher Ledford, "No more election bets for me."*

HCSD 1957 QB Shelnut, Avery Cantrell, C W 'Bo Bo' Wilson, Sheriff Cal Wilson, Dorsey Peek, Harry Morris, Mr. McDougald.

HCSD c.1957 Ft Row: Virgil Mooney, CW Bo Bo Wilson, Sheriff Cal Wilson, Q B Shelnut, Phillip Moore, Dorsey Peek. Bk row: Buddy Martin, J. R. Manus, Harry Morris, Pete Doster

BETTY WILSON ALLEN

Betty Wilson Allen, youngest daughter of Cal Wilson served as his secretary while he was in office. One of her duties was tag sales, and as you can see, she had the honor of getting the first one.

1957 Betty Wilson is busy issuing tags. A. L. Carlin is the Clerk. Note: Hall County is number 11, according to population. The tag sales began January 2nd, and ran until April 1ˢᵗ. Two auto mechanics, Sandy Pitchford and Millard B. Kelley (author's father- in-law), 2ⁿᵈ and 3ʳᵈ in tag line, who worked for Clark Morgan's garage in downtown Gainesville, took a break from their work to buy tags. Mr. Kelley, a WWII veteran, always wore his cap bill turned up. He came home from the war, went to school under the GI bill and became a mechanic, raised a large family including four daughters and three sons, and later worked in his own shop on Browns Bridge Road at the family home where Mrs. Evalou Kelley still lives. His sons Richard, Ronald and Mark still continue the auto repair business there. Mr. Kelley passed away on May 5, 2005.

When Betty Wilson Allen learned I was working on the history of Hall County Law Enforcement, I didn't have to contact her — she called me. She is the daughter of Sheriff Cal Wilson and is extremely proud not only because he was her Dad, but because of his terms served as Sheriff of Hall County.

Betty is the widow of Harold Allen and is retired from the City of Gainesville. She was the youngest of her parents' four children, and was secretary for her Dad during his terms as Sheriff.

Betty allowed me to go through a very detailed and well organized scrapbook she had kept of her Dad's activities in while he was in office. Betty has a thorough knowledge of how the Sheriff's Department was run and the changes which took place while Sheriff Wilson was in office. She explained how all Hall County officials were placed on a salary system instead of the fee system beginning January 1, 1957.

For the first time, the county purchased the patrol cars and paid the deputies' salaries. Legislation passed requiring the county commissioners to furnish the Sheriff with the number of men and patrol cars he requested in order to patrol the county and perform their necessary duties. The county commissioners purchased four 1957 Fords and uniforms for six deputies. The Sheriff's salary was $10,000 per year, which was set by legislation and determined by the population of each county. All the deputies and one secretary were paid $300 per month. The Chief Deputy was paid $325 per month. All employees worked for the same monthly salary for four years without an increase. They received no overtime pay, and were off only one weekend per month and one day per week. However, when court was in session, no one was off duty.

Sheriff Wilson served as Hall County Tag Agent (Irvin Lawson was the first Sheriff to begin this practice) beginning January 2, 1957. The county received $.50 commission on the first 4,000 tags sold and $.25 on the remaining tags for the year. Hall County furnished two clerks to sell tags for three months. The Sheriff and his secretary sold the tags the remainder of the year. Prior to the Sheriff acting as Tag Agent, tags had to be ordered by mail from the State Capitol. The Sheriff, therefore, was merely doing this as a service to the people, certainly not because of the proceeds earned.

Betty said that the patrol cars were lettered "Hall County Sheriff's Department" for the first time in 1954, but the Sheriff's car remained unmarked. She said her Dad gave all his men a uniform for a Christmas present in 1955. Furthermore, he made Mrs. Sally K. (S.T.) Higgins the first known woman special deputy because of her duty as a Hall County

Visiting Teacher — she was in charge of school truancy. Sheriff Wilson knew some of the areas she had to work could put her in a dangerous situation. Mrs. Higgins received her badge and commission in 1954. These gave her the power to make an arrest if needed.

Betty Allen told of the long hours her Dad put in as Sheriff. During this period, the Sheriff was a working sheriff and was on call 24 hours a day, seven days a week. The Sheriff was personally involved in many of the arrests and raids conducted within the county. Betty was well versed in the activities in the Sheriff's Office as her Dad's personal secretary, and assumed many of the duties while her Dad and his deputies were out in the county. The Sheriff had to be a worker instead of an administrator during this time in history.

In talking with Betty Allen, she makes you believe that Cal Wilson was the best Sheriff this county ever had — and that he was the best father any daughter ever had. And that's the kind of respect any secretary/daughter should have!

Betty Wilson Allen — 2010

Betty Wilson Allen, a lifelong resident of Gainesville and Hall County, GA, graduated from Airline High School in 1953. While in high school, Betty was a cheerleader and she also helped her father, Sheriff Cal Wilson, in his office.

Her first job after graduating high school was with a local attorney and then with the Hall County Board of Education. On January 1, 1957, Betty became her father's full time secretary in the Hall County Sheriff's Office during his tenure in office. After the civil service test, Betty was hired on January 1, 1962, as a tax clerk for the city of Gainesville. At the time, she was the youngest employee in the office.

Betty worked the same job for thirty years, retiring in 1992, at the age of 57. On her retirement, Betty said, "the biggest regret in retiring from the city was missing the people." Betty enjoys people and history, and she has played a role in the history of Gainesville and Hall County during her life. She was very helpful during the writing of the first edition of this book, and she has been such an asset during the revision.

Thank you, Betty, for your service.

WILBURN L. REED, JR.

(1965 – 1972)

Wilburn L. Reed was Sheriff of Hall County for eight years. He served more than a quarter of a century in law enforcement. Reed was employed by the Georgia State Patrol and the Georgia Bureau of Investigation from 1942 to 1964 when he resigned to run for Sheriff.

Reed was married to Ruby P. Reed and they had one son, William Frank. Sheriff Reed was a member of the Sheriff's Association, Peace Officer's Association and Lakewood Baptist Church.

After his career in law enforcement, Reed ran a cattle farm in northern Hall County. He passed away at age 60 on October 4, 1978, of a heart attack while working on his farm. Hall County can be proud to have had a man of Wilburn Reed's caliber serve as Sheriff.

RET. PATROL CAPTAIN CARL MATHIS

Capt. Carl Mathis

Carl Mathis was married to Marguerite Mathis for 67+ years, and they had one son, Phillip. Marguerite died in April, 2009. Carl is now 96 years old and lives alone with his favorite puppy dog.

Carl started his career as a security guard during the building of Camp Gordon Military Base during WWII. He then worked 19 years delivering gas to the residents of South Hall County. While delivering gas, he got to know the people and the road network of the southern part of the county. In 1965, after Sheriff Wilburn Reed was elected, Mathis and Henry Delong had a job interview with the new Sheriff. Hubert Crow, Jr. had just been hired as Sheriff Reed's Chief Deputy. Carl Mathis and Henry Delong were the next two deputies hired for the new administration.

Carl said that in the old days, there was no job security for the deputies under a previous Sheriff; if the Sheriff lost the election, so did all the deputies who worked for him! The new Sheriff would bring in his own deputies, and if he wanted to, he would then re-hire some of the old ones – but it was entirely at his option.

Neither Mathis nor Delong had ever been in law enforcement. They had to purchase their own guns, ammo, belts and handcuffs – the department furnished the uniforms. The salary was very low – you had to really want that job!

Henry Delong lived and worked in the southern part of Hall County, which also gave him knowledge of the residents and roads. They were assigned to patrol that part of the county. Cody Bone and Ron Attaway were responsible for patrolling the northern part of the county. When Sheriff Reed was elected, all the patrol cars had high mileage and poor maintenance. There were many mechanical problems with the patrol cars. They had two-way radios and a female dispatcher who worked out of the Sheriff's office in the old courthouse. According to Mathis, she did an excellent job! Mathis said that Sheriff Reed was an excellent Sheriff and he enjoyed working for him. The deputies had to learn their jobs by on the job training. They didn't have to attend a police academy or qualify on the range with their weapons. They practiced on their own – if they wanted to.

Capt. Mathis said that Tom Whelchel and Sylvia Ladd, both former deputies, were rehired by Sheriff Reed because they had experience. In later years, all the old deputies were grandfathered in and were certified without having to attend the police academy because they already had years of road experience. Sheriff Reed lost the election after four years, and Sheriff England became the Sheriff for the second time. Mathis said that Sheriff England started job security by allowing all deputies to keep their jobs if they wanted to remain in the department. This was a smart move because the deputies were already trained and made a better qualified and efficient department.

Mathis rose to the rank of Patrol Captain and was very proud to say that all his men were like family. They all enjoyed working and being together – no personnel problems whatsoever. Every so often, Capt. Mathis invited the patrol shift out for a steak dinner at his expense. Having good harmony among his men enabled them to do a better job. According to Mathis, even in the 1970's, there was still just a north, south and local car. Two deputies per car for the north and south, and he rode local and was back-up when needed. He never asked his deputies to do anything that he wouldn't do. He led by setting the example.

Capt. Mathis retired in 1978; he personally feels that he had the happiest and best patrol shift. He has always been proud of his career with the Hall County Sheriff's Department. He was my first patrol shift leader when I was hired in October, 1974. I was a rookie and it was wonderful to have a seasoned Captain like him to teach me how to become a good officer. Capt. Mathis was like a father to all of us. We knew he enjoyed his job and he always put his men first. Retired Patrol Capt. Carl Mathis is a role model for many to follow. Thank you, Capt. Mathis, for your dedicated service to Hall County, GA.

RET. LIEUTENANT
BOYD HULSEY

Retired Lieutenant Boyd Hulsey

Boyd Hulsey was a lifelong resident of Hall County, raised in the Sardis area. He was a veteran of WWII, serving in the European theater. While he was home on furlough, Boyd saw Dessie Andrews at the home of a relative - she was to become his wife of 63 years.

After the war, Boyd returned to Hall County, where he worked for many years at Gainesville Mill. During this time, he jointly owned and operated a garage and two gas stations with his partner, O. J. Roberts, at the corner of Railroad Avenue and Atlanta Highway.

In 1965, Boyd was hired by Sheriff Wilburn Reed as a Hall County Deputy. He quickly rose to the rank of Shift Commander – a position he held until his retirement in 1988. He gave Hall County twenty-three years of professional leadership and dedicated service, and served under three

Sheriffs: Wilburn Reed, Ed England and Dick Mecum. His leadership traits will always remain in the Hall County Sheriff's Department. Boyd was known to be one of the best patrol car drivers in the Department during his tenure.

Boyd and Dessie's long marriage produced two sons, Larry Bryson Hulsey, who died in February, 1968, while serving in the U S Army in Viet Nam, and Eddie Hulsey, who once served as a Gainesville Police Officer.

Boyd Hulsey passed away on March 4, 2010, at the age of 84, and was buried at Memorial Park Cemetery with full law enforcement ceremonial honors including a 21 gun salute and the playing of 'taps', conducted by the Hall County Sheriff's Department Honor Guard.

Boyd was a dedicated Christian officer who served his country and the citizens of Hall County well, and was a member of his church, Community Baptist, for over fifty years.

To complete three generations of law enforcement officers, Boyd's grandson, Chad Hulsey, was sworn in as a Hall County law enforcement officer on the day his grandfather was buried.

RET. FBI SPECIAL AGENT SARAH PICKARD

Sarah Pickard receives her FBI credentials and badge after graduation from the FBI Academy in May, 1982.

Sarah Pickard was born in Chapel Hill, NC. Sarah's parents divorced when she was two, and she lived with her paternal grandmother and father in Chapel Hill. Her father sold fire trucks for American La France and his territory was the Southeastern US - Florida, Georgia, North Carolina and South Carolina. During a visit to the Gainesville Fire Department, one of his firemen friends set him up on a blind date. It was a match! They married and Sarah's father brought Sarah and her grandmother to live in Gainesville with her new step-mother, step-sister and step-brother.

Sarah graduated from Gainesville High School in 1971, and a family friend, Mrs. Jenny Broxton, knew she needed a job. She recommended Sarah to Sheriff Wilburn Reed who hired her as a clerk in the Sheriff's Office in 1972. Mrs. Broxton taught her the ropes.

Later Sheriff Reed lost the Sheriff's election to Ed England. Just prior to Sheriff England taking office, Sheriff Reed transferred Sarah to the Detective Division as a secretary; this was done to better her career.

Sarah was eager to learn more than clerical skills. She knew she had to advance in Civil Service to make more money, so she asked to become a matron along with her clerical duties, and was allowed to do so. Sarah assisted the detectives with drawing up search warrants, going on raids, and searching and interviewing female victims, witnesses, arrestees and prisoners. She helped transport female prisoners to court and treatment facilities, and she interviewed rape victims, family violence victims and female victims of other crimes.

Sarah attended any law enforcement training or seminars available. She was able to convince Sheriff England to send her to the Georgia Police Academy in Atlanta, GA, making her a certified Deputy Sheriff. During this time, the dress code for female employees in the Sheriff's Department was skirts. After an incident at the jail, when a matron either fell or was pushed to the floor, Sarah and others convinced Sheriff England that pants would be better suited for their work. The Sheriff agreed, but with a stipulation – they could wear pants, but they must also wear a white shirt with patches on both shoulders and a tunic over the shirt that covered their hips.

During the time Sarah was with Hall County, she graduated from the Gainesville (Junior) College with an associate degree in Criminal Justice.

Around that same time, Gainesville had two local FBI agents, Jim Burris and Dave Phillips, and they sometimes worked their cases out of the Hall County Detective's Office. Sarah was always available to assist them if they needed some immediate clerical work, since their typing pool was in Atlanta.

Upon their recommendation, Sarah approached Sheriff England about attending the FBI National Academy in Quantico, VA. As always Sarah succeeded, and in 1979, was the first female in the State of Georgia to graduate from the FBI National Academy. And she also made the Atlanta Journal in a write up for this accomplishment. Sarah's hard work and dedication was beginning to be noticed.

While in the FBI National Academy, Sarah received credits for her course work through the University of Virginia, which were transferred to

Brenau (College) University where they helped her receive a BA degree in Criminal Justice.

Sarah was hired by the Atlanta office of the FBI in May, 1982, and went back to the FBI Academy for Special Agent training from May to August, 1982. Then she returned to the Atlanta office and awaited her first assignment as an FBI agent. When it came she was flabbergasted. Her first assignment was in Honolulu, Hawaii!

The FBI already had one female in Honolulu, so Sarah was the second female FBI agent to be assigned there. She later learned that headquarters felt that the first agent needed a peer, so they asked, "What female has just graduated from the Academy and has some experience in law enforcement?" Turned out it was Sarah — that's how she got her first assignment.

Sarah reported to Hawaii in the early part of 1983. Since Hawaii is not part of the conterminous United States, she didn't get a house hunting trip but the agents in the office there found her a temporary apartment before she got there and had picked up her car from the ship it had traveled on and had it serviced and ready for her when she got there. Upon her arrival, she was met at the Honolulu airport by the other female agent, with whom she became good friends, and her new supervisor. Sarah worked white collar crime and civil rights cases while in Honolulu. She worked undercover on a drug case and learned that undercover work was not for her!

Sarah was on the way to a picnic on the beach on July 4th, 1984, when she got a call saying she was being transferred. Where? She was not happy to find out it was New York City. Moving from Hawaii to New York City was not accomplished as easily as moving to Hawaii. At the time, New York was the largest field office in the FBI and it was very impersonal. Because the squad she was going to was getting a new supervisor, no one called from New York to offer her any help in moving. She found her own temporary quarters long distance by picking one out of a travel guide. In the fall of 1984, she boarded a plane in Honolulu, at 11:00 PM, with everything she owned. She arrived in New York the next day at 6:00 PM.

At the airport, she and all her earthly belongings wound up on a curb waiting for a taxi. In her own words, she was 'so overwhelmed' she just sat down on her trunk and cried. A taxi pulled up to the curb and the driver loaded her belongings into the trunk and asked her where she wanted to go. Through her tears she handed him a piece of paper with the address. He kindly patted her on the back and said, "You'll be OK".

And you know she was! She stayed in New York five years, working white collar crime. She was the case agent in charge of the FBI fraud investigation of former Philippine President Ferdinand Marcos and his wife, Imelda. She traveled to the Philippines, Japan, Hong Kong, and France and recovered much of the artwork and personal property purchased by the Marcoses with money stolen from the Philippine and United States Governments. In 1989, soon after the indictments in the Marcos case were obtained, she was promoted to Supervisory Special Agent (SSA) - Office of Professional Responsibility (OPR) and assigned to FBI Headquarters in Washington, DC.

She was one of five SSAs responsible for overseeing or personally conducting all investigations regarding alleged criminal and serious misconduct of all FBI employees. This was one of Sarah's most sobering and rewarding assignments within the FBI. People working in the law enforcement community sometimes make bad decisions and, when that happens, there are a lot of outsiders who want to know why and whether the bad decision was of the heart or of the mind. Sarah worked just as hard ferreting out every bit of mitigating evidence in every case as she did proving or disproving the allegations. She said she feels like she helped some good people keep their jobs but she helped rid the FBI of some bad employees as well.

It was while Sarah was in this position that she reviewed the case of the first FBI agent ever charged with murder. She received all of the local law enforcement agency's paperwork on the case, read it and mulled over it, and told her superior "He killed her." The FBI opened a criminal investigation and worked it jointly with the Kentucky State Police. It was in the coal mining country of Pikeville, Kentucky, that the agent was convicted of murdering his pregnant informant with whom he had had an affair. After he pled guilty, he told where her body could be found. It was almost one year to the day after he killed her, that her body was recovered from a ravine beside a dirt mining road.

After the OPR, Sarah worked as an FBI inspector, checking field offices and FBIHQ divisions for compliance and adherence to performance standards.

Then in October, 1993, she was promoted to Field SSA in Springfield, Illinois, where she supervised a squad of Special Agents in Springfield and two resident agencies in Moline and Peoria. She remained in Springfield for about three and one-half years and was promoted again in 1997.

This time she became the Unit Chief of the Crimes Against Children and Indian Country Unit, a brand new unit in the Violent Crime Section of the Criminal Investigative Division at FBIHQ. The FBI has primary investigative jurisdiction on all federally recognized Indian Reservations. Agents assigned to investigate Indian Country crime are like local police officers - they investigate burglaries, thefts, murder, rape and the physical and sexual abuse of children, one of the most prevalent crimes in Indian Country. In her position as Unit Chief, Sarah wrote the FBI's investigative policy for all matters involving crime in Indian Country and crimes against children. Her Unit interacted with Congress regarding laws and procuring funds for personnel and non-personnel resources to fight the crimes under her oversight.

During this time, the Innocent Images National Initiative (IINI) was launched. Congress added $1 million to the FBI's budget annually specifically for the investigation of the sexual exploitation of children over the internet. It was Sarah's job to come up with policy and guidelines for conducting the investigations and utilizing the appropriated funds. Task forces were established in FBI field offices across the United States. Using these funds, agents were set up in these offices and specially trained for the explicit purpose of combating this crime. Everything pertaining to the IINI was paid out of these funds — personnel benefits, technical equipment, vehicles and their maintenance, and training.

The advent of the internet has led to an explosion of the crime of sexual exploitation of children. At the same time, however, the internet has become a major means of fighting this crime by using computer forensics.

From 2000 to 2003, Sarah was the Senior Assistant Special Agent in Charge of the El Paso, TX, division which sits on the border of Mexico across from Juarez. International drug smuggling was the most significant crime problem in the office and Sarah supervised all of the FBI's organized crime (OC) and drug investigations in El Paso. The majority of the agents in the El Paso Office worked tirelessly to identify and investigate drug trafficking organizations, develop informants and intercept international drug shipments. It was not uncommon for agents to intercept a tractor trailer load of marihuana and cocaine, take it to a secure location, completely unload and unpack a ton to two tons of drugs, photograph, test and weigh them, then repack the drugs and return the drugs to the smuggler. The agents would then follow the load of drugs across the country to its final destination so that the domestic drug trafficking side of the smuggling operation could be identified and arrested. Needless to say, there were a lot of federal laws and Bureau rules and regulations to comply with and a lot of coordination with other FBI offices, the DEA and local and state law enforcement agencies.

In 2003, Sarah was transferred to the Los Angeles Division, where she was the Assistant Special Agent in Charge of all OC and drug investigations in the division. Although Mexican drug trafficking was still an important part of her job, she had to learn about a whole new area of crime - Russian OC. Alone at home again on a big holiday - Thanksgiving 2003 - in a new city, trying to decorate a new house, it suddenly hit Sarah, "If I was home, I'd be with my family today." So she retired and came home after a 22 year career. Although her career wasn't one that movies would be made about, she went places and saw things and met people that she never thought a girl from the hills of North Georgia would do.

Now she gives back! She works for her church, First Presbyterian of Gainesville where she is a deacon, chairperson of the flower guild, and on the worship and operations committees. She helps her sister with their parents, plays cards, rides horses with her sister in law, walks and plays with her cocker spaniel every day and says she is the happiest she has ever been.

My interview with Ret. FBI Special Agent Sarah Pickard was impressive and extremely interesting. While her goal at the beginning was simply to work and make a living, this hard working and determined woman launched a successful career in a world where few women had gone before. Sarah, thank you for your work ethic — and thank you for your service to our country.

DEPUTY JOHN CRONIC

John graduated from Oakwood High School where he was a star basket-ball player. That's where he also met his wife, Doris, in study hall. Doris graduated and went on to nursing school at Crawford Long and became a registered nurse. John and Doris married and raised three children in the Chestnut Mountain area – Jan, Steve and Russ Cronic.

In late 1965, John was hired as a deputy sheriff in the patrol division under Sheriff Wilburn Reed. His first riding partner was Boyd Hulsey who had been hired a few months before him. John and Boyd were responsible for patrolling the northern part of the county – Murrayville, Clermont and Gillsville. They worked the night shift, twelve hours a day, with one day off a week. In addition to their regular job responsibilities, they also had to attend court, grand jury hearings, etc. with no extra pay or sleep. John said that some nights, after being in court during the day, he would be extremely drowsy, making it a long night on the job.

During the early days, one of his best friends and riding partner was Darrell Farmer. They enjoyed their jobs and working together; they had full trust in one another. John told of a time when he and Darrell went to arrest an escapee. A family member opened the door and threw out a pail of liquid on them – and then closed the door. Darrell got the brunt of it – a pail of Clorox! They had white spots all over their clothing and hats. Quick reflexes, naturally ducking their heads, allowed the rims of their hats to protect their eyes. Yes, they did arrest the escapee, who was hiding in the attic. They were fortunate to escape serious injury.

Another time, John and his partner walked into a situation when the arrestee reached over and picked up a loaded weapon and stuck it into John's ribs. John's partner then stuck his own gun into the side of the arrestee's head. So there they stood – a domino effect of loaded guns. Just picture the Three Stooges. Who would shoot who? Any way you went, someone was going to be injured or killed. According to John, he put his silver tongued talking ability into action. He told the criminal to drop his gun – and the arrestee complied! On that occasion no one was hurt.

During the early days the officers didn't have portable radios to call for back-up, so they had to rely on their partner and their own initiative. John saw just about every situation during his long career as an officer. In 1975, John Cronic and Charlie Tipton were awarded the American Legion Certificate of Commendation – Officer of the Year – Hall County Sheriff's Department. John Cronic carried himself with dignity and pride. He was a hard worker, his conduct was above reproach, and he served as a positive role model for all. He was instrumental in teaching young rookie officers the ropes; we did not have training officers. I was one of those rookies who learned a great deal from him. John always had a good attitude and was an excellent communicator. He knew how to defuse out of control situations. In the early days, the experienced officers would help new officers. They didn't go to the shooting range – they taught themselves to shoot on their own time.

John could not remember his salary when he started in 1965, but it was low. One had to want to serve; it wasn't for the money. After 15 years as a deputy, John ran for sheriff in 1980, against Fred Perra, Dick Mecum, Ron Angel, and Ed England. Dick Mecum, a Republican, won the race.

After that, John went to work for his brother in the security business, and later became the owner. He worked 19 years, 7 nights a week. He was on his way to work one night during this time and came upon a vehicle that had wrecked and was engulfed in flames. Disregarding his own safety, he pulled three little girls out of the burning vehicle. His action saved their lives. John was recognized for his heroic action by the Sheriff of Hall County and others.

John and Doris both now enjoy their retirement in northern Hall County. A special thanks and salute to you, John, for your service.

DEPUTY DARRELL FARMER

Darrell worked as a Hall County Deputy for about four years and left in 1973. He later worked for 31 years with General Motors. He and John Cronic had a close bond as riding partners; they still are very close friends. Darrell said that John Cronic was a well trained officer whom he trusted with his life, and that he really enjoyed having him as a riding partner. Darrell mentioned the escapee from the PWC and the pail of Clorox.

While riding together, he and John encountered many difficult situations, but by being a solid team, they managed to come out of all of them without any serious injuries. Darrell has high praise for his former riding partner — and John says the feeling is mutual.

DEPUTY CHARLIE TIPTON

June 1, 1975 Charlie Tipton and John Cronic receiving Officer of Year Award

Charlie was retired from the U S Army, and was the top pistol shooter in the Army. He had won numerous awards in competition, and he brought that experience to the Hall County Sheriff's Department.

We went to the police academy together and he shot a perfect score. The instructor asked him to help out on the firing range. He won Officer of the Year along with Officer Cronic in 1975, and he later served as Chief of Police of Oakwood, GA.

Charlie passed away several years ago at an early age.

Thanks, Charlie for your service.

SHERIFF EDWARD LEE 'ED' ENGLAND

1961 – 1964, 1973 – 1976, 1977 - 1980

Ed England was in law enforcement for nineteen years, twelve of those as Sheriff of Hall County. Many changes occurred in the county during those years, primarily due to the growth of the population. Sheriff England's ambition was for the county to be a safe and protected place for its residents.

Ed England was a lifetime resident of Hall County, born to the late Raymond John England and Maude (Ward) England. He joined the Air Force during WWII, where he served with the 8th Air Force in the European Theater and was honorably discharged in 1945. His grandfather, H. W. "Henry" Ward served as Deputy Sheriff for the late W. A. Crow, Sr. during his years as Sheriff.

England first entered into law enforcement on July 21, 1950, when he was hired by Hall County Sheriff Cal Wilson as a deputy, and later served as

Chief Deputy. He then joined the Gainesville Police Department in 1952, under Chief Hoyt Henry and served there until 1954.

Ed England was first elected Sheriff of Hall County on November 23, 1960, and took office on January 1, 1961, at the age of 39, making him one of the youngest Sheriffs in Georgia. When he took office, the Hall County Sheriff's Department had fourteen deputies and seven patrol cars. The patrol cars had long two-way radio antennas on the rear with a large silver star painted on the front doors. None of the patrol cars had air conditioning.

At the end of his first term as Sheriff in December, 1964, England went to work for the Flowery Branch Police Department as Chief and stayed there for twenty-one months. On December 28, 1972, England was again elected Sheriff of Hall County. He was re-elected on December 17, 1976, serving two consecutive terms — a total of twelve years as Sheriff of Hall County.

England was opposed in the Democratic Primary on August 5, 1980, by Fred Perra, Gene Cape, John Cronic and Ron Angel. England always had only one platform — to give honest, fair and impartial law enforcement to the citizens of Hall County. He and Angel were the top vote getters and faced each other in a runoff on August 26, 1980.

Angel, a former GBI Agent and U. S. Marshal, received 7,980 votes to England's 6,268, placing him on the General Election ballot against Richard V. "Dick" Mecum, the Republican candidate. Mecum won the election, and England ended his law enforcement career, saying he would not seek office again.

Ed England loved all of his officers and could always be recognized by his shiny black Buick and big white John B. Stetson hat — it had been a tradition down through the years for the Sheriff to wear a big white hat.

True to his word, Sheriff England did not run again and enjoyed his retirement, going on fishing trips to Florida with his friends. At the end of his last term, the Sheriff's Department had eighty-six personnel and fourteen patrol cars.

Sheriff England was a family man who loved his wife, Ardella, and daughter, Michelle Thrasher, and never forgot about the members of the Department. He had a total of nineteen years in law enforcement — twelve as Sheriff of Hall County. Along with Andrew J. Mundy, England served the second longest term of any Sheriff of Hall County.

Sheriff Ed England passed away on January 30, 2008, at the age of 86. He was a member of the Georgia Sheriff's Association and a member of the Gainesville Masonic Lodge #219. He was buried at Memorial Park Cemetery with full honors by the Hall County Sheriff's Department Honor Guard.

Hall County is grateful for the service Ed England gave to his country and to Hall County. After Ed England, the county would not see another Sheriff with a big white hat.

CHIEF DEPUTY S. R. "RON" ATTAWAY

Ron Attaway, Chief Deputy under Ed England's administration, felt strongly about training and how it upgraded the caliber of law enforcement officers.

Ron Attaway was born May 24, 1929, and was a life long resident of Hall County. He graduated from Lyman Hall High School, and served twelve years in the Army National Guard.

Ron began his law enforcement career with the Hall County Sheriff's Department on January 1, 1965, when Wilburn Reed took office as Sheriff of Hall County. After about a year as a patrolman, he was soon promoted to detective, and, after six years, became Chief of Detectives.

On April 4, 1967, Lt. Ron Attaway, at age 38, was the first Hall County Officer to be recognized as Officer of the Year for outstanding contributions to law enforcement. When Ed England took office as Sheriff in 1973, Ron was promoted to Chief Deputy.

When Attaway came to the Sheriff's Department, there were eight patrolmen, one detective, three jailers, the Chief Deputy, one secretary and the Sheriff. They worked six 12-hour days with no overtime pay and no extra pay for court appearances.

Chief Attaway remembered the trend of crime in the mid-60's as being largely auto theft and burglary. He felt that the lack of certain laws on the books contributed to the widespread auto theft problem. For example, possessing a vehicle with altered vehicle numbers or without a number was not against the law, so cars could be stolen, numbers altered and the officers didn't stand a chance to positively identify the automobile. There were some large auto theft rings operating in adjacent counties, Attaway recalled.

Ron Attaway felt that law enforcement education was important, and he had extensive training for his job. Perhaps the most outstanding of these was the eleven week session at the FBI Academy. He felt that decisions handed down by the Supreme Court during those years had dramatically changed the qualifications and caliber of the law enforcement officers of that day. There were stricter standards to go by, thereby requiring better trained people to accomplish the mission. In the later years of Chief Attaway's tenure, he said he had noticed a vast improvement in the quality of personnel as well as the training they receive. He felt the Sheriff especially must be knowledgeable as to the laws and guidelines for officers. "Either he (the officer) has to know the law or he's not going to do anything, because he's going to be afraid to act if he doesn't know what he can or cannot do", he said.

Attaway recalled that the office of Sheriff began its gradual change back in the mid-60's when the Sheriff became more of an "office sheriff" than an "arresting sheriff." He felt that the major responsibility of the Sheriff was setting policies and procedures, requiring familiarity with all law enforcement guidelines and standards.

Referring to the old jail on Bradford Street, Attaway cited the poor design as being the major obstacle to any efficiency of management there. In our interview in 1980, he said "If we built a new jail today exactly like it, it would be obsolete according to federal guidelines and standards". Even though it was originally designed to house 120 males and 8 females, its condition at the time of the interview would not allow that capacity. The arrangement of the cells, the inaccessibility of maximum security cells as well as poor observation sites for security were just a few reasons it was difficult to provide sufficient security there. Studies conducted of the old facility found that the strength and soundness of the outside walls would make it economically unfeasible to renovate it at the time. Attaway felt the design of the Main Street jail allowed its operation with the same complement of personnel or even fewer.

Even though there is a great deal of stress on any law enforcement officer, the Chief Deputy's position carries an even bigger burden of responsibility. He is on duty at all times, continually receiving phone calls and other demands of his time, and he must make decisions and act on behalf of the Sheriff most of the time. Chief Deputy Ron Attaway said he worried about the welfare of his personnel, which added more stress. There was no standard shift for him — he usually staggered his work hours and always tried to be on the scene when there was a major crime. It was imperative that he, like any law enforcement officer, had a wide knowledge of the law.

In his position, Attaway tried to maintain an outward appearance of calm, even if there was turmoil inside. He realized that decisions he made could affect the safety and welfare of his personnel as well as the public. He also felt strongly that good communication with his personnel came only through maintaining a good rapport and relating to them on their level.

In November, 1991, at the age of 62, Capt. Ron Attaway retired from the HCSD as Commander of the Detective Division with 26 years of dedicated law enforcement service. His career encompassed patrolman, detective, Captain over the Detectives, Chief Deputy and Commander of the Detective Division. He was a model officer who hired and trained many new officers.

Ron and his wife, Flossie, had four children, two of whom, John and Tim, also had successful law enforcement careers. Hall County was fortunate to have a man of Ron Attaway's knowledge, qualifications and level-headed judgment leading the personnel of the Sheriff's Department during his tenure.

Ron Attaway passed away on March 10, 1995, and was buried at Memorial Park Cemetery with full ceremonial honors by the Hall County Sheriff's Department. He was instrumental in making Hall County a better place to live, and Hall County is grateful to him for his service.

AGENTS HIT UNDERGROUND STILL SITE

Georgia revenue agents and Hall County Sheriff's officers raided a large underground moonshine operation at Chestnut Mountain near Gainesville on Saturday afternoon.

Officers said the 3,000 gallon capacity still, capable of producing some 300 gallons of white lightning per day, was located in the backyard of a residence located just off the Winder-Gainesville Highway.

The installation was camouflaged with pine needles, officers said, and was destroyed by dynamite. One person was arrested at the scene, but he was not immediately identified by arresting officers. Agents said the still appeared to have been in operation about two months.

- Daily Times, December 13, 1964

Officers Tom Whelchel and Sylvia Ladd inside house
where supplies were kept for underground still.

SCENES OF UNDERGROUND STILL OPERATION

Scenes of underground still operation

(Marijuana Raid in Hall County – January 18, 1976)
(L to R) Sheriff Ed England, Chief Ron Attaway &
Chief of Detectives Carlton Stephens

MOONSHINE STILL DESTROYED - 1980

On Friday, February 8, 1980, a thirty gallon capacity whiskey still was located and destroyed off Graham Road, east of Price Road in northern Hall County. The raid was led by Hall County Sheriff Ed England and assisted by Gainesville Police Chief George Knapp. Also, Captain Marion Darracott and other members of the Vice, Intelligence and Narcotics (VIN) Unit participated in the destruction of the still. Sheriff England was handy with a double bladed ax. This is a prime example that moonshine is still being made, but not like in the old days.

NOTE: Moonshine got its name from the fact that the whiskey was manufactured and run(moved) at night so that law enforcement officials could not see the smoke from the operation — made in the moonshine under cover of darkness.

LIEUTENANT JUDY FREE

Judy left the Gainesville Police Department and was immediately hired by Hall County Sheriff Ed England in April, 1974, as a clerk matron. She was responsible for caring for all the female prisoners while working all the jobs in the jail and detective office. She helped transport female prisoners to any location required – to prison, hospital, court or wherever needed. She was accepted by everyone in the Sheriff's Department.

Judy's husband, James (Porky) Free, was also a Hall County patrol deputy. He already had an application in with the Sheriff's Department when she applied, but she was hired before him. Later, when he was hired in the patrol division, Sheriff England didn't want a husband and wife to work in the same division. However, in later years, the ruling was rescinded, which allowed her a better chance for advancement.

Sheriff England gave Judy the opportunity to attend the police academy in 1975, and later she received her certification. She felt that Sheriff

England knew that it was the time to let women hold the same positions as men, and be eligible for promotion as well. He then began to send other women to the academy and allow them to branch out into other positions in the department. Sheriff England was the first Hall County Sheriff to send a female to the police academy.

TRIP TO MARYLAND

Sheriff England sent Judy and her husband, Porky, to Annapolis, Maryland to pick up a suspect who had robbed Gem Jewelry in Gainesville and was apprehended in Maryland. The Sheriff gave them $100.00 and told them to complete the trip in three days. On the first day the $100 was gone – spent on motel, food, etc, so they had to go into their own funds. When truckers saw an out of state patrol car moving on up the interstate, they fell in behind it – and Judy and Porky took a convoy of trucks with them to Maryland.

They picked up the suspect and headed toward Gainesville when they had a blow-out. The prisoner, in handcuffs, volunteered to change the tire. Later they stopped in Lexington, NC, and, after placing the prisoner in the local jail, got a motel and settled in for the night. The next morning they had to hustle to get back within Sheriff England's time frame. They were running over the speed limit and looked back to again see a convoy of truckers hooked up with them, driving the same speed as the patrol car. They brought the prisoner (along with the trucks) back to Gainesville safely and Sheriff England reimbursed them for their out of pocket expenses.

In 1988, a riot and fire broke out in the jail at the new Detention Center, but it was at night – not on Judy's shift. The SWAT team from Alto Prison was called in and stopped the disturbance.

Sheriff Dick Mecum promoted Judy to the rank of Corporal, the first female Corporal in Hall County. Finally, women were placed into the same promotional ranks as men! Sheriff Mecum promoted on qualifications and merits, not by gender. Later she was promoted to Sergeant and then to Lieutenant, day shift leader of the Hall County Detention Center. She worked the night shift, too, for a short period! Judy's career encompassed 30 years in law enforcement, wearing many hats – police traffic cop, clerk/matron, corporal, sergeant, and lieutenant. She was instrumental in training many new officers because, in later years, all new deputies started their careers by working in the jail before moving to patrol and other divisions if they wished.

Lt. Judy Free dedicated her life to law enforcement and has set the example for others in loyalty, integrity, ability, appearance, and participation in training programs which exceeded most other officers in her pay grade. She has a folder full of diplomas and certificates of training. Lt. Free accomplished all this through hard work, leadership and having the desire to serve the citizens of Hall County. She has blazed the trail for female officers to follow. Thanks, Judy, for your fortitude and service!

HORSEPLAY ON THE JOB!

Lt. Judy Free said she was written up twice for things that happened that she was not aware of. In the Sheriff's Department, a leader was responsible for what their employees do or fail to do. It wasn't funny to her then, but she talks about it now with a smile.

Some of her officers were involved in handcuffing one of their fellow officers to the plumbing in the bathroom, leaving him there to be found by the next shift. Of course, it was reported and Judy was called in to stand accountable.

Then there was another incident when some of her officers handcuffed a comrade to the rear gate at the Detention Center. The gate was electrically operated by an officer in the control room while monitoring a camera. The control room officer would playfully open the gate, and the attached comrade would have to run along with the gate. Then he would close the gate – and the unlucky officer would have to run or be dragged back. This game went on for a while. The handcuffed officer got his daily exercise.

Thanks, Judy, for sharing these stories.

Judy Free is also listed in the Gainesville Police Dept. section in Part IV.

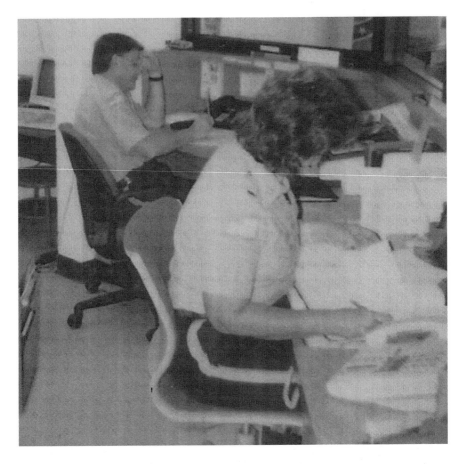

Judy & James (Porky) in the jail on Main Street

WHO RAIDED THE PIE CABINET?

In the 1970's, Hall County deputies could eat at the jail at no cost. During the day shift, they would take turns and eat lunch in the jail dining room. Most of the time Sheriff England and other high ups would be there, too. At night, O'Dean McDougal, the jail food/kitchen supervisor, would leave out food for us – bread, eggs and bologna most of the time, but sometimes ham, etc. The night shift would drop in between midnight and 1:00 am for their nightly sandwich. Someone would fire up the grill and most of the time the meal consisted of eggs and bologna sandwiches.

On this particular night, some of the hungry patrol officers stopped by for their sandwich. One of the alert deputies discovered that the pie cabinet was full of freshly baked pies. This ring leader was believed to be Porky Free! The next morning, McDougald, head of the kitchen, opened the pie cabinet to admire his work. He was shocked to discover that all the pies were gone – nothing left but pie plates and a few crumbs! It was obvious that someone had eaten up all the evidence. McDougald was not happy, and he immediately went to see Sheriff England – bad news for the night shift boys. McDougald's report went over like a lead balloon; there would be no sweets for the noon meal at the jail.

After a very short internal investigation, it was evident that the night shift guys were responsible for the loss of the pies. By this time, the whole department was laughing – everyone except Porky and his crew. Oh, yes, and McDougald! Porky and his night shift commandos ended up getting a butt chewing by the Sheriff, and he put the pie cabinet totally off limits to deputies. Sheriff England's face was firm about this incident, but underneath the surface he still loved all the pie eaters, along with all the rest of us.

NICKNAMES WERE COMMON IN THE 1970S

In 1974, many of the Hall County deputies were known by nicknames. It was difficult to know their actual name without checking their nameplate. I'll list a few of the names:

Big Ed	Sheriff England
Gray Fox	Ron Attaway
Strawberry	Dean Tipton
Big Eyes	Dale Sutton
Big Foot/Big Mac	Bob McMahan
Soul Brother	Fred Stringer
Malfunction	James Harper
Butch	Edward Strayhorn
Fireball	Willard Langdon
Mighty Mouse	David Garrison
Stan the Man	Stanley Bullock
Pork Chop	James Free
Lee Bug	Lee Grissom
Quick Draw	Jan McGraw
Jake the Snake	Jake Wofford
Double Ought	Randall Long
Boss Hog	Boyd Hulsey
Perkins	Ricky Armour
Roscoe Rules	Danny Cantrell

Even Sheriff England used them: "Is Malfunction working today?" he asked one day. We knew exactly who he was referring to – James Harper. Most of the deputies had name tags made with their nicknames; they wore these on holidays.

THE BASKETBALL GAME BETWEEN THE FLAMES AND B'S

In February, 1975, Sheriff England challenged the Hall County Fire Department (Flames) to a basketball game with the Sheriff's Department B's. The Sheriff did this to raise money for the Georgia Sheriff's Boys Ranch. The game was played at the South Hall Gym. Tickets were 75 cents with a musical half-time show! When the Flames came onto the court, they were announced by their names. But when they featured the lawmen — B's, they were fielding a team that was reminiscent of a bunch of renegades. They were announced by their everyday work names such as: "Mighty Mouse", "the Clown", "Pork Chop", "Taco", "Malfunction", "Big Foot", and "Soul Brother". The charity basketball game was a success, and Sheriff England was well pleased. The competition between the Flames and B's was high — both teams did an outstanding job, and the Georgia Sheriff's Boys Ranch was the winner!

The teams had a rematch later on at Brenau College Gym, for the same cause and just as successful.

DALE SUTTON

(CHIEF JAILER)

Dale Sutton, Chief Jailer, had many tales to tell about happenings around the Hall County Jail on Bradford Street.

Captain Dale Sutton was born August 22, 1923, and for the most part, was a life long resident of Hall County. He volunteered for the U. S. Army on April 25, 1942, and served until December 29, 1945, as a paratrooper with the 503rd Airborne Infantry Regiment. He made three combat jumps with his regiment: One during the battle for New Guinea (1943 – 1944), one during the battle for Noemfoor Island (July 2 – August 31, 1944), and one during the famous second battle for Corregidor (February 16 - 26, 1945). According to Sutton, on the day of the Corregidor jump, the wind was blowing at 35 MPH over a treacherous, rocky drop zone.

My initial interview with Dale was in 1980, when I was working on the first edition of this book. Dale was 57 then with approximately twenty years of law enforcement experience at that time.

Capt. Sutton began his career on January 20, 1956, when he was hired by Gainesville Police Chief Hoyt Henry as a motorcycle officer. His daily motorcycle riding partner was Officer Phillip Moore. They rode Harley Davidsons with the kick start, which would send the rider flying over the handlebars if not properly done.

Sutton advanced to the rank of Sergeant in the Traffic Division, but he left the department on June 29, 1967, when he moved to Florida. Later he returned to Gainesville, and on January 20, 1970, he was hired by Hall County Sheriff Wilburn Reed as a deputy.

When Sheriff Reed was defeated by Ed England in 1972, Sutton was promoted to the rank of Sergeant (Patrol Division). Then in October of that year, he was promoted to Captain and given a position in the Hall County jail, an office he held for most of his remaining career.

The old jail on Bradford Street was built in 1935, originally having a capacity for 120 males and 8 females. The meals were prepared by the prisoners under the supervision of the cook, O'Dean McDougald. The laundry was also done by the prisoners, supervised by the inside security personnel. Captain Sutton was responsible for eight security personnel who were under the direct supervision of Corporal Jack Porter, four outside jailers (including one female matron), and three shift sergeants. McDougald, the cook, was also under Sutton's supervision.

One of the inside security personnel, Mr. Sylvia Ladd, who retired once from law enforcement and then came back, was a big asset to the Hall County jail due to his knowledge and experience in jail procedures. Mr. Ladd was a good example for the younger jailers.

In my conversation with Captain Sutton in 1980, he recalled many episodes which had made his life at the jail interesting to say the least. One prisoner, who was drunk when he was incarcerated, was seen by a doctor but died while in jail. The old Hall County jail was famous for its 'fan club' which was responsible for its share of jail breaks. The fan club originated when prisoners found a way to break out through a ventilation system installed to improve the air circulation in the jail. Finally, when Dick Mecum was elected Sheriff, one of his first orders of business was to stop this escape route by having steel screens welded over the fans, and to change the jail procedure that enabled prisoners to get close to the fan.

Capt. Sutton also told how prisoners would dress up in different clothing and attempt to walk out during visiting hours. Visiting hours were twice a week on Wednesdays and Sundays. At that time, due to a lack of manpower and funding, there were no security personnel on duty from 10:00 pm to 6:00 am. There was only one officer at the desk who was kept busy on the phone and radio.

Dispatch was previously located in the jail, moved to the Detective's Office, and then on October 1, 1979, Central Dispatch went into service. Chief Paxton with Rural Metro Fire Department, and Chief Deputy Ron Attaway were instrumental in getting the system initiated. At that time, the Central Dispatch personnel were employed by the County Administrator and no longer had any connection with the Sheriff's Department. Supervisor Elaine Barnes had nine years dispatch experience with the Gainesville City Police Department and the Hall County Fire Department before coming to Central Dispatch. There were two dispatchers on duty at all times, one on the Sheriff's Department radio and one on the Fire Department and ambulance radio. There were seven full-time dispatchers – all females. Any emergency calls, whether Sheriff's Department, Fire Department or ambulance calls, went through Central Dispatch.

In 1980, Central Dispatch was responsible for any emergency calls in the county. Elaine Barnes, Supervisor, is on the far left.

Because there was no inside security at night in the jail, the specified prisoners (turnkeys) maintained a key to the inside lock. However, they had no way to get the outer door open.

Sutton recalled one incident when they took that key, made an imprint of it in a bar of soap, then the next day took a metal plate off a window and made a key which would unlock the door. The jail was housing federal prisoners at the time and five of them escaped. They sawed a hole large enough to get their hand through and unlocked the door to the cell. They went back to the bullpen area, and by tying one end of a blanket to a table and the other to a bar , then taking a broom and making a wench type pulley out of the blanket, they snapped the bar out, then escaped out the window. Sutton still had that roughly hewn key in his possession.

For many years, Sutton operated the jail with only one security man for the morning shift and one for the afternoon shift. To solve the problems created by a lack of security at night, the day shift man was moved to the 10:00 pm to 6:00 am shift. Sutton commented that manpower shortage had been a major problem at the jail down through the years. Sutton said then, "Now we employ more people at the jail than they used to have in the entire Sheriff's Department!"

The old Hall County jail was extremely difficult to maintain, according to Sutton, because of its solid concrete structure from ground level through three stories, including the roof. Most piping was built into the walls as they were poured, making it difficult to get into them for repairs. At the time the jail was built, galvanized pipe was used for all water and steam connections. After a number of years, it was prone to rust through completely. Sutton said when a bath facility was repaired in one cell block, a leak was sure to appear the next day in another area.

Times had changed by 1980, so that prisoners didn't go out on work details as they had in previous times. Therefore, because of their presence, it was difficult to give the jail a thorough cleaning. With the aid of modern (for 1980) pest control methods, however, roaches and other bugs were not the problem they had been in the past.

Dr. Hartwell Joiner, the physician for the Hall County Sheriff's Department, came by five days a week to check any prisoners who needed medical attention. Any prisoner needing dental treatment was transported to the dentists by deputies. Occasionally, a prisoner would need further medical treatment, such as x-rays, etc., and would be taken to the hospital. The jail personnel were also responsible for seeing that prisoners appear in court at their appointed times.

According to Sutton, the Hall County jail had three floors with a basement for a laundry and a boiler room. On November 12, 1980, the day of my conversation with Capt. Sutton, there were 99 people in jail. The year-round average number of prisoners (according to a survey conducted by Bill Huff) was 75. The number of female prisoners was variable. At that time there were no female inmates in jail, but there had been twelve females incarcerated the prior month.

Dale Sutton had over twenty years in law enforcement. At the later part of his career, he transferred to the Warrant Division. Within just a few years of our interview, Dale retired because of his health.

Captain Dale Sutton was the spark that kept gloom from entering the Hall County jail. He never seemed to run out of jokes, and was jolly and friendly in an atmosphere that could otherwise have been considered dark and dismal. He was my number one morale booster.

Sutton and his wife, Ruth, were married in 1968, and had five children. They enjoyed the summers during their retirement years at their vacation camper in Cherokee, N.C. Most days during inclement weather, he could be found at Lakeshore Mall chatting with old (or new) friends including his old partner, Phil Moore.

Dale passed away on December 19, 2000, and was entombed at Sawnee Memorial Gardens in Cumming, GA with full ceremonial honors by the Hall County Sheriff's Department Honor Guard and other local law enforcement officers.

Dale will always be remembered for his many years as Chief Jailer at the old Hall County jail, and for his humor he shared with everyone. Dale, old friend, thanks for your service to your country, city and county.

HALL COUNTY SHERIFF'S DEPARTMENT – 1973

ED ENGLAND – SHERIFF

John Adams
Jim Ash
Chief Deputy S. R. 'Ron' Attaway
Billy Barnes
Sgt. Charles Berryman
Capt. Cody Bone
Sgt. James Brookshire
Horace Buffington
Cpl. Stanley Bullock
James Cantrell
Gene Cape
Tony Carter
Bobby Cobb
Gene Colonna
John Cronic
Homer Davis
Henry Delong
Sgt. John Dyer
Harold Farr
Larry Fuller
David Garrison
Jack Gillespie

Arthur Jetton
Wanda Kemp
Sylvia Ladd
Randall Long
Robert Marchbank
Capt. Carl Mathis
O'Dean McDougald
Barbara McFarland (Walls)
Bob McMahan
Robert McQueen
Ira Pitchford
Jack Porter
Boyce Simmons
Gary Simmons
George Smith
Edward Strayhorn
Judy Strickland (Mecum)
Fred Stringer
Capt. Dale Sutton
Willie Thomas
Cpl.Dean (Strawberry)Tipton
Ricky Tumlin

David Griffin
Lee Grissom
Capt. Boyd Hulsey

52 total employees

Buddy Waldrep
Jerry Walls
Tom Whelchel
Jake Wofford

ERNEST EUGENE (GENE) EARLS, SR.

Ernest Eugene (Gene) Earls, Sr.

After twelve years with the Gainesville Police Dept., Gene joined the Hall County Sheriff's Department in the mid 1970s. Stories of actual police calls handled by Gene Earls and Willard Langdon (riding partners) follow.

Wild Man in the Trailer Park
(Officers Earls and Langdon)

One night we got a call to S T & T Trailer Park regarding someone running through the park acting like a wild man. Looking back, we should have known that anyone with a name like Jim-Bob would mean trouble! When Gene Earls and I got to the scene, the culprit was easy to find; he came running toward us like a crazed gorilla - yelling and screaming. We both jumped on him and started to handcuff him. Gene got one handcuff on his left wrist and that was it. Gene had one arm and I had the other. Jim Bob was high on something and he was lifting our feet off the ground. We did not have portable radios back then, and couldn't turn him loose to get back to the car radio. Luckily, someone in the trailer park saw our dilemma and called dispatch, telling them that we needed help. In a matter of minutes, a convoy of county and city patrol cars arrived. We finally got the guy handcuffed, but couldn't get him in the patrol car! He had long legs and big feet, and he would use them to push off from the side of the car. He was not getting tired, but by this time we were exhausted! Pepper spray did not affect him at all.

When we finally got him in the patrol car, we thought it was all over. Wrong! Jim Bob started turning flips and kicking the inside of the car. By the time we got to the jail, he had kicked both rear windows out of the patrol car, and was trying to crawl out. With the help of other officers, we got him into the holding cell. We were told by the jailer to leave the handcuffs on him. Breathing sighs of relief, we were thinking that this was finally over. Wrong again! He got up on the bench in the holding cell and dove head first into the steel jail door, splitting his head and face open. We had to get another patrol car – with windows – and take him to the emergency room. After crashing into the cell door, and with the help of the county physician and his well placed sedative, some of Jim Bob's energy had dissipated. All this happened during the first two hours of our shift, and we still had six more hours left to work!

"Help, Brothers, Help!"
(Officers Earls and Langdon)

One night a domestic violence call came in from the south side of Gainesville and Gene Earls and I responded. A man had hit his girlfriend on the side of her head with such force that her eye ball had jumped out of the socket. We called for medical help and got her enroute to the hospital, and then we turned our attention on the perpetrator. He started fighting us but we succeeded in handcuffing him, thanks to Gene's strong arms. When we got him to the patrol car, he started planting his feet against the side of the car and kept pushing us off. It was a dark quiet night, and the guy started yelling at the top of his lungs: "Help brothers help, help brothers help", on and on.

People started coming from all directions and we were soon surrounded – and they started tightening the circle! We were still fighting the subject and couldn't call for backup – still no portable radios. Out of nowhere a big (275lb) woman (whom Gene and I had helped before) appeared on the scene. She started cursing at the crowd and physically knocked down two or three of the men there.

By this time Gene and I had the arrestee in the car and quickly left the area. We went back the next day, thanked the lady for her help, and told her to call us if she ever needed help.

Just say the "S"
(Officers Earls and Langdon)

It was a beautiful sunny day, and we received a call to transport a mentally unstable person to Georgia Mental Health Institute in Atlanta. Gene Earls was driving, and we were set for a routine trip to Atlanta – this was going to be a good day on the job! We picked up the patient and, after handcuffing him, put him in the backseat of the patrol car.

Up to this point the patient hadn't caused any problems and everything was just fine. A few miles down I-985, the patient suddenly yelled out in a piercing voice "just say the 'S'! He kept yelling, "just say the 'S'! This went on for a while before he really went ballistic, yelling "I said say the 'S'! He was screaming, turning flips and kicking the windows.

Gene put the pedal to the metal and the speedometer was bumping 100 mph with blue lights and siren. I called GMHI and told them to have a straight jacket ready with help outside once we got there. I kept them posted on our location. I looked back and, to my horror, saw that the patient had broken the handcuffs! Then he kicked out the back window of the car, then both side windows. The wind was rushing through the car, but Gene was an excellent driver and didn't let up. The only thing that kept the man from jumping out of the car was his large size.

Shortly thereafter, we pulled into GMHI. Hospital employees helped us get him out of the car and into the straight jacket. At this point, I gained a lot of respect for those who worked in mental health facilities. Again, this was the start of the shift; we still had most of the day to go!

Redneck Drag Racing
(Officers Earls and Langdon)

Gene Earls and I were about to make our late night stop at the Hall County jail for our bologna and egg sandwich. It was around 1:00 AM when dispatch gave us a drag racing call on Gillsville Highway near the highway barn. We took off to the scene and found a bunch of rough looking, long haired types sitting in some souped up vehicles. No reason to be there, but they were parked as if everything was normal. We checked the hoods of the cars and it was obvious that the cars had been running hard. We told them of the report of drag racing and that if we had to come back, someone was going to be arrested.

We left, but as soon as we got back to town, we had the same call. So we returned to the scene — same thing, bunch of cars with hoods red hot, smoke and steam coming from some of them, and people just sitting there as innocent as could be. Gene told one of the drivers to get out of his car. The driver — a greasy, long haired specimen of Southern manhood — refused verbally to get out and used the 'N' word. Gene professionally asked him again to get out of the car; again the driver refused by using the 'N' word. I saw a look of pain come on Gene's face like I'd never seen - I knew something bad was about to happen. At that time, Gene Earls was well built and strong as a mule. He reached through the open window with both hands, grabbed two hands full of hair and clothes and snatched the driver out of the car — through the open window — and stood him up on the ground.

Once out of the car, the driver realized he had gone a bit too far with the 'N' word and had a change of attitude — his knees were knocking Yankee Doodle. Long story short, there was no more drag racing that night. We then went back to the jail and got our bologna sandwich.

I personally apologized to Gene — I was so saddened to know that my race was still using the 'N' word, especially to an experienced law enforcement officer.

Things like this did not happen all the time, but rest assured, there is never a dull moment in law enforcement. Lots of people have misinformation on the duties of a police officer. Some think that officers just ride around in a new patrol car and eat doughnuts all day. These stories show that officers never know what the next call will be like — what kind of danger they may walk into.

NOTE: A full biography of Officer Earnest Eugene Earls is listed in the Gainesville Police Department Section.

RET. LT. ART JETTON

Art Jetton

Art Jetton was 22 years old when he was hired by Hall County Sheriff Ed England on April 1, 1973. He was assigned to Capt. Carl Mathis' shift; then, after the Police Academy, Sheriff England selected him to be the Community Relations Officer for the Department.

Deputy Jetton worked in the Hall County schools teaching the children about law enforcement officers and the Junior Deputy program. Years later, many of these children have become police officers. Art taught safety programs, drug prevention, neighbor watch programs and first aid.

Starting pay for a deputy at that time was $485.00 per month. There were three rotating shifts, and everyone was friendly and enjoyed their jobs. If there was ever any friction within the shift, Capt. Mathis solved it. There was care and respect for each other.

At one point, Chief Ron Attaway needed a diver to search for stolen property thrown into Lake Lanier, so he told Art that if he would become dive qualified, he would try to get him a 5% pay raise. With the help of then Hall County Fire Chief Larry Williams and Dive Instructor Grady Youngblood, Art got his dive certification. However, the 5% pay raise never materialized.

Art was still glad to do this additional task. In 1979, the Hall County Fire Department had a few volunteer certified divers who dove if there was a drowning. However, the Hall County Commission abolished the county operated fire department and approved a contract with the privately owned Rural – Metro Fire Department, Inc. of Scottsdale, Arizona. Rural – Metro was the first fire department in the state that was not operated by a government or a non-profit corporation, according to C. H. Wofford who was executive director of the Georgia State Firemen's Association as the time. Rural – Metro began operations in Hall County on March 1, 1979, and they did not have a dive team.

So, as of March 1, 1979, Art Jetton was the Hall County Sheriff's Department Dive Team. Art recruited a few guys to join his team, and the Sheriff's Department paid for their training. They used actual drowning sites to conduct live training exercises – still using the same two instructors, Larry Williams and Grady Youngblood. The new dive team members were Randall Long, David Garrison, John Attaway and Jim Ash. The divers were ready and available 24 – 7. If someone needed them, they came – some even in their private vehicles. They used some of the dive equipment from the former fire department and had barely enough equipment to do the job, but they were a dedicated group.

I was a patrol deputy and on occasion provided security on the bank while these young, brave daredevils would submerge themselves in the lake searching for drowning victims. I remember once when a man climbed to the top of the highest point - the middle support - of the Dawsonville Highway Bridge and dove off. Art and his team stayed underwater searching for so long, I started to panic. I really thought they had run out of air. Finally, Randall Long surfaced along with the other members of the dive team – and they had recovered the body. These guys were young and did not fear danger. By the way, no hazardous duty pay for them – they were just dedicated officers. According to Art, Lake Lanier was always zero visibility; they had to search by feel.

Art Jetton led the Hall County Dive Team from its inception in 1979, and oversaw the recovery of more than 100 drowning victims from Lake Lanier before his retirement on April 1, 2003, after 30 years of service.

Art was also a member of the first Hall County Sheriff's Department SWAT team, headed by Bob McMahan. It was like the dive team, with very little equipment available to do the job. In the early days, these guys did the job with what they had. The first dive team used patrol cars and an old Army surplus vehicle to get their equipment to the drowning site. Looking back on the situation, they did an outstanding job with what they had.

Ret. Lt. Art Jetton was always friendly and willing to help in any situation. After his retirement from the Sheriff's Department, he served as a campus police officer at Gainesville State College.

In the early morning hours of Valentine's Day, 2009, at age 58, Art fell down 13 steps at his Gainesville home and broke his neck and fractured his skull. He later suffered a stroke that left him partially paralyzed. He continues to recover at home with the help of therapy. I took this interview by phone and Art seems in good spirits. Hopefully this dedicated officer will have a successful recovery from his injuries. Art, thanks for your service.

1976 ORIGINAL S.W.A.T. TEAM

GIB CRONIC	BOB MCMAHAN	DAVID GARRISON
ART JETTON	RANDALL LONG	GEORGE SPAIN
	DALE BARRETT	

Original Hall County SWAT Team - 1976
Top row (l to r): Gib Cronic, Art Jetton, Team Commander Bob
McMahan [A retired US Army Ranger], David Garrison. Bottom row:
Randall Long, George Spain, Dale Barrett. John Attaway and Jim
Ash are not pictured; they were in Sniper School.

Members were trained by Sgt. Bob McMahan based on his military experience as a Combat Ranger, and later members had the opportunity to attend the FBI SWAT training in Quantico, VA.

Later, under Sheriff Dick Mecum's tenure, SWAT team Commander Bob McMahan was the first Training Officer for the Hall County Sheriff's Department.

POLICE CHASE ENDS
IN FIERY CRASH

It was Friday, November 3, 1979, and my riding partner David Griffin had called in sick. We had just been assigned a brand new 1979 Dodge patrol car. The new car had a Plexiglas safety protector between the front and rear seats, which replaced the old wire cage.

Since I was a one man unit that day, my supervisor assigned me to ride locally and be available to back up the other units. It was a beautiful afternoon and it had been a fairly quiet day.

Then a call came in to the Gainesville Police Department that there had been a wreck on Atlanta Highway, and the people involved were fighting. Gainesville Police Officer Randall Scroggs and his partner responded to the call.

I was on routine patrol on Highway 129 South near Monroe Drive and was listening to the radio traffic. When Officer Scroggs and his partner got to the intersection of Broad and Dorsey streets, they observed two off duty state troopers trying to head off the suspect's car. James Beck, the driver of the car, was drunk! Beck had left the first accident on Atlanta Highway and was involved in another wreck at Broad and Dorsey. Officer Scroggs told Beck to pull over, but instead Beck hit the gas and fled down Broad Street, sideswiping several cars.

The city officers chased Beck and were joined by Hall County Sheriff's Deputy, Gene Cape. The city and county patrol cars pursued Beck onto the Athens Highway where, after dodging some traffic, Beck broke into the clear and increased his speed to over 70 miles per hour.

I had positioned myself on Monroe Drive in case the chase came out my way. I blocked one lane of 129 South with my patrol car, leaving two lanes open. I called the units in the chase and advised them of my location at 129 South and Monroe Drive, and I also told them which lane I had blocked. Shortly afterward I saw the fleeing vehicle approaching at a high rate of speed.

Beck had two open lanes so I just knew he was going to switch lanes at the last moment and maneuver around me. Wrong! Due to his intoxicated state and preoccupation with attempting to flee and elude the other officers, the suspect did not notice that the very lane he was driving in at 80+ mph was blocked by my patrol car!

The thought occurred to me that he was playing chicken – wrong again!

Beck's car struck the right rear of my new patrol car, causing a big explosion and fire ball. The patrol car spun around in the air 360 degrees, landing back near its original position. The gas tank had exploded and flames engulfed the entire vehicle. The police radio, mounted in the trunk, flew out and was found alongside the roadway approximately 150 yards away.

Initially I was knocked unconscious and awoke to see flames lapping from the rear of the car all the way over the hood. The Plexiglas protector behind the front seat kept most of the flames in the back seat area. If I had been in another patrol car with the old type wire cage, I would have been burned alive.

I had extra ammo in the vehicle in case I ever got in an extended firefight – and it began to explode! The fire and the smoke, along with the heat, were so intense that backup officers could not get near the car. Still dazed, I attempted to get out and then realized I was still in my seat belt. I finally managed to get the belt unfastened and jumped out of the car. After a few steps I fell to the ground.

When the fire department got there, the rear tires and the ammo in the car were exploding — fellow officers thought I was still inside the car. The firemen also thought I was still in there, but soon they found me in the grass face down. I survived with a mild concussion, a few small burns and singed hair.

The firemen were heroes! They disregarded the exploding ammo and put the fire out. Beck's car ricocheted to the left and came to rest facing south in the median between the lanes. The driver was thrown from the vehicle and landed in the grassy median. We were both taken to Northeast Georgia Medical Center and treated and released. I was allowed to go home and Beck went to the Hall County jail!

Chief Ron Attaway was responding to the scene, coming down I – 985 at a high rate of speed. His right front tire blew out, but he kept driving. He arrived on three wheels — afterwards, his car had to be towed, too. To put it mildly, there were some officers who were very unhappy with Beck, but they were professional and arrested him without any undue force. The looks on their faces told their feelings.

I got hugs from every officer there, including the firemen! Officer Gene Cape said he was almost ready to take serious action when Beck's car hit my patrol car. He said that if Beck had gotten through, he would have had to put a few holes in Beck's car. He said, "Some people might not agree with that, but are you going to let him go out and hit a carload of kids?"

City and county emergency vehicles had converged on the scene in a matter of minutes. This beautiful November afternoon had turned into a nightmare because of a drunk driver.

Thanks to all my city and county comrades for coming to my rescue.

Because of this incident, I was later nicknamed "Fireball".

DETECTIVE LEE GRISSOM

Deputy Lee Grissom was wounded in the line of duty as a Hall County Deputy.

Hall County Deputy Lee Grissom was a Vietnam veteran who was severely wounded while serving with the U. S. Navy Seabees. Lee had a big scar on the back of his neck and shoulder blade, and walked with a limp. He could have drawn disability for his wounds, but instead he worked a regular shift as a patrolman and later as a Sergeant – Detective. Grissom was a 16 year Hall County law enforcement veteran who had special skills in solving burglaries and thefts – he was the best.

Lee had been with the Sheriff's Department for a few years when, on the night of February 27, 1974, he and his partner, Bobby Cobb, answered a disturbance call to a trailer at Greenway's Mobile Home Park in Rabbittown on Highway 13 North.

When the two officers approached the trailer, Deputy Grissom was shot in the abdomen by a suspect armed with a .22 caliber rifle. Cobb wounded the suspect in the shoulder with a shotgun blast while he was attempting to escape out the back door of the trailer. Then, aided by other officers, Cobb arrested the suspect, who later received a five year sentence for shooting an officer.

Officer Melvin Long of the Gainesville Police Department was the first back-up officer to arrive at the scene, even though it was out of his jurisdiction. Officer Long rushed Deputy Grissom — code 3 — in his city patrol car to the Northeast Georgia Medical Center for treatment. Officer Long was instrumental in saving his fellow officer's life. It was six weeks before Grissom recovered from this wound.

In the latter part of his law enforcement career, Lee developed melanoma cancer, and died on October 7, 1986, at the young age of 44. He had pain every day from his war injuries, but he never complained, friends said. As he was fighting the cancer that would end his life, his friends again said that he did not complain.

Lee Grissom was a dedicated officer who was liked by all his peers. He was a hard worker and gave his job 100 % at all times. He served his country and Hall County in an honorable and brave way. Lee, a job well done; you will always be missed and remembered by your fellow officers and the citizens of Hall County, Georgia.

PERSONNEL LISTING – HALL COUNTY SHERIFF'S DEPARTMENT

November, 1980

E. L. (Ed) England, Sheriff

S. R. (Ron) Attaway, Chief Deputy

JAIL

CHIEF
Dale Sutton

SERGEANTS
Billy Barnes
Stan Bullock
Dean Tipton

JAILERS
Rudy Bromley
Bobby Cobb
Judy Free
James Jackson

SECURITY
Robert Acree
Joe Cooper
Gib Cronic
Sylvia Ladd
Curt Lance
Jack Porter, Cpl.
Loy Priest
Richard Robertson

PATROL DEPUTIES

CAPTAINS
Cody Bone
Boyd Hulsey
Ed Strayhorn

SERGEANTS
Lee Grissom
Randall Long
Bob McMahan

DEPUTIES
John M. Adams
Rickey Armour
James Brookshire
Danny Cantrell
David Dearman
Donnie Edge
Harold Farr
James Free
Kenneth Freeman
David Garrison
Lanier Gilmer
Charles Haley
James Harper
Gene Hodge
Darrell Ivey
Randall Kirsh
Willard Langdon
Robert McQueen
Phil Moore
Jimmy Motes
John Murphy
Robert Pilgrim
Dennis Seymour
Gary Smith
George Spain
John Tullis
Rickey Tumlin
Sonny Turner
Steve Tyner
Jackie Wimpey
James Wofford

DETECTIVES

CHIEF
Carlton Stephens

CAPTAINS
Tony Carter

SERGEANT
Steve Howard

DETECTIVES
Barbara McFarland
Sarah Pickard
Tommy Mefferd
Jerry Walls

VIN
Jim Ash
John Attaway
Dan Bishop

RECORDS CLERKS
Rebie Brown
Wilda Southers
Thelma Tweedell

COURTS & CIVIL

CHIEF
Tom Whelchel

CAPTAIN
Buddy Waldrep

SERGEANT
Charles Berryman

CRIME PREVENTION
Art Jetton, Sgt.
H. C. Moore

STEP
Dale Barrett
David Griffin
Carlton Sosebee
John Sisk

COOK
O'Dean McDougald

PROPERTY OFFICER / ADM. ASST

James Cantrell

Hall County Sheriff's Department December, 1980
(Sheriff Elect Mecum on lower left)

RON ANGEL

Ron Angel defeated Sheriff Ed England in the Democratic Primary of 1980

The stage was set and all the cast lined up for what was to be one of the most exciting Sheriff's races in Hall County history. The participants included incumbent Sheriff Ed England and his four Democratic opponents Fred Perra, John Cronic, Gene Cape and Ron Angel. On the sidelines, waiting for his part in the action, was Republican candidate, Richard V. (Dick) Mecum. The Democratic Primary on August 5, 1980, produced two candidates for a runoff – Ed England and Ron Angel.

Angel, a former GBI agent and U. S. Marshal, conducted a door to door campaign, promising to bring to the Hall County Sheriff's Department a more professional and organized approach to combating crime in the area. He offered 22 years of experience in the field of law enforcement, most of which was spent in investigative work. Angle had the support of defeated Democratic candidates Fred Perra and John Cronic.

Sheriff England ran on his record, as he had been in office for three terms, a total of twelve years. But on August 26, the day of the runoff, Angel easily defeated England with 7,980 votes to England's 6,268 in a heavy turnout of more than fifty percent of Hall County's eligible voters. Sheriff England said this marked the end of his law enforcement career, having served the second longest term of any Sheriff in Hall County. He wished Angel the best of luck and said he would not seek office again.

At this point in the race, Dick Mecum, who had been campaigning in the background, came on stage to square off with Angel for the final act – the general election. Both men conducted a door to door, person to person campaign, answered questions during forums (one was a broadcast on radio sponsored by the Gainesville – Hall County League of Women Voters). Angel and Mecum ran a clean and professional race, both highly qualified and trained for the office they were seeking.

On November 4, 1980, it was election day in Hall County – time for the final curtain call. As with all races, there can be only one winner, and Angel was defeated by Dick Mecum by 3,137 votes, bringing to Hall County their first Republican Sheriff.

SHERIFF RICHARD V. "DICK" MECUM

1981 - 1992

Dick Mecum - Hall County's first Republican Sheriff

On May 30, 1980, Richard V. 'Dick' Mecum paid his qualifying fee of $750.00 to run for the office of Sheriff of Hall County, Georgia. He didn't know it, but he was about to make history, and change the sheriff election system forever in Hall County. He was seeking office as the first Republican Sheriff of Hall County, GA.

Immediately, he hit the ground running, working from daylight to late evenings. Mecum was seeing approximately 200 citizens a day; this increased to about 400 citizens by the end of the campaign. You could see him on the street corners waving at the passing motorists, with signs reading "Me for Mecum".

Mecum ran unopposed in the August 5th Republican Primary. Throughout past history, Democrats had always controlled the Sheriff's race – until this time. On November, 4, 1980, Richard V. 'Dick' Mecum became the first Republican Sheriff of Hall County, Georgia. Mecum, age 40, defeated Democratic nominee Ron Angel with a vote tally of 11,671 to Angel's 8,534, as 66 percent of the eligible voters turned out for the election.

Mecum carried 21 of 31 precincts, while Angel, who defeated incumbent Ed England in the Democratic Primary runoff, won the Friendship, Polkville, Clinchem, Gillsville and Flowery Branch precincts. According to Dick Mecum, organization was the key to his victory, and he pledged he would "take that kind of organization to the Sheriff's Department".

Dick Mecum was born October 2, 1940, in Galesburg, Illinois, to Clark and Gertrude Mecum. His family moved to Fort Collins, Colorado in 1950, where he grew up and attended school. He is married to the former Judy Clark of Gainesville.

Before winning the Sheriff's race, Mecum had been in law enforcement for 13 years. Starting in Colorado as a patrolman and rising to the rank of major, he also had been a major with the University of Georgia Police Department, Director of the Northeast Georgia Police Academy, and supervisor with the Georgia Police Academy. He is a U. S. Navy veteran with four years of service.

After being transferred to Athens, GA, in his employment, Mecum attended the University of Georgia and earned a Bachelors degree in Business Administration in 1977. In 1987, he completed a Master's degree in Public Administration from Brenau College.

Dick Mecum was the first Sheriff of Hall County with a college degree, and the first Sheriff in the State of Georgia to hold a Masters degree. Therefore, with his training, education and experience, Hall County voters elected the most qualified Sheriff in the history of the county. Sheriff

Mecum was equipped with the managing skills to make the Sheriff's Department into a professional and organized law enforcement agency by utilizing modern and scientific methods of fighting crime. The time had come in Hall County history for the department to be upgraded and modernized in order to accommodate the growing population and the changing times.

When Dick Mecum took office as Sheriff of Hall County at midnight on January 1, 1981, he had a total of 83 total personnel, three patrol cars on duty with two-man units, two patrol districts – North and South, and a shift supervisor riding local as backup. The jail had approximately sixty male inmates – no females.

The department leaders were as follows: Chief Deputy Ron Attaway, Chief of Detectives Capt. Carlton Stephens, Cmdr. of the jail, Dale Sutton, and Court Services Capt. Tom Whelchel. There were three (8 hour) patrol shifts that rotated each month.

One of the first items on Sheriff Mecum's agenda was to eliminate the well known "fan club" at the old jail. Inmates had been escaping frequently through the large ventilation fans on the second and third floors at the back of the building by tying bed sheets together and rappelling to the ground. This practice was stopped by having steel screens welded over the outside fan openings, and inmate rules and enforcement regulations were also changed. That took care of the problem.

In addition, Sheriff Mecum implemented photo I. D. for all members of the Department and created a new policy and procedure manual. He began procuring modern equipment such as portable radios for patrol deputies. For the first time, they had immediate contact with dispatch while outside their patrol car. He changed the rotating shifts that had been a hallmark of the department for years to permanent eight hour shifts, and he was the first Hall County Sheriff to allow females to become patrol officers. In March, 1981, Mecum purchased ten new Chevrolet Impala patrol cars, and put one deputy in each. Now one deputy was doing the same work as the former two-man patrol units.

L to r: Sheriff Dick Mecum & Capt. Ken Grogan,
certified Hall County divers, preparing for a dive

Dick Mecum was the first Sheriff of Hall County to be a certified diver. He was a hands on sheriff who was present at major crime scenes in order to provide his subordinate leaders with any assistance needed. Plus, at times he participated with the dive team in recovering drowning victims. He knew when to manage the office and when he was needed in the field. At the end of his tenure, the department had grown to approximately 240 personnel.

Sheriff Mecum did so much to improve the department, it is almost impossible to list everything. I will attempt to list some of his accomplishments during his 12 year tenure as Sheriff of Hall County:

❖ Established a law enforcement radio frequency for the Sheriff's Department. Prior to 1981, the Hall County Sheriff's Department shared a radio frequency with the Gainesville Police Department.

❖ Increased the patrol districts from two districts to ten districts to provide Hall County with greater concentrated patrol and to respond more rapidly to calls for service.

❖ Stated the first law enforcement precinct stations in Hall County at Flowery Branch and Clermont in order to keep patrol units closer and more responsive to their patrol districts.

❖ Established a Training Division, and started the Field Training Officer Program for the training of newly hired Deputies; upgraded training for Departmental In-Service, advanced and specialized training courses; and established the Law Enforcement Training Network (LETN) to give the Department exposure to national training and procedural methods.

❖ Established a Property and Evidence Division to handle all property and evidence recovered by Deputies and to maintain a chain of custody for court case evidence.

❖ Established operational divisions in the Department for Detention Center, Courts, Detectives and Patrol.

❖ Started a Juvenile Division to work closely with the County Schools, Juvenile Court and the Department of Family and Children Services in the handling of juvenile offender and abuse crimes committed against children.

❖ Established a bookkeeping/accounting system to provide accurate record of monies received by the Department.

❖ Started highly trained SWAT and Hostage Negotiation Teams that have been instrumental in numerous high-risk situations requiring their abilities. In national competition these teams have consistently had high rankings.

❖ Began an escort by Deputies of High School bands and ball teams to games and events held outside of Hall County.

❖ Established school crossing guards to free up Deputies to be more responsive for calls for service and patrol.

❖ Established a Traffic Enforcement Division to concentrate on traffic problems; a Lake Patrol to increase patrols in our lake parks and the neighborhoods around the parks; a Community Oriented Policing to develop a closer working relationship between the community and law enforcement; a Grid Patrol to analyze criminal activity for a more proactive patrol effort.

❖ Upgraded the Recovery/Rescue Dive Team with new equipment and dive boat. Much of the equipment and the boat were acquired at no cost to the taxpayer.

❖ Began programs for inmates at the Detention Center involving GED, reading, and several other learning and educational programs.

❖ Began the "Buckle up Bear" safety programs in the county schools to educate children on the need for seat belt use. This program has received State and National recognition for its education success.

❖ Established the Multi-Agency Narcotics Squad (MANS) in conjunction with the Gainesville and Oakwood Police Departments. MANS has been recognized as one of the more effective illegal drug repression units of its kind in the State.

❖ Computerized all Sheriff's Department records and reporting systems and all of the Detention Center's arrest/booking procedures and all inmate activities, increasing greater information flow and access.

❖ With the cooperation and assistance of the Hall County School System, the Drug Abuse and Resistance Education (DARE) Program was established. This has proven to be a very successful program.

❖ Established a computerized fleet maintenance program that has been used to significantly reduce costs of maintenance and upkeep of all Department vehicles.

❖ Worked to become the first law enforcement agency in the nation to implement the new FBI crime reporting system with both written and computer reporting.

❖ Established the Crime Scene Technician Division to bring increased amounts of skill, expertise and technology into evidence gathering at crime scenes.

❖ Became the first law enforcement agency in Georgia to establish an inmate Work Release facility. Also, a House Arrest Program was started. Both programs have paid for themselves and provide inmates an opportunity to repay victims and to support their families while in jail. This has become an example of alternative sentencing visited by several local government organizations throughout the Southeastern United States.

❖ Increased security requirements for the Hall County Courthouse.

❖ Was instrumental in getting new laws passed to strengthen the Hall County Civil Service to increase the job protection for all Hall County employees working for Constitutional Officers.

❖ Worked for, designed, and established one of the most modern law enforcement and Detention Centers in Georgia. The Detention Center is now capable of housing over 500 inmates.

- ❖ Started inmate medical programs in the Detention Center with annual inspections by the Georgia Medical Association.
- ❖ Established a Polygraph Section to assist in criminal investigations.
- ❖ Established a Medical Examiner in Hall County to provide increased investigative knowledge in criminal investigations.
- ❖ Increased Deputy safety and protection by providing bullet proof vests, portable radios, and upgrading their revolvers to semi-automatics.

Sheriff Mecum served three terms (12 years) as Sheriff, and retired at the end of 1992. During his tenure, the inmate population at the jail increased from 60 to nearly 400. Calls for service increased from 12, 400 in 1980 to nearly 40,000. The population of Hall County increased 30% during that time; the overall crime rate – burglary, theft, robbery and auto theft – remained lower than the crime rate of fifteen years prior.

Through his hard work and leadership, Dick Mecum shaped the Sheriff's Department into a modern, elite department, second to none. When he left office, the Hall County Sheriff's Department was recognized throughout Georgia as state of the art.

NOTE: Richard V. Mecum was appointed by President George W. Bush as the United States Marshall for the Northern District of Georgia following U. S. Senate confirmation on August 12, 2002. Currently, he is still serving in this capacity.

DICK AND JUDY MECUM

*Sheriff Dick Mecum and Captain Judy Mecum made up the first
Sheriff and wife team ever to serve the citizens of Hall County.*

Holding an Associates Degree in Criminal Justice, Judy Mecum began her career in the early 1970's as a secretary in the sheriff's office and retired after a successful career in 1997. She worked directly for the Sheriff and, in addition to clerical duties, she was responsible for the collection and accounting of all monies paid.

In 1977, Judy attended the Northeast Georgia Police Academy in Athens and became a certified deputy sheriff. After attending the academy, Judy returned to her clerical job with the Hall County Sheriff's Office.

It was during her training at the police academy that she met her future husband, Dick Mecum, an instructor at the academy, and they were married January 28, 1978. They each brought four children into the marriage; six girls and two boys.

Dick Mecum was elected Sheriff of Hall County in 1981. That same year, Judy transferred to the Detective Division and established the Hall County Sheriff's Juvenile Division. Later the division was expanded to include five investigators. While head of Juvenile Investigations, she was involved in numerous high profile child abuse and child molestation cases. Judy also established community awareness programs in child abuse prevention for teachers, parents and children.

In 1989 Judy became the first Juvenile Investigative Sergeant, and created a "Seat Belt Safety Program," teaching second graders the theme of "Bear to Buckle Up" — and received State and National recognition for its educational success. This program was the first to allow officers into the school system for educational purposes.

She became the first female Juvenile Lieutenant (1990), and the first female Captain over the Criminal Investigative Division (1992).

After Sheriff Mecum's third term ended in 1992, he chose not to run for re-election. Judy returned to the Juvenile Division in February, 1993. Judy received many certificates and honors for her loyal service to the Hall County Sheriff's Department. She was a member of the Georgia Women in Law Enforcement and she was one of six nominees for Woman of the Year — 1990 among Georgia Women in Law Enforcement.

She was recognized by the VFW Auxiliary for the State of Georgia for working with young people in presenting her programs for safety in the area of drugs and child abuse.

Judy ran for sheriff in 2000, but lost to Steve Cronic, making her the second female to ever run for the office of Sheriff of Hall County and the first female to run as Republican.

Judy has devoted her life as a public servant and protector, especially to helping the children of Hall County. This distinguished officer has been instrumental in making a change in the male dominated police force. She is a seasoned officer who broke down barriers which will benefit many who will follow her.

Thank you, Judy Mecum, for your service to the citizens of Hall County.

(Photo Courtesy Milton Martin Toyota & The Times)

Hall County Sheriff's Department Leaders – 1986
(l to r) Capt Ron Attaway, Capt James Ash, Major Tony Carter, Capt Buddy Waldrep, Capt E. E. Strayhorn, Jr.

(Photo Courtesy Milton Martin Toyota & The Times)

Hall County Administrative Division

Ft Row – Sandy Bell, Debbie Seabolt, Connie Dearman.
2nd Row – Rebie Brown, Barbara McFarland, Linda Mauney, Jimmy Forrester,
Charlie Berryman. Bk Row – H C Moore, Ed Barfield, James Brookshire,
Ricky Tomlin, Capt Buddy Waldrep.

(Photo Courtesy Milton Martin Toyota & The Times)

Hall County Detective Division

Ft Row — Hope Micolli, Judy Mecum, David Dearman, Ron Attaway. Bk Row — James Harper, John Murphy, Jerry Walls

(Photo Courtesy Milton Martin Toyota & The Times)

Hall County STEP and DUI
(Lt to Rt) Sgt Gib Cronic, Jackie Wimpy, Dale Barrett, Frank Sosebee.

(Photo Courtesy Milton Martin Toyota & The Times)

Hall County Sheriff's Patrol:
A Watch
(Lt to Rt) Ed Clark, Wilburn Turner, Lourdes Bruce, Jimmy Motes, Terry English,
Randall Kersh.

(Photo Courtesy Milton Martin Toyota & The Times)

B Watch Sheriff's Patrol
Ft Row — Robert Pilgrim, Lt Robert McQueen, Jim Henson.
Bk Row — Sgt Dennis Seymour, Wilda Southers, Trent Dubose, David Sullivan,
Eddie Troutman, Carl Dietrich, Jessie McGee

(Photo Courtesy Milton Martin Toyota & The Times)

C Watch Sheriff's Patrol

Ft Row – Avery Niles, Thomas Slayton, Bobby McGee. 2nd Row – Ron Bridgefarmer, John Canfield, David Bramlett, David Gazaway. Bk Row – Sgt Jeff Strickland, Lt Bob McMahan, Kerry Alexander, Gerald Couch.

(Photo Courtesy Milton Martin Toyota & The Times)

D Watch Sheriff's Patrol
Ft Row — Buck Jones, Terry Conner, John McHugh, Sgt David Garrison. Bk Row —
Lt Boyd Hulsey, Steve Tyner, Robin Ramsey, Marty Nix.

(Photo Courtesy Milton Martin Toyota & The Times)

A Watch –Detention Center
Ft Row – O'Dean McDougald, Betty Hughes, Mike McKeithan, Greg Dobson. Bk Row – Robert Loggins, Cpl Glenn Canada, Mike Richardson, Jeff Hubbard.

(Photo Courtesy Milton Martin Toyota & The Times)

B Watch – Detention Center
*Ft Row – Cpl Valerie Clark, Mike Cooper, Sgt Bobby Cobb. Bk
Row – Keith Bangs, Eddie Reeves, Don Smith, Tim Ivey.*

(Photo Courtesy Milton Martin Toyota & The Times)

C Watch – Detention Center
*(Lt to Rt) Sgt Stanley Bullock, Ken Alexander, Cpl Vickie Gable,
Cynthia Roper, Dwight Turner, Curtis Kesler, Joe Shelton.*

(Photo Courtesy Milton Martin Toyota & The Times)

D Watch – Detention Center
Ft Row – John Rucker, Kenny Thompson, Kelly Thompson. Bk Row – Steve Carey, Marvin Hall, Sgt Ricky Fagge, Cpl Greg Bennett.

RET. LT. BOB MCMAHAN

Bob McMahan is a retired Airborne Ranger Instructor. He had two tours of combat duty in Viet Nam, and was also awarded a Purple Heart for wounds received during one of these tours. McMahan was one of the best Mountaineering Instructors at the Ranger Camp – always calm and was a natural teacher/instructor, always confident in himself.

After 20+ years as a US Army Ranger, Bob joined the Hall County Sheriff's Department on February 1, 1973. He was assigned to Capt. Cody

Bone's shift, and attended the Atlanta Police Academy along with fellow officers Robert McQueen and Gary Smith. After the three week course, McMahan was assigned to regular patrol duty.

Sheriff England needed two officers to help find and incarcerate the hundreds of people who had outstanding warrants against them, and to transport out of state prisoners. These officers had to meet certain criteria – they must be tall and strong and they must have been on the force a while; no room for inexperience here. The Sheriff chose Harold Farr - a tall confident deputy, and one of the best patrol car drivers in the department, and Bob McMahan - the highly skilled former Army Ranger, who was about the same stature as Farr.

Harold and Bob worked their own schedule when they thought they could apprehend these warrant dodgers. It wasn't long before Harold and Bob started filling up the jail! They would bring them in, Wanda Kemp would book them, and the team was back on the road. One day Harold and Bob arrested 18 or 20 people! The stack of warrants started to get smaller, but there were still plenty left. These officers had to be able to look these people up, arrest them, and be able to defend themselves in the meantime.

I had just joined the Department, a green rookie, scared of my own shadow, not knowing anything about law enforcement when Harold and Bob made the news. They had a felony warrant for a well known local criminal and the Sheriff wanted him in jail.

The boys got lucky and spotted the subject one night in a 1970 Chevrolet convertible traveling west on Industrial Blvd. Harold was driving and the subject refused to stop for the blue lights. A police chase was on! From Industrial Blvd., the fleeing suspect turned left just before A-1 Junction, crossed the railroad tracks and came out at the Gainesville Airport. He made a left onto Airport Blvd. and was heading back toward Queen City Parkway. By this time, pursuit driving was in full force: engines roaring, siren screaming, blue lights flashing, and tires squealing.

The fleeing suspect acted as if he was running for his life! McMahan took the pump shotgun, hung out the passenger window during all these maneuvers and started shooting. He shot four times with double ought buckshot. He shot out both rear tires – and the suspect kept going. Harold said, "Get the gas tank!", and McMahan shot two holes in the gas tank. The suspect was still flying with one hole in the bumper and two flat rear tires.

Heading for the interstate, he attempted a right turn at Queen City Parkway and spun out, making a 180 degree spin facing backward. Simultaneously, the patrol car had a head-on collision with the suspect's vehicle. The impact caused the trunk lid to fly open on the suspect's car. McMahan jumped out and snatched the subject out of the vehicle.

After the news got out about this episode, the crooks knew better than to try and outrun these determined hunters. Looking back, in the old days deputies did not have any hard and fast rules pertaining to when they could fire their weapons. I don't know about you, but I like this type of realistic action; this time no one got hurt, but the suspect's car needed two tires and some body and paint work. Bottom line, these two seasoned officers got their man, gave him an attitude adjustment, and demonstrated to all of us rookies just how to get the job done.

Another time, Bob McMahan was directing traffic on Highway 60 at Yellow Creek Road in Murrayville. The little church right on Hwy 60 was on fire, and the Fire Department had water hoses running across the highway. A Ford Mustang approached the scene and, disregarding Bob's signal to stop, down-shifted and gunned it. McMahan jumped out of the path of the vehicle – and shot the right rear tire down. Yes, the Mustang did stop! He had to protect his own life along with those of the fire and rescue workers. The point is that officers must make split second decisions in doing their jobs every day.

When Dick Mecum became Sheriff, Bob was selected as the first Training Sergeant for the Hall County Sheriff's Department, and he started Hall County's first SWAT team. Bob and I were both Ranger Instructors in the US Army Ranger Department, and I helped Bob conduct hand-to-hand combat training for the deputies at the Gainesville College Gym. This training was to teach them to work together and learn how to protect themselves; everyone enjoyed it fully. They really got into the hip and overhead throws! The young officers had trust and respect for Bob; he taught them well! Shortly after that training, a suspect got a deputy down, but the deputy used his training. He grabbed the suspect by the throat and slammed his head into the ground; that saved the deputy's life.

The SWAT team had only minimal equipment to begin with – shotguns, a couple of sniper rifles, vests, a surplus State Department of Transportation Carry All with two seats, and a surplus military Gama Goat, which was used mostly for show at the schools.

McMahan also took the SWAT team and others to Yonah Mountain for mountain climbing and rappelling training. The SWAT team used patrol cars (and sometimes their personal vehicles) to get to the scene fast. They later got an Uzi Submachine gun – 9mm – to train with. By being a former Ranger Instructor, even without advanced equipment, McMahan molded the team into a well trained unit. They learned to think alike and knew how to work together as a team; this made up for the lack of equipment. They were young daredevils and trusted one another – they were tough! Most of all, they trusted McMahan who had previous combat experience, and was a solid leader.

The first SWAT team members were: Sgt. Bob McMahan, Randall Long, Jim Ash, Dale Barrett, Gib Cronic, David Garrison, John Attaway and Art Jetton. They received no hazardous duty pay – just dedicated officers. McMahan and Randall Long attended SWAT training at the FBI Academy in Quantico, VA. While at the school McMahan taught the instructor a better technique in throwing a grappling hook through a window – the way Rangers do it!

McMahan started the first Memorial Service Firing Squad for the Department. This was before the Honor Guard, and was used initially at Deputy Acrey's funeral – a 21 gun salute with McMahan giving commands and seven members, all in Class A uniforms, white gloves and stainless steel pistols, firing three volleys. The second time they were used was at the funeral of Deputy Lee Grissom – the former Navy SEAL received a 21 gun salute. From that, Hall County later formed an Honor Guard for the Department.

One time the SWAT team was called out at night and McMahan responded from his home in civilian clothing, with SWAT gear over the top. Members of the team went inside and arrested the suspect – who was high on drugs. When the two SWAT officers brought the suspect out, he looked up and saw McMahan in civilian clothing and said, "Who are you?" Mac replied, "I was running coons along the creek, heard all the commotion, and came up to see." The suspect replied, "Oh, OK", and proceeded to be placed in the patrol car.

Another time, an officer responded to a domestic disturbance call in Flowery Branch. The female had a track record of being mentally unstable. The officer wasn't alert and the suspect grabbed his .357 pistol out of his holster and drew down on him. The officer had no choice but to turn and run for his life while the suspect was firing at him with his own weapon! She then went inside and the SWAT team was called. Police negotiators were talking to her by phone while she was lying on a bed with a knife. The police revolver was on a table next to her. McMahan and his team could see her through the window. On the count of three, they crashed through the door, yelling like Rangers. They scared the perpetrator stiff, as Mac hit her twice with a stun gun. They recovered the deputy's pistol and the knife.

While placing her in the patrol car, McMahan apologized for having to hit her twice with the stun gun; she replied, "That's OK, darling"! This was a teaching point — an officer must protect his pistol at all times!

One dark night, one of Sgt. McMahan's patrol deputies was checking a small road off Monroe Drive that went down a steep grade. The officer came to the end of the road and applied his brakes, but the patrol car began to slide as if it was on ice — but it was summertime. The wheels were spinning and unable to get any traction. Then the officer noticed a breath taking odor. A septic tank truck had illegally dumped a full load of waste at the bottom of the hill.

The list wrecker reluctantly towed the patrol car to safety. The front man at the jail washed and detailed the patrol car from top to bottom many times, but an odor was still there when the car was retired. They never discovered who was responsible for the illegal dumping.

McMahan was on Boyd Hulsey's shift and he and Randall Long were patrolling the lake one night. Out in the lake, a distance from a boat ramp, were head lights shining from underneath the water. Investigation showed that a vehicle had gone down the boat ramp, and was deep in the lake with its head lights on. The weather was very cold, but Long quickly undressed and dove into the lake. After a while he surfaced and gave the all clear — no one was in the vehicle. Randall got back in the patrol car, shaking like a leaf from the cold water. When the list wrecker got to the scene, Randall again dove into the cold lake and hooked the cable to the vehicle so it could be winched out; it turned out to be a stolen telephone company truck.

Mac told about the story of a murder in Hall County. The suspect fled and his whereabouts were unknown.

Some time later, Bob and his wife went to Las Vegas for a vacation. They were walking down the street in Vegas when McMahan saw an individual jay walking. The police officer in him made him notice — "that guy is jay walking." As they got closer, Bob recognized the man. At the same time, the man recognized Bob. It was the murder suspect from Hall County! The suspect turned and fled. McMahan contacted Chief Ron Attaway who contacted Las Vegas authorities, and they arrested the suspect. According to Chief Attaway, it was a common practice for someone who committed a crime in Hall County to flee to the west coast. This is just an example of how officers are alert at all times, even off duty on vacation. Mac violated the Vegas rule — what happened in Vegas did NOT stay in Vegas!

McMahan was later promoted to Lieutenant and was on the night shift for about five years. Later, during Sheriff Vass' administration, he transferred to the day shift. Later still, he was Asst. Patrol Cmdr., and then retired (after the Olympic Games) in October, 1996, with 23 years and 9 months service. After his retirement, he served on the Civil Service Board for eight years — the maximum time one could serve.

Currently Bob McMahan and his wife, Dixie, own and operate the Rucksack Military and Police Supply Store at 2407 Old Flowery Branch Road in Gainesville (behind Ryan's Restaurant). Bob and Dixie have been married for 53 years. He is a founding member of the Mountain Ranger Association and a member of the Peace Officers Association.

Thank you, Bob McMahan, for your dedicated service to your country and to the Hall County Sheriff's Department. You opened a lot of doors for others.

JAMES HARPER, JR.

JAMES HARPER IS PICTURED WITH HALL COUNTY DETECTIVES – 1986

James (Jimmy) Harper, Jr. is a second generation law enforcement officer. His father, James Harper, Sr. was Captain over the traffic division of the Gainesville Police Department and retired with 25 years of service. Jimmy was hired by the Hall County Sheriff's Department on July 13, 1974, by Sheriff Ed England when he was just 21 years old. Sheriff England had worked with Jimmy's father when they were both police officers for the City of Gainesville under Chief Hoyt Henry.

Jimmy started his law enforcement career on a Saturday, and later attended the first session of the Northeast Georgia Police Academy in Athens, GA, located across the street from the Varsity. Dick Mecum was one of his instructors. Attending with him were Danny Cantrell, Dennis Seymore, James 'Porky' Free, and Dick Taylor from the Fire Department. They drove from Gainesville and left early each day in order to get to Athens on time for the training.

Jimmy came out top shooter in his class with the pistol. Charlie Tipton was on top the next year, and John Attaway the next year – three consecutive years of top shooters from the Hall County Sheriff's Department.

Jimmy then was assigned to work in the Hall County Jail, working for Capt. Dale Sutton. He stayed at the jail for about two years. He was very intelligent and was good with the paperwork, but he was still a very young, green rookie.

On one occasion, all the jail officers went upstairs to eat in the dining room with Sheriff England, and left Jimmy assigned to the radio (dispatch was at the jail then). Think about it – all the seasoned officers upstairs eating and a rookie on the dispatch radio! The bank alarm for First National

Bank of Oakwood sounded. The bank was being robbed! Jimmy miscued and sent all the patrol units to the First National Bank on Browns Bridge Road. The officers ran into the bank with weapons drawn, and the employees yelling, "You have the wrong bank – it's Oakwood!" So all the officers quickly left for the Oakwood branch bank. From then on, some of the older officers started calling the rookie 'Malfunction'. The nickname stuck. Jimmy said that later he did a few more awkward things that pounded the nickname home.

A while later, Chief Ron Attaway was attempting to select an officer for a detail while talking on the radio. He wanted to send Jimmy, but couldn't think of his name. So he said, "You know who I'm talking about – ah, uh, Malfunction!" That was it; Jimmy has been 'Malfunction' ever since. He said he's been testifying in court, and some of the defense attorneys have referred to him as 'Mal'.

Jimmy was a good sport and accepted his nickname with pride. He proved to all that he was an efficient, dedicated, intelligent police officer. He just had a bumpy start – like most of us rookies. The fact is if an officer makes a mistake, regardless of what it is, everyone knows it and he just has to live with it – it can't be erased. This is what makes the job so difficult.

Jimmy was selected by Sheriff England to be Crime Prevention Officer. He served in this position for about one year. Jimmy was then assigned to Capt. Boyd Hulsey's night shift 11p – 7a. He has the highest respect for Capt. Hulsey; so does everyone else!

For a while, Jimmy threw a low profile in the department, just doing his job with nothing exciting happening. Everything was going well – just routine stuff. Then 'Mal' made headlines within the department again.

Jimmy and Danny Cantrell were riding together. Danny was driving and Jimmy was carrying a Mini 14 rifle with special ammo. You can see this coming, can't you? A gentleman called in and reported his pickup truck stolen and gave the description. Danny and Jimmy spotted the stolen pickup on Queen City Parkway. The fleeing vehicle almost hit Officer Homer Davis, turned onto Industrial Blvd., left on Bradford, right on Myrtle Street, tried to run over another officer, and then turned right on Spring Street toward New Holland. There were no houses in that area at that time, and no other traffic on the road.

Danny and Mal were hot on his trail in a high speed police chase. The suspect had no intention of stopping. With blue lights and siren screaming, Jimmy leaned out with his Mini 14 (remember he was an ace shooter) and shot one tire out, but the suspect kept going. Then he shot 3 or 4 more times hitting the fleeing pickup. All the while, they were going at a high rate of speed. In the curve at New Holland, near East Main Street, Danny tapped the suspect's vehicle with his bumper and spun him out.

Dale Barrett was filling in on the dispatch radio that night. After this fierce chase, Dale called the owner of the pickup truck and advised him that he had some good news and some bad news. The good news was that they had recovered his stolen truck; the bad news — it had numerous bullet holes. The ammo Jimmy was using was so powerful that it made more than one hole. Later on, Sheriff England was somewhat concerned about the ammo.

The suspect was found guilty and sentenced in Hall County Superior Court. Jimmy's shift captain was off duty that night, so he just went with his training.

In February, 1981, Jimmy and John Sisk scored the highest on the detective test, and they were promoted to detectives by the new Sheriff, Dick Mecum. Jimmy served as detective for the remainder of his career — approximately 23 years. He was taught detective work by Ron Attaway and Jerry Walls; Jimmy praised Ron Attaway on his police knowledge as a detective and the way he communicated with others. He credits his outstanding law enforcement career to those officers — including Bob McMahan. He also credits Sheriff Richard V. Mecum with modernizing the Hall County Sheriff's Department, bringing it to a level comparable to any other department in the state.

Jimmy retired in October, 2004, as a detective sergeant with 31 years service. He then began work with the White County, GA Sheriff's Department and is now a sergeant in the civil division, working with more former Hall County deputies: Jimmy Motes, John Murphy, Keith Bangs, Ret. Capt. Buddy Waldrep and Capt. Debbie Waldrep, who is Jimmy's supervisor.

James Harper is a professional officer who has dedicated his life to serving Hall County as one of the top investigators, working on all types of cases during his long career. He will be remembered for his outstanding service, but most of all for his famous trademark nickname: Malfunction.

Court House Admin Division — c1990s
Ft row (L TO R): W Stinson, L Mauney, Cpt B Barnes, M Cooper,
B Walls, C Schroeder. Bk row: T Miller, Jimmy Forrester, R Kersh,
C Matthews, D Cheney, Cynthia Roper

HCSD Honor Guard late 1990sFt row (l-r): Dallas Van Scoten, Brad Rounds, Ramone Gilbert, Gary Kansky 2nd row: Jimmy Motes, Gary Buffington, Chris Matthews, Maurice Gregory   3rd row: Mike Fielding, Robert Puckett, Don McDuffie, Avery Niles, Bill Sharp

Demolition of the old jail on Bradford Street in September, 1999 — before and after. The jail was built in 1935, and withstood the 1936 tornado with very little damage. The 122nd Infantry Regiment of the Georgia National Guard, commanded by Col. Thomas L. Alexander, set up headquarters and an aid station at the jail.

Dedication
of
Hall County Detention Center

March 12, 1982

Architects:
Bailey, Vrooman
and Alligret
Atlanta, Georgia

Hall County Detention Center
622 South Main Street
Gainesville, Georgia

Detention Center - Main Street

RET. LT. CODY BONE

Dick Mecum and Cody Bone at Cody's retirement.

Cody Bone was born in 1917, and lived in Hall County all his life, except for time spent working in Michigan in a war plant during WWII. Upon his return to Hall County, Cody worked at New Holland Mill from 1946 – 1965.

On January 1, 1966, he was hired by Hall County Sheriff Wilburn Reed and began his second career as a Hall County deputy, and was a shift supervisor most of his career. Cody worked for three Hall County Sheriffs: Wilburn Reed, Ed England and Dick Mecum.

By the time of his retirement from the Sheriff's Department on March 10, 1984, Cody had accumulated eighteen years of dedicated service to the community.

Cody Bone passed away in November, 1993, leaving behind his wife Roberta and son Michael. Michael is a second generation law enforcement officer with thirty-four years with the DNR as a Conservation Ranger. He is now enjoying his retirement.

1ST. SGT. CURTIS L. KESLER

1ST Sgt Curtis L Kesler and his Spartanburg County, SC patrol car

Curtis L. Kesler is a native of Hall County and graduated from Johnson High School in 1984. While in high school, he worked at a fast food restaurant, and moved to a management position after graduation. In the restaurant he often talked with Sgt. Stan Bullock of the Hall County Sheriff's Department, and Sgt. Bullock began to encourage Curtis to come to work for the Department.

With a good word from Sgt. Bullock, Curtis applied at the Hall County Sheriff's Department, and was hired by Sheriff Dick Mecum on June 20, 1986. As with all new hires, he went to work in the jail, and stayed there thirteen months until Under Sheriff Tony Carter asked him to go on the road. He trained on the day shift under Lt. Robert McQueen and then attended the Police Academy in Athens, GA in the fall of 1987. When he completed the Academy, he went on patrol on the night shift under Lt. Boyd Hulsey.

In 1993, Curtis' wife, Shanna, graduated from the University of Georgia and was recruited by Milliken and Company in Spartanburg, SC. They moved to Inman, SC, and Curtis immediately applied with the Spartanburg County Sheriff's Department and was hired. Curtis and Shanna both started their new jobs on the same day – April 12, 1993.

In Spartanburg, Curtis was assigned to the desk until he could complete a three week SC Academy course on SC laws, etc., then went to Uniform Patrol on the third shift. He worked in the Resident Deputy Program – Community Policing in 1997, and was promoted to Sergeant in 1999, and again went to the third shift. In June, 2007, Curtis was promoted to 1st Sgt. – night shift, and in 2008, he became Shift Commander.

Sgt. Kesler credits his success in his law enforcement career to the sound teachings of his mentors in the Hall County Sheriff's Department, Sgt. Stan Bullock and Lt. Boyd Hulsey. He says that Lt. Hulsey not only taught him good enforcement techniques, but he taught him to do his job in a Christian manner.

Lately, he has decided to try something new and moved to day shift, for the first time in twenty four years.

1st Sgt. Kesler was named Community Police Officer of the Year in Spartanburg County in 1998, and Supervisor of the Year in 2001. He and his wife, Shanna, have been married for twenty years and have two children, Brittany and Matthew.

THE DRUG SNIFFING DOG

Several years ago, after I had left the Sheriff's Department and became a probation officer, my wife and I took our big black lab, Lex Luther, on a walk from our house, across Browns Bridge Road, and on down toward the lake. The dog had a chance to play in the water, and then we headed back through the woods in a round about way toward home. We came out of the woods into the back yard of a house trailer, meandered through the yard, and out onto Keith's Bridge Road.

As circumstance would have it, my step-son, Curtis Kesler, worked as a Hall County Deputy at that time, and he happened to be patrolling the area. He saw us coming out of Keith's Bridge Road onto Browns Bridge Road, and pulled over. Since we'd already had quite a long walk through the woods, we accepted his offer of a ride home. We put the dog into the back seat and crawled in behind Curtis.

A few days later during an office visit to the probation office, one of my probationers told me about some of her friends and how they had come very close to being caught with drugs. They had been alert, and from their trailer window had seen the team of detectives with a drug dog come out of the woods and across their back yard.

They quickly got rid of the evidence by flushing all the drugs down the toilet. They felt lucky that the drug dog never did alert on their trailer – but they did see the team and the dog being picked up by a Hall County deputy. It was a very close call, they told their friends, but they had outsmarted the detectives.

I advised the Sheriff's Department afterwards; there had been drugs in the trailer at that particular address – but not any more! I never did let on that the 'drug team' was actually me and my wife just taking our dog out for a walk.

CORPORAL RICKY TUMLIN

(RICKY TUMLIN IS INCLUDED IN THE GROUP PHOTO OF HCSD ADMINISTRATIVE DIVISION 1986)

Ricky Tumlin started his law enforcement career on June 1, 1972, working in the Hall County jail. Later he worked on the road, but mainly worked in Court Services in the Hall County Court House.

While still in Court Services, Ricky retired on December 1, 2004, with thirty-two and one-half years of faithful duty to Hall County.

SHERIFF ROBERT G. 'BOB' VASS

1993 - 2000

All that is necessary for the triumph of evil is that good men do nothing.

Edmund Burke

Bob Vass was apparently thinking of this quote when he decided to run in the Democratic Primary for the Office of Sheriff of Hall County in July of 1992. He was someone who wanted to do something about it. He won the election with one of the largest margins (90.4%) for the sheriff's race in the history of the county. He ran unopposed in the general election in November, 1992, and assumed command of the Hall County Sheriff's Department at midnight on January 1, 1993.

Robert G. (Bob) Vass was born May 4, 1934, in Atlanta, GA, the son of Ted Dawson and Mary Brown Vass. He graduated from Brown High School and attended Presbyterian College in Clinton, SC on a football scholarship, graduating in 1956. While in college he was a track and field star and set a broad jump record of 24' 2".

As Sheriff, his goal was to maintain and improve the department with new ideas and leadership. Sheriff Vass' dream was that someday the citizens could walk the streets of their community at all hours without fear – and that their children could walk to school without being approached by drug dealers. He was confident that with everyone's support, this dream could be a reality.

Sheriff Vass was concerned about two areas of crime – illegal drugs and gang activity. He started a Gang Task Force to focus on and confront gang activity in the county, and he expanded the Drug Abuse and Resistance Education (DARE) program to include all fifth graders in the county. This proved to be a very successful program. He also began the School Resource Officer Program, placing armed uniformed deputies in all middle and high schools in the county. He selected the best officers for this duty – someone who could work, interact and communicate with school staff and students. This officer would be the link between the school and law enforcement.

According to Sheriff Vass, he saw the success of this program firsthand when he was visiting one of the schools. He noticed during the changing of classes that as they passed the School Resource Officer in the hall, each student would reach out and touch him. This showed the respect they had for the officer. He reflected that this was one of his most rewarding decisions – placing these officers in the schools. Their cars were painted black to stand out as School Resource Officers.

Sheriff Vass' pride and joy was expanding the DARE program. There were 135 DARE graduations during his tenure as Sheriff, and he personally spoke at 133 of them, missing only two. He became a little teary eyed as the story was told of a disabled boy who had to be carried into one of the DARE graduations. According to the Sheriff, the DARE program was a special program for special kids. He was proud of the special units: SWAT, DIVE, Honor Guard and STEP. He started the RED DOG (Run Every Drug Dealer Out of Georgia) Squad with everything in black – uniforms, weapons, etc. A special team of officers made up this unit, and their mission was to do exactly as the name implied.

While Sheriff, he initiated a program to allow patrol deputies to drive their cars home. This served to increase visibility of deputies on patrol both on the roads and in their neighborhoods and it shortened response time. It also acts as a deterrent to criminal activity.

In 1995, Sheriff Vass, along with nine other law enforcement officers, visited Budapest Hungary. Their mission was to demonstrate Western forms of law enforcement to that country. In preparation for the security of the 1996 Olympic Games Rowing Venue held in Hall County, the Sheriff was invited to Israel to study terrorism for 14 days.

Sheriff Vass was known for his open door policy for everyone – employees as well as citizens of Hall County. Well liked and always friendly, he made the Sheriff's Office approachable for anyone with needs or concerns.

At the end of his second term as Sheriff of Hall County, Vass was presented with a Ruger pistol by the department at his retirement.

Sheriff Vass has served in the criminal justice system for a total of 40 years: 6 years as a State Probation Officer working State and Superior Courts in Fulton County, GA.; 21 years with the Department of Justice and the US Courts - Federal Probation Officer, Northern District of Georgia; 8 years as Sheriff of Hall County and 5 years as a board member of the Georgia State Board of Corrections, appointed by the Governor.

Sheriff Vass is now enjoying full retirement. He is a member of the First Baptist Church, Georgia Sheriff's Association, Georgia Peace Officers Association and various other organizations. He has four daughters: Vicki, Jan, Cindy and Bonni and three grandchildren.

Sheriff Vass has devoted his life as a public servant in many levels of law enforcement. During our interview, he spoke of his philosophy on being Sheriff. He said, "to be a successful Sheriff, in one hand you must grip the hilt of the mightiest sword, and in the other caress the hand of the smallest child."

Hall County Sheriff Bob Vass discussing the crime situation with Crime Dog McGruff

HALL COUNTY SHERIFF'S DEPARTMENT - 1995

Sheriff
Robert G. Vass

Undersheriff
Tony Lee Carter

Captains
James Ash
Edwin Barfield
Jack Canupp
Kenneth Grogan
Buddy Waldrep

Lieutenants

D. Bishop	J. Free	B. McMahan
T. Conner	D. Garrison	R. McQueen
G. Cronic	R. Gilbert	J. Mecum
R. Fagge	L. Gilmer	M. Nix
J. Forrester	T. Ivey	E. Strayhorn, Jr.
	A. Jetton	J. Walls

Sergeants

J. Attaway	M. Gregory	D. Newbern
M. Bandy	N. Harkins	A. Niles
K. Bangs	C. Hewett	R. Puckett
J. Carter	D. Ivey	D. Seymour
D. Daniels	G. Joy	D. Smith

D. Edge
V. Gable

G. Lanich
R. Loggins
C. McNeal

G. Smith
J. Wimpy
D. Woods

Corporals

E. Bingham
G. Buffington
R. Cates

A. Dover
M. Fielding
K. Nix

W. Southers
J. Strickland
M. Teems

Personnel

K. Alexander
W. Anderson
V. Andrews
T. Ashley
N. Badwell
C. Barrett
G. Bennett
M. Blihoode
T. Boggus
W. Boyd
L. Bragg
M. Bragg
J. Brown
D. Buchanan
S. Bullock
T. Burnett
V. L. Burrell
V. S. Burrell
B. Burton
S. Carey
H. Carroll
T. Casper
D. Cheney
E. Clark
P. Clark
D. Cole
F. Collins

B. Dillashaw
R. Dobbins
B. Dunagan
C. Durham
D. Ellis
T. English
J. Evans
C. Farmer
H. Farr
E. Flalthmann
C. Forrester
J. Free
M. Free
M. Frost
J. Fry
D. Fuller
R. Garletts
K. Garrison
K. Gazaway
R. Kersh
M. Kogod
K. Lane
K. Langford
C. Le Doux
S. Lilly
S. Loggins
D. Long

L. Mauney
D. McDuffie
P. McFarland
J. McHugh
R. McManaway
C. Mealor
D. Miller
T. Miller
C. Mooney
G. Moore
J. Motes
J. Murphy
J. Mustin
M. Myers
D. Nipper
M. Nix
R. Nix
A. Norman
T. Orr
K. Palmer
M. Palmer
M. Parson
P. Payne
R. Phillips
S. Pickens
R. Pike
R. Pilgrim

M. Cooper
D. Corn
G. Couch
S. Couch
T. Couch
J. Covington
S. Dailey
M. Dalton
A. Dial
L. Didio
C. Dietrich

B. Lawther
M. Lusk
L. Mahaffey
S. Marillet
T. Maloney
J. Marshall
C. Martin
S. Martin
W. Massey
C. Matthews
D. Matthews, Jr.

R. Ramsey
R. Rayner
B. Reed
E. Reeves
S. Reynolds
E. Roach
B. Roberts
M. Robertson
P. Robinson
B. Rounds
D. Ruiz

Personnel (continued)

K. Sargent
G. Savage
R. Sena
B. Sharp
V. Shepherd
J. Shoemaker
K. Shope
J. Shull
B. Sims
R. Smith
D. Sneed
M. Spears
C. Speed
I. Spendola
W. Stinson
D. Sullivan
J. Tapiox
D. Thompson
R. Thompson
W. Thompson
J. Tredway
R. Tumlin

L. Tyler
S. Tyner
B. Uriegas
D. Usher
D. Van Scoten
J. Von Esson
H. Wade
J. Wade
K. Wade
D. Waldrep
E. Wales
B. Walls
K. Watkins
S. Watson
D. Weaver
S. Welsh
R. West
A. Wiley
S. Wilkerson
B. Williams
B. Wilson
W. Wofford

Pride – K-9

Total of 243 employees plus K-9

Hall County Red Dog Squad
Front row (l TO r): Gary Buffington, Bonner Burton, Murray Kogod. 2ⁿᵈ row:
Donald McDuffie, Wes Anderson, Shawn Jackson, M Nix, Tammy Crawford, Scott
Lilly, Paul Payne. In window: Paul House and Jeremy Grindle.

Hall County Dive Team – Spring, 1997
Front row (l to r) - Ron Dobbins, Steve Tyner (Asst. Commander),
Lt. Art Jetton (Commander), James Giles.
Back row - Mark Robertson, John Marshall, Jeremy Grindle,
Cory Barron, Gary Buffington.

HALL COUNTY SHERIFF'S DEPARTMENT– 2000

SHERIFF
Robert G. Vass

UNDERSHERIFF
Tony Carter

CHAPLAIN
Jeff Benefield

CAPTAINS

James Ash
Ed Barfield
Jack Canupp
Ramone Gilbert
Murray Kogod

LIEUTENANTS

D. Barrett	L. Gilmer	R. McQueen
D. Bishop	D. Ivy	A. Niles
T. Conner	T. Ivy	M. Nix
G. Cronic	A. Jetton	G. Smith
D. Daniel	M. McGinnis	D. Spillers
R. Fagge	C. McNeal	J. Strickland

SERGEANTS

J. Attaway	G. Joy	K. Nix
S. Bullock	R. Kersh	R. Ramsey
V. Gable	K. Lane	D. Seymour
I. Griffin	G. Lanich	B. Sims
K. Head	C. Matthews	S. Tyner
J. Hubbard	M. Myers	J. Wimpy
T. Johnson	K. Neece	D. Woods

CORPORALS

N. Bagwell	R. Nix	K. Sargent
C. Forrester	R. Pilgrim	K. Schoonover
L. Mahaffey	K. Ramsey	W. Southers
	B. Rounds	

SCHOOL RESOURCE OFFICERS

W. Anderson	J. Crisp	S. Reynolds
B. Burton	R. Dobbins	E. Roach
Sgt. J. Carter	S. Jackson	I. Spindola
	P. Payne	

REGULAR DEPUTIES

A Abercrombie	T. Casper	C. Durham
D. Allen	E. Clark	A. Edison
G. Allen	P. Clark	A. Edwards
T. Anderson	M. Combs	K. Edwards
R. Ansbro	M. Cooper	D. Ellis
M. Bandy	G. Couch	R. Ellis
C. Barrow	T. Couch	T. Ellis
K. Bartunck	M. Crook	T. English
C. Basham	S. Dailey	J. Evans
J. Beal	M. Dale	C. Farmer
S. Beverly	S. Dalton	H. Farr
D. Black	M. Davidson	C. Fields
M. Blihovde	T. Davidson	V. Finley

W. Boyd
S. Bradburn
L. Bragg
D. Buchanan
G. Buffington
V. Burrell
S. Carey
P. Carpenter
D. Gazaway
V. Gazaway
C. Giaquinta
S. Gilbert
J. Giles
J. Gonzalez
A. Gooch
G. Goodman
N. Grant
T. Grizzle
S. Guyton
R. Haefele
J. Haney
J. Harper
D. Harris
R. Henslee
L. Hestand
C. Hewett
J. Higginbotham
S. Hightower
J. Hooper
P. House
J. Hunnicutt
R. Hunter
C. Ivey
M. Jackson
D. Jarrard
C. Johnson
C. Jones
M. Kelley
D. La Rocque

S. Day
J. Deaton
S. DeLuna
A. Dial
C. Dietrich
E. Dorsey
A. Dover
B. Dunagan
A. Martin
S. Martin
C. Mattox
A. McClure
S. McCusker
D. McDuffie
P. McFarland
I. McIntosh
C. Mealor
J. Middleton
D. Miller
V. Mink
L. Moore
M. Moore
J. Murphy
J. Newton
M. Nix
J. Owens
W. Parks
D. Parrish
B. Parton
T. Pass
P. Peppers
B. Phillips
S. Pickens
R. Pike
S. Polston
K. Preston
M. Raines
A. Ramey
K. Rayner

B. Foster
F. Foster
D. Franklin
J. Free
M. Friedrich
D. Fuller
K. Garrison
M. Gaudio
C. Sharpe
J. Shelton
L. Shipley
J. Shull
J. Simmons
J. Smith
L. Smith
M. Smith
R. Smith
S. Smith
L. Souders
M. Speas
W. Sproul
S. Spurlin
D. Sullivan
R. Suttles
J. Tapia
M. Taylor
J. Thomas
M. Thomason
C. Thompson
M. Thompson
T. Thompson
R. Toppins
T. Traynor
J. Thedway
R. Tumlin
D. Tyner
R. Vickery
J. Wade
M. Walker

K. Langford	B. Reed	B. Walls
C. Le Doux	E. Reeves	G. Watson
D. Long	J. Reeves	R. Watterson
B. Libow	B. Roberts	D. Welsh
B. Lowther	M. Robertson	R. West
H. Magnus	R. Rungruang	T. White
J. Manley	C. Schroeder	T. Wilbanks
J. Marshall	I. Sepulveda	S. Wiley
B. Williams	B. Wilson	M. Wurtz
	W. Worrell	

DETECTIVE DARRELL IVEY

Darrell is a lifelong resident of Hall County in the Belmont Community. He and his wife Judy have been married for 40 years. They have one son, Jay, and two daughters, Kelly and Lori.

In January, 1966, at the age of 19, Darrell was drafted into the Marine Corps, along with another Gainesvillian, former Police Chief Jerry Forrester. During his career in the Marines, he served a combat tour in Vietnam.

On June 20, 1968, Darrell joined the Gainesville Police Department and was assigned to the traffic division. He served eight years with the Department before resigning on June 30, 1976.

After taking some time off from law enforcement, Darrell was hired by Sheriff Ed England on April 1, 1978, as a Hall County Deputy. He served with the Sheriff's Department for 22 years, retiring April 1, 2000, as a Shift Lieutenant. During his 30 year career in law enforcement, Darrell wore many hats: traffic division with the city, patrol deputy, Sergeant, ten years as a Detective, and Patrol Lieutenant. Most of the time he worked evenings/ night shift. During most of his career, he worked a second job, sometimes two. For years he worked sixteen hours a day, seven days a week in order to support his family. Police work was a low paying job when he first started. Initially Darrell was hired by Chief Hoyt Henry. He served under two police chiefs and three sheriffs.

As a detective, Darrell worked homicides for years, and worked for a while with Det. Lee Grissom, who had been shot in the line of duty and severely injured. Grissom had a unique way of getting information. One time an informant had promised to bring them some information, but later reneged. Darrell and Lee saw the informant through the window of a local pool room. The informant thought he was safe and sound inside the building and shot them a bird. Grissom solved that problem — he called some of the guys outside and told them something in private. They went back inside and beat the daylights out of the informant. Lee then put the patrol car in gear and drove off. As they looked back, the fight was still going strong!

Darrell said he never questioned Lee on how he got his information for search warrants — Lee always had plenty of evidence. He was a special kind of detective; he would fight fire with fire — and he got the job done.

During Darrell's career, this seasoned officer experienced every situation imaginable — you name it and he saw it. He devoted his life serving his country as a combat veteran and a law enforcement officer, and has the highest respect from all his peers.

Darrell's son, Jay, has followed in the exact footsteps of his father. He served six years in the Marines with a tour of combat duty in Iraq, became a city policeman and presently is a Hall County Deputy as a K-9 officer.

Darrell is enjoying his retirement, playing his guitar and making regular visits to the Grand Ole Opry in Nashville, TN. Thank you for your service, Darrell. Your footprints in law enforcement will benefit many who will follow.

(l to r) Dale Barrett, David Garrison, Darrell Ivey

RET. CAPT. BUDDY WALDREP

As a young man, Buddy Waldrep applied for a job with the Hall County Sheriff's Department, and a little while later got the surprise of his life. He was out mowing his lawn when he saw a shinny, black Buick pull into his driveway. The gentleman driver was wearing a big white hat. It was none other than the High Sheriff of Hall County, Ed England. The Sheriff asked Buddy to sit in his car with him, and when the Sheriff left, Buddy had just been hired as a Hall County Deputy.

Buddy reported for work on May 1, 1963, the beginning of a successful thirty-four year career. There were fourteen people in the Department when he started! He began as a patrol deputy for a short period, and then volunteered to work in the jail as a jailer. Soon afterward, he became the Chief Jailer – working in the old jail on Bradford Street.

When Sheriff Mecum was elected, he promoted Buddy to Captain – Commander of the Administrative Division, i.e. Courts, Warrants, Civil and Courthouse Security. Captain Waldrep held this position (except for a short period as Commander of the Detention Center) until his retirement in August, 1997.

After his retirement from the Sheriff's Department, Buddy Waldrep worked for ten years as a Campus Security Officer for Gainesville State College. Later he moved to White County and is a Reserve Officer with the White County Sheriff's Department.

During his tenure in law enforcement, Captain Waldrep has gained a great deal of experience while working in the jail and in his position as Administrative Commander.

Late one evening after court, Captain Waldrep went down to check the prisoner holding cell in the basement of the Hall County Courthouse. The elevator malfunctioned when he got ready to leave, and he was locked in the basement holding cell. He couldn't call out because his portable radio wouldn't transmit from that area. He thought he'd be there all night, so he simply took out his paperwork and started to work.

But as luck would have it, Sgt. Charlie Berryman felt nature's call and ran down to the bathroom in the basement. He heard Buddy calling for help. Yes, they did get the elevator repaired, and Buddy was rescued.

Captain Waldrep is known to be a hard worker. For example, he was always working – serving civil papers, court documents, FIFA's, etc., even while enroute to and from work. He was a very dedicated and conscientious officer, and he worked for three Sheriffs: Ed England, Dick Mecum, and Bob Vass. He also worked in both jails – Bradford Street and Main Street.

Retired Captain Buddy Waldrep has forty-seven years of experience in law enforcement. He is enjoying his retirement with his wife, Captain Debby Waldrep in White County, GA.

CAPTAIN DEBBY WALDREP

Debby Waldrep receiving White County Officer of the Year Award.

Hired by Sheriff Dick Mecum, Debby Waldrep began her law enforcement career in December, 1985, as a secretary in the Hall County Sheriff's Department. After about six months, she moved to Court Services.

In 1986, Debby attended the Athens Police Academy and returned as a certified deputy sheriff. Her career encompassed clerical, Court Services, Supervisor of Records and Warrants (1993 – 1997).

In October, 1997, Debby took a three month leave of absence to pursue a career in the White County, GA Sheriff's Department. She was hired by White County Sheriff Neal Walden, and never returned to Hall County. She was hired as a patrol deputy, and rode alone for about a year. During that first year, she was involved in helping with the victims of the tornado that struck on the Hall/White County line with thirteen fatalities. This work lasted approximately 45 days, helping residents of both counties recover from the tragedy. She found a rewarding career in White County that she enjoys very much.

Debby was promoted to Sergeant in 1998, and began working Court Services – warrants, civil, courts and transport. In 2004, she was promoted to Captain of Court Services. Currently with twelve years service to White County, Captain Waldrep has six deputies working for her – James Harper, Keith Bangs, Jimmy Motes, Tina Couch, Thomas Lucas, and Christopher Davis – all experienced and certified officers. She is also a training officer for the White County Sheriff's Department.

Captain Debby Waldrep has twenty four years in law enforcement with twelve in Hall County and twelve in White County up to this point. She began her career in law enforcement when it was difficult for women to succeed above secretary/matron. However, she had a desire to be a certified officer so that she could best help others in need. With hard work, leadership ability and a desire to serve, she started at the bottom and worked herself up to her current position.

Captain Debby Waldrep, thank you for your service to Hall County. In addition, White County is fortunate to have you.

RET. LT. JIMMY FORRESTER

Jimmy Forrester retired in 1996, with approximately 30 years in law enforcement where he worked for five different Hall County Sheriffs. He also has an honorable discharge from the U. S. Army Reserve. Jimmy started his law enforcement career with Sheriff Cal Wilson in the later part of his term in 1959.

During this time, Sheriff Cal Wilson's department had grown to thirteen employees. They drove 1959 Chevrolets with big motors and they would fly! The deputies worked twelve hour shifts, six days a week for $300 a month. In the early days, most offenders pled guilty, cutting down on time waiting in court to testify.

Still, if a court appearance was necessary, deputies testified on their own time. Deputies were required to furnish their own weapons and ammunition, and the department furnished uniforms which were not always in the best of condition. Deputy Forrester said he was so broke when he was hired that Sheriff Wilson loaned him his personal snub-nosed .38 caliber pistol until he was able to purchase his own. Deputies had to be dedicated and wanting to serve – it was difficult to live on the low salaries.

When Sheriff Wilson lost the election, Jimmy quit law enforcement for a short time and drove a gas truck, but later returned to the Sheriff's Department.

Sheriff England was the new Sheriff, but Jimmy quit again for a short time, and then returned to duty. That's when Sheriff England put his foot down and told him that if he quit again, he would not be hired back. Deputy Forrester took him at his word and made law enforcement his lifelong career.

Jimmy was a graduate of the Atlanta Police Academy, and has a substantial number of diplomas and certificates of law enforcement training. There was no guarantee of a continuing job when he went into law enforcement under Sheriff Wilson. Each newly elected Sheriff brought in his own deputies, making certain everyone was on his team. Real job security for deputies didn't come until the department came under Civil Service rules and guidelines.

When Sheriff England took office in his first term, deputies wore green uniforms and Jimmy didn't like them at all. Later they changed to tan uniforms and western hats, then on to the Smokey Bear hat.

Jimmy remembers his first pay raise. Sheriff Reed raised the pay for deputies to $100 per week - $400 a month – WOW! When the department went under the Civil Service system, the schedule changed to three eight hour shifts, rotating each month, working forty hours per week, but still no extra pay for going to court. This changed in later years.

Jimmy Forrester served in two divisions during his career; Patrol Division and Court Services – retiring as a Lieutenant in Court Services. During my interview with Jimmy, I could tell he was fond of Captain Carl Mathis and Sheriff England by his many kind words of praise for them both. They seemed to be very special in his career.

Jimmy was a highly skilled officer who helped many new officers during his tenure. I was one of those officers. I had been with the department for about two years and was assigned to Jimmy as his riding partner. We used to look forward to going to work each day because we were a solid team. I had initially been trained by my previous partner, Gene Earls. I was fortunate to have the opportunity to work with another skilled officer who kept on teaching me the ins and outs of law enforcement – there is a lot to learn! We were confronted with everything in the book, but Jimmy had the experience to make things easy. I was always relaxed because I knew Jimmy had already faced many difficult situations in his career, and we could take care of whatever we came across.

One dark night, Jimmy and I were routinely patrolling when we came upon a one car accident. The vehicle ran off the road at a high rate of speed and crashed. It was a sports car and was folded up like a crushed tin can, with steam and smoke spewing from the front. We jumped out and the only sign of the driver we could see was one foot underneath the bent metal; it was a mess!

We immediately called for medical help, but we had a difficult decision to make. We could hear the driver moaning inside the mass of crushed metal, and we also noticed the strong odor of gasoline as well as alcohol. If the gasoline ignited, there was a possibility that the injured driver would be burned alive. At that time our patrol cars were not equipped with fire extinguishers. We made the decision to get him out of the vehicle one way or another — expecting the vehicle to explode at any moment. I began trying to lift the car and Jimmy got a firm grip on the driver's one foot that was barely visible. I heard Jimmy straining and grunting while pulling on the leg, and then the driver started screaming. Suddenly Jimmy shot backward down in a ditch and disappeared. I ran down the embankment and there stood Jimmy holding a leg complete with sock and shoe! He said, "Willard, I pulled his *#@%$! leg off!" Per Jimmy, I replied, "The hell you say!" After checking a bit further, we discovered that it was an artificial leg. It had detached from the driver as Jimmy pulled and yanked on it. We then went back and finally found some other body parts to pull on and extricated the drunken driver. The fire department arrived and extinguished the fire. By that time, medical help had arrived and the victim was taken to the emergency room.

Later, when we walked into the ER, Jimmy set the artificial limb up on the head nurse's desk. The nurse asked, "What is this?" To which Jimmy replied, "The rest of the body parts of this guy we just brought in." Miraculously, the driver escaped with no serious injuries. He was treated and released, and he and his still detached artificial leg were transported to Hall County jail. Needless to say, this is Jimmy's favorite story.

On a sunny afternoon, we got a call regarding a man beating his wife. A man was out in the yard beating his wife to death — get there quickly. Dispatch advised of a possible rifle in the gun rack of the man's pickup. Jimmy was driving — he was an excellent driver. We went down Hwy 129 South wide open, and turned onto Gillsville Highway with blue lights and siren. The big motor in the patrol car was roaring. Jimmy had the pedal to the metal and tires were screaming in all the curves. Jimmy's driving experience was paying off! We slid into the yard with heat vapor coming off the hood of the car.

The large built man had his wife down on the ground and her face was beaten unbelievably. We drew our pistols and yelled for him to stop or we were going to blast him. At that point he stopped beating the woman and began reaching into his pickup. I took a position behind the patrol car with my pistol resting on the hood, while telling him that if he pulled a gun, he was history.

Jimmy was in a bind; he was caught out in the open. The only cover available was a skinny poplar tree about 5" in diameter. Jimmy jumped behind the tree with his pistol trained on the subject. He had his torso sucked in tight – he looked as stiff and straight as a bullfighter. As he was trying to get his body hidden, the subject changed his mind about his gun and started a head on charge toward us, like he was about to tackle the quarterback.

Jimmy and I holstered our weapons and immediately went into hand-to-hand combat. We knocked him down and he fell face first into a pile of gravel. – producing a good bit of rash! Even though he was highly intoxicated, we had a time getting him handcuffed – his strength was unbelievable. He was taken to jail and his injured wife was transported to the hospital. It was all about alcohol – the man was a hard worker but could not handle his drinking. Later, he ended up solving his drinking problem and his wife remained with him. I told the whole department about Jimmy sucking in like a bullfighter behind that sapling.

We had many difficult situations but neither of us ever received a serious injury. Jimmy retired as Lieutenant and he is one of the finest officers I have ever met. Thanks, Jimmy, for the many dedicated years serving Hall County. Jimmy retired and worked about eight years as a bailiff for Superior Court Judge Andrew Fuller. He is now fully retired, living with his wife in northern Hall County and enjoying his family.

Jimmy Forrester's 1996 retirement at the courthouse. Jimmy is flanked on the left by Willard Langdon and former Sheriff Ed England on the right. Sitting: lt. Randall Kersh, center ? , and rt. Louise Tolbert.

RET. SGT. STANLEY G. BULLOCK

Stan Bullock began his law enforcement career in 1965, after having served as a Seaman in the Merchant Marines. Most of his career was in various supervisory positions at the jail – he spent seventeen years working in the old jail on Bradford Street before the move to the Main Street Detention Center.

Sgt. Bullock was a dedicated officer who liked to help people in need. He gave his job one hundred percent, and was fair to everyone. All the young rookie deputies depended on Stan to show them the ropes, and he was a great teacher. Sheriff Ed England depended on Stan Bullock and Dean (Strawberry) Tipton to keep things in order at the jail.

Stan was the kind of person people wanted to be with; he was friendly and enjoyed telling a joke.

When I was a deputy, a story was personally told to me by the victims' relative that I asked Stan about. He confirmed it in his usual unpretentious manner. Late one night in the 1960s, at the old jail on Bradford Street, Stan was at the desk and received a distress call from a victim. After relaying information to Stan, the victim dropped the phone.

Three escapees had broken into a business, not realizing that people were living upstairs. A confrontation ensued, and the robbers caused harm to the family, but one of the victims had managed to get the phone call made.

Sgt. Bullock got on the police radio and telephone and sent out information about the criminals to all the surrounding sheriff's departments, even into the state of South Carolina. In the 1960s, communication was limited and the phone service was somewhat primitive. Bullock used his experience and quick thinking, and called the local telephone operator who connected him with all the different law enforcement agencies. He was persistent and stayed on the phone until the BOLO was disseminated to departments hundreds of miles from Gainesville.

In the meantime, the criminals had stopped to break into Greenway's Grocery in Rabbittown on their way out of town. They were apprehended a few hours later by a Cornelia police officer near the Habersham County line. Without Stan Bullock's quick action, they may never have been caught. This is just one example of the outstanding work this seasoned officer did for the citizens of Hall County.

Stan Bullock retired in June, 2000, after a successful career with the Hall County Sheriff's Department. He had 34 years on the job — more longevity than anyone in the Department! He loved his job and was well respected by all his fellow employees. Stan's footprints will always be present at the Hall County Sheriff's Department.

Sgt. Stan Bullock passed away on December 23, 2007, leaving behind a loving family. He was buried at Memorial Park Cemetery with honors by the Hall County Sheriff's Department Honor Guard.

DAVID AND INA GRIFFIN

David and Ina Griffin are both former Hall County deputies. David Griffin started his career with the Sheriff's Department in March, 1973. After attending the Atlanta Police Academy, he was assigned to the patrol division. After a suitable time on the road, he was selected as a detective – investigating homicides, burglaries, thefts, etc. Later, Sheriff England and Chief Attaway selected him and Carlton Sosebee, both seasoned officers, to initiate the first Selective Traffic Enforcement Program (S.T.E.P.) in the Hall County Sheriff's Department. They were the first officers qualified to run radar. The STEP unit concentrated on speeding, DUI, and hazardous driving practices. Their mission was to reduce traffic accidents, deaths and injuries in Hall County. The department received a grant from the Office of Highway Safety to supply two officers and one vehicle with supportive equipment to set up the STEP Unit, with salaries paid by the STEP grant.

David and Carlton were immediately deterrents in the troubled areas of Hall County. Many drivers were surprised to see a county unit running radar. Later in David's career, he returned to the patrol division and picked up a new riding partner – Willard Langdon! David and I rode together for about two years; I had about four years experience when we started. We made a good team and enjoyed working together. Together, we felt like we could handle anything, and we enjoyed coming to work.

After Dick Mecum became Sheriff, we were furnished a portable radio per deputy and the units became one man units assigned to a designated zone. I hated being separated from my riding partner. On the other hand, it was exciting to operate alone, especially after we had all the new equipment.

After riding as a one man unit for years, David left the department for another career in 1985. David and I were among only a few who had a four year college degree. David landed a job as a State Parole Officer, and after four years of duty, he was transferred to the Gainesville Parole Office and worked there until he retired. David was a well trained deputy and parole officer who devoted his life to serving in the US Army in Vietnam, Hall County Sheriff's Department and the Georgia State Parole Division. He is a very pleasant person and a great friend. One of David's prize possessions is the badge of former Sheriff Ed England. Sheriff England had two badges inscribed with his name, and he gave David one of them after he left office. Our friendship today is just as strong as it was many years ago. Thanks, David, for your service.

Ina Griffin started her career in the Sheriff's Department in 1981, and rose to the rank of Sergeant. She first worked as Major Tony Carter's clerk, and later became Sheriff Mecum's secretary. After a short break in service, she was a work release detention officer, Training Sergeant and later the property Sergeant. She was always available to do any job that helped the department.

Ina spoke highly of Sheriff Mecum, indicating that he was an excellent leader. Through his leadership, he brought the Sheriff's office up to modern standards.

Sergeant Griffin opened many doors and broke the ice for other females to follow. She was the first female to handle male blocks in the jail, and the first female Training Sergeant. Good luck, Ina, and thanks for your fortitude and service.

Though retired, David and Ina have a new career as the owners of "Pet Pleasers Bakery, Inc." where they make treats for our pets! Their store is located at 4324 Mundy Mill Road in Gainesville. They are both enjoying their new career. My puppy really enjoys his visits to Pet Pleasers!

David Griffin holds the badge given to him by former Sheriff Ed England

RET. DETECTIVE JERRY WALLS

Jerry and Barbara Walls have a total of sixty-four years
of law enforcement experience between them.

Retired Lieutenant Jerry Walls began his law enforcement career with the
Gainesville Police Department on October 1, 1966. He was hired by Chief
Hoyt Henry and worked as a patrolman until September 15, 1969, when he
was hired by Sheriff Wilburn Reed as a Hall County deputy.

Jerry and James Cantrell were riding partners as patrol deputies on Capt.
Boyd Hulsey's shift. They enjoyed their work together and were a great
team, accomplishing a great deal. Jerry and James were the first uniformed
deputies to work a homicide and get a conviction. Sheriff Reed was having
a Department Christmas party and Jerry and James volunteered to work and

cover all calls for the county. The murder occurred that same night during the party, so they worked the case without asking for assistance.

When Sheriff Ed England took office on January 1, 1973, Jerry and James were transferred to the detective division. There Jerry was assigned another riding partner, Detective Homer Davis. Davis was an old moonshine detective from the old school of law enforcement. They worked the night shift and worked all types of crimes, but most often worked on drug related crimes, thefts and homicides. After several years and much experience, Jerry attained the rank of Lieutenant - the first Lieutenant ever in the Hall County Detectives.

The Gainesville Optimist Club honored Lt. Walls on May 11, 1987, as an Outstanding Law Enforcement Officer for the year 1986. The eighteen year veteran was recognized for a job well done in the community. In 1988, Detective Jerry Walls was chosen Officer of the Year by the Hall County Sheriff's Department.

Lt. Walls was second in command of the Hall County Detectives Office, and he worked as an investigator from 1973 until 1989. Then he was transferred to the Detention Center as the Lieutenant over the Warrant Division and worked there until his retirement on July 5, 1998, under Sheriff Bob Vass.

Lt. Walls worked under one Police Chief and four Sheriffs during his thirty-two year career in law enforcement. Jerry speaks very softly, but 'carries a big stick' as the saying goes. He is a professional and dedicated public servant to the citizens of Hall County. His precise knowledge of criminal justice enabled him to be a very efficient investigator. He is always available to help a friend, and gives sound advice if asked. Jerry, thanks for your years of faithful service to this county.

Retired Lt. Walls is presently working part time in security work, and is enjoying his retirement and his life with his wife, Barbara, their three daughters and seven grandchildren with number eight expected in the fall.

Lt to rt: GBI Agent Tommy Mefferd, George Spain, Art Jetton, Detective Jerry Walls, Bob McMahan, David Garrison, and Steve Tyner – Hall County Sheriff's Department recovered stolen trailer that had been cut up and thrown in river in Dawson County.

RET. DEPUTY BARBARA WALLS

Just out of school, Barbara was hired by Sheriff Wilburn Reed in November, 1972, and began doing clerical work in the Hall County Sheriff's Office. She worked with Mrs. Jenny Broxton, the Sheriff's secretary, who was very helpful to her and who was greatly admired by not only Barbara but by all of those who knew her.

After Ed England was elected Sheriff, Barbara continued in her same position, and in 1977, she was allowed to attend the Northeast Georgia Police Academy in Athens, GA, becoming a certified Deputy Sheriff. She then returned to her clerical duties in the Sheriff's Office.

In the early 1980's, Deputy Walls was transferred to the Detective Office working as a general detective. When Sheriff Dick Mecum was elected, she moved back to the court house, working in Court Services, transporting prisoners, in Hall and other counties for court, serving civil processes, and working all the courts within the courthouse.

In 1989, Barbara worked in the Warrants Division, working out of the old Detention Center. And in 1992, she transferred back to the court house and worked as Court House Security (door) for a while as well as continuing to perform the duties of the Court Service Officers. She continued there until her retirement as a Corporal under Sheriff Steve Cronic on November 30, 2004.

Cpl. Walls has spent her life serving the citizens of Hall County with 32 years experience in the Hall County Sheriff's Department. Barbara was the first female Officer of the Year for the Hall County Sheriff's Department in 1998. She has set the standards high and has been instrumental in breaking down gender barriers for other women in law enforcement.

Since December 1, 2004, Barbara has worked as a State Court Bailiff for Judge Gene Roberts, and when Judge Larry A. Baldwin, II was appointed she became his Chief Bailiff, a position she very much enjoys.

Thank you, Barbara, for your hard work and dedication.

SHERIFF STEVEN D. CRONIC

2001- PRESENT

Steve Cronic is a native of Hall County, Georgia, growing up in the Chestnut Mountain area and graduating from Johnson High School. The son of former long time Hall County Deputy John Cronic and his wife Doris, Steve, a middle child, has an older sister and a younger brother.

Possibly from the influence of his father's profession, Steve fostered an early interest in law enforcement. At the age of twenty, he began his career as an Enforcement Officer for the Georgia State Department of Transportation. From there he went on to the City of Gainesville as a police officer and continued his career as an investigator for the District Attorney's office, Northeastern Judicial Circuit of Georgia. He then went into private industry as a corporate security manager and a Regional Fraud Supervisor with a large insurance company.

Sheriff Cronic received both his B. S. Degree in Criminal Justice and his Masters Degree in Business Administration from Brenau University. He is a graduate of the Georgia Police Academy, the F. B. I. National Academy in Quantico, VA., the National College of District Attorneys Major Crime School and Special Investigation School, and a graduate of the International Association of Arson Investigators Arson School.

In 2000, Cronic announced his candidacy for the Office of Sheriff as a Republican, and he won the election, making him the second Republican Sheriff in the history of Hall County. He is also only the second Sheriff in the history of Hall County to have a Masters Degree.

Sheriff Cronic took office at midnight, January I, 2001, with two major goals in mind for the Sheriff's Office — to maintain and increase the level of professionalism and service, and to achieve State Certification and National Accreditation for the office.

In June, 2001, in an effort to gain a more cohesive relationship between the Sheriff's Department and the community, Sheriff Cronic established a summer camp for kids. It was the D.A.R.E. to Dream Camp with 300 kids from Hall County participating. The camp was later renamed the Advance Summer Camp for Kids, and is funded by donations from business owners in the community.

In an effort to reduce vandalism, a program was developed to allow citizens to report gang graffiti so that it could be removed and cleaned up. Sheriff Cronic has worked hard to eliminate gang activity, and to prosecute those involved in gang related crimes.

The county now has fifteen districts, which gives blanket coverage for protection of citizens, reduces response time and promotes increased visibility of patrol officers. The department now is approaching 500 employees and is the sixth largest Sheriff's Department in Georgia. Further, about 240,000 service calls are answered annually. In order to more efficiently answer these calls and expedite the crime solving process, the Sheriff maintains close working relationships with Federal Agencies including the FBI, DEA, and ICE, as well as law enforcement agencies from surrounding municipalities.

Sheriff Cronic replaced the radio system of the department with a state of the art 800 megahertz system. Over a period of time, 24 new deputies were hired through grants, providing the best patrol coverage in the history of the Department with precincts in the northern, central and southern parts of the county.

Sheriff Cronic implemented a Victim Service Program which provides immediate and long term support of victims and families of violent crimes and traumatic events. This program is funded by a grant from CJCC and staffed with two employees. He also implemented the Teen Driver Program, which is conducted during the summer months at each of the six high schools. Licensed students are educated, through the use of specialized goggles and golf carts, on the dangers of operating a motor vehicle while impaired. The course is operated in cooperation with the Hall County Board of Education and is funded mostly by local business owners.

Sheriff Cronic started a Hall County Sheriff's Officer Reserve Unit, beneficial to both the department and the community. It is made up of experienced former law enforcement officers who volunteer their time to work on major events such as parades, rowing competitions and other functions requiring a large law enforcement presence, leaving full time officers to continue their regular duties.

Also, during summer months, Park Marine donates a pair of jet skies that are used by the Reserve Unit to patrol activities on Lake Lanier. Through Homeland Security grants, Sheriff Cronic purchased a lake patrol boat, a SWAT response vehicle and an incident command vehicle. The patrol boat is used daily and is especially helpful during peak summer months.

Since three-fourths of Lake Lanier is located in Hall County, an underwater search and recovery team is required to recover drowning victims and evidence. Sheriff Cronic secured a state grant of $35,000 to purchase side scan sonar to aid divers.

The Hall County Honor Guard competed in the National FOP Honor Guard competition in Washington, D. C. in 2007, and placed third. Each Memorial Day, at the veterans section of Memorial Park Cemetery, the Honor Guard marches the entire 24 hours of the holiday period as a tribute to the veterans of Hall County.

Due to overcrowding at the old detention center, Sheriff Cronic converted the vacated Regional Youth Development Center into Hall County's first female work release, providing a rehabilitation program for female offenders while collecting living expenses from employed female inmates. Also, female inmates who are incarcerated for drug related charges can continue out-patient drug abuse treatment while serving their sentence — a first for female inmates.

Sheriff Cronic created the Hall County Sheriff's Office Citizen's Academy. Scheduled twice yearly, the Citizen's Academy was developed to provide opportunities for citizens to work directly with deputies and investigators through classroom presentation, hands-on training and ride-a-longs.

Through partnerships with private enterprise, the Sheriff's Office has received donations that help support specialized functions - the donation of a Toyota pickup truck from Milton Martin Toyota for ADVANCE officers, and donations from Fieldale Farms that helped fund the canine (K – 9) units, one K – 9 for each shift.

Sheriff Cronic secured private donations to purchase four drug dogs assigned to School Resource Officers. The Sheriff also initiated a reward program in the Hall County School System for information leading to drug arrests or seizures. The program allows students to confidentially provide information on drugs or drug activity to School Resource Officers in middle and high school. In exchange for this information, the student may be eligible for a reward of up to $200. This money is paid from funds seized from other drug dealers.

Hall County serves as the lead agency for the Multi-Agency Narcotics Squad or MANS UNIT and the Gainesville Hall County Gang Task Force. Several years ago Hall County was one of the major clandestine drug lab counties in North Georgia. Through investigative efforts and strategies, the labs have almost become extinct.

Sheriff Cronic broke ground in March of 2006, on a $54 million jail for Hall County. On November 15, 2007, the new Hall County jail, located on Barber Road opened for business. It was completed on time and under budget. Through the leadership of Sheriff Cronic, the 500+ prisoners from the old Detention Center were moved without incident in three days. Additionally, since the facility was built to meet future needs, there were approximately 400 open beds slated for future use. Since most of the costs for the jail are "set costs" the sheriff used this as an opportunity to board excess inmates from other counties and generate over 5 million dollars annually to help off set the costs of housing our inmates.

In 2005, Sheriff Cronic was appointed by Governor Sonny Perdue to the County and Municipal Probation Advisory Council. Sheriff Cronic was selected the county's most popular official two years in a row by Lanier Magazine. Also in 2005, he was chosen by Brenau University, his alma mater, to be inducted into the Alumni Hall of Fame.

Sheriff Cronic is very active in the Georgia Sheriff's Association, and he has a special place in his heart for the Sheriff's Youth Homes. He makes good use of Hall County Government's TV 18 to relay important issues to citizens concerning crime prevention and other law enforcement activity. He serves and supports a number of civic organizations and boards including the Edmondson-Telford Center for Children, the Hall County Commission for Children and Families, the Northeastern Judicial Circuit's Domestic Violence Task Force, the County and Municipal Probation Advisory Council, and was appointed by the Lieutenant Governor to the State Board of Public Safety, covering the GBI, State Patrol and the Police Training Center at Forsyth, GA. The Governor also appointed him to the Sheriff's Retirement Fund Commission.

Sheriff Cronic is currently in his third term as Sheriff, and ran unopposed in the last two elections. He was the 2006 recipient of Georgia's Public Safety Award for Outstanding Contribution to the Profession. He was also the Georgia Sheriff's Association 2007 Sheriff of the Year for the State of Georgia. He is a member of the Northeast Georgia Police Academy Advisory Council, Regional Vice President of the Georgia Sheriff's Association – Region 3, the Official Chaplain for the Sheriff's Association for the State of Georgia.

Under the leadership of Sheriff Steve Cronic, the Hall County Sheriff's Department has reached a new level of efficiency and quality of law enforcement. The Hall County Sheriff's Department is now a State Certified and Nationally Accredited Agency – the first ever for Hall County. The Department ranks among the top agencies in the state of Georgia.

During my interview with Sheriff Cronic, he spoke at length praising his employees for their teamwork and devotion to duty. He also spoke about what he felt were the keys to success – the power of prayer and the hard work of his employees. He is extremely proud of all the members of the Sheriff's Department. According to Sheriff Cronic, it is his job to make promises to the citizens of Hall County; however, it is the brave and devoted men and women of the Department who make it happen. Sheriff Cronic is a dedicated, hard working leader and Hall County is fortunate to have him as Sheriff.

Sheriff Steve Cronic and his wife, Kathy, have been married for thirty two years and they have two children, Melinda and Cody. They are members of Lakewood Baptist Church where he serves as a deacon.

Scene of northern Hall County off Shirley Road

HALL COUNTY SHERIFFS DEPARTMENT - 2010

Administrative Division

Steve Cronic, Sheriff

Col. Jeff Strickland, Chief Deputy

Major Terry Conner, Div. Cmdr.

Becerra, Linda Elena
Blan, Brandy Michelle
Bollinger, Melissa S.
Brewer, James Camp
Buffington, Anita Kaye
Burns, Angela Marie
Burton, Allen Bonner
Collison, William Scott
Crawford, Tammy Renee
D'Anna, Deborah Ann
Dover, Angela Lavon
Gazaway, Larry David

Gilbert, Stephanie Laurie
Groover, Joseph Allen
Kemp, Jr., Robin Lee
Moore, Jennifer G.
Myers, Michael A.
Nordman, Robin Cay
Peters, Bertha L.
Shoemaker, Jeffery Sean
Tyner, Donna Lynne
Wilson, Betty Jo
Young, Malinda Lipscomb

Sheriff's Services

Major Ramone Gilbert, Commander

HALL COUNTY SHERIFFS DEPARTMENT - 2010

Court Services Division

Capt. Chris Matthews, Div. Cmdr.

Acrey, Richard Layne
Allen, David Jonathan
Anderson, Edward Allen
Beverly, Steve Michael
Blalock, Raymond Sentell
Boyle, Debra Marie
Bridgette, Robert C.
Buffington, Joel Brian
Cook, Perry K.
Couch, Timothy Lee
Crowell, William J.
Edwards, Kevin Wayne
Garrett, Sandy J.
Gaunt, Chris D.
Harmon, Jr., Kenneth Ray
Hubbard, Jeffery Ray
Knapp, George S.

Larocque, Dorothy Jean
Lee, Weda A.
Lomax, Robert G.
McElreath, Randall Eugene
Mink, Vivian Sue
Mitchell, Mark Dana
Orlikowski, Richard J.
Parks, Raleigh Thomas
Pitzer, Wesley Jacob
Ramsey, Kristy Lynn
Rungruang, Russell Nopporn
Smith, Lisa Kimberly
Tapia, Jose Rogerio
Toppins, Randy Lee
Turner, Larry Lee
Watt, Jennifer Ann
Wurtz, Monica Lynn

HALL COUNTY SHERIFFS DEPARTMENT - 2010

Criminal Investigation Division

Capt. Woodrow Tripp, Div. Cmdr.
1st Lt. Kevin Head

Alexander, James Kerry
Ansbro, Richard Steven
Ayala, Maritza Alejandra
Bales, Kimberly Bess
Barron, Corey Benjamin
Buffington, Brandi M.
Campa, Alondra
Corn, David Daniel

Long, James Dale
Mariotti, Joseph Edward
Matthews, Jr., Douglas W.
Mazarky, Michael Allan
McCusker, Sean Patrick
McDuffie, Donald Louis
McMillan, James Madison
Migliore, Heath Brian

Couch, Gerald Jay
Crisp, Jason Daniel
Day, Seth Forrest
Durham, Cameron Groves
Franklin, Jr., Lindon Dan
Gaudio, Matthew Earl
Grindle, Jeremy Paul
Head, Kevin Roy
Henderson, Brian Mason
Higginbotham, John Stephen
House, Paul Clifton
Ivey, Casey Shane
Klein, Steven Robert
Lane, Roger Douglas
Lilly, Jeffery Scott

Miller, Angelyn Lauren
Mills, Nathaniel West
Moore, Gary Bart
Neece, Kenneth Raymond
Payne II, Paul Donald
Sargent, Kiley Mitchell
Scalia, Donald Michael
Shull, Jeffrey Todd
Smith, Jason Wesley
Speed, Billy Carlton
Sproul, Wayne Charles
Thomason, Mark Anthony
Trinkwalder, Richard Francis
Van Scoten, Christy Nicole
Ware, Christopher Scott
Wiley, Anthony Scott

HALL COUNTY SHERIFFS DEPARTMENT - 2010

Jail

Capt. Mark Bandy, Div. Cmdr

Adams, Debra Louise
Alexander, Corey Justin
Alford, Christopher Brian
Ashley, Jeffrey Glenn
Ashman, Dexter Gene
Ayers, Joel Clifton
Ayers, Leah Anne
Bachelor, Christopher Jay
Baines, Terry Lee
Banks, Trina Letorrie
Barnes, Glen Patrick
Barnes, John Robert
Basham, Craig Steven
Belgrave, Augustus
Bennett, Stephanie Renee
Benson, Sandra G.

Channell, Sabrina Dale
Chavez, Isabel
Chisholm, Alicia Dawn
Clark, Johnathan Boyd
Cleveland, Dustin Lee
Colella, Dani Bree
Combs, James Michael
Compton, Jamie Eric
Cooke, Cheryl Ann
Cooper, Michael Doyle
Cordell, Judy A.
Cowan, Alisha Susan
Cruz, Ana Karen
Cuffy, Deborah Maria
Cunningham, Holly Noel
Daniel, Dwayne Richard

Betancourt, Bonnie Joy
Bonds, Justin Lee
Bridges, Kimberly Ann
Brown, James Newt
Brown, Jonathan Derek
Buffington, Jeffry Scott
Burger, Christi Dawn
Burson, Rayshia Arlyce
Byers, Kaeshawn Tyrelle
Calderon, Jesus Rodolfo
Cannon, Stephen Gary
Cantrell, Phillip Randall
Cape, Brent Wesley
Cape, Spencer Ryan
Cash, Carrie Dawn
Chaffer, Marlana Kaye
Chandler, Kenneth Dustin
Fields, Jena Celeste
Flowers, Leon
Forrester, Charlotte
Fortson, Rhonda Curry
Foster, Melissa Carvetta
Froelich, Anita Paulette
Gable, Cheryl Lynn
Gandara, Mercedes Margarita
Gaston, Kimberly Lynn
Gentle, Alphonso
Gober, Marcus Gabriel
Gonzalez, Brian
Goudy, Egera Susan
Griffeth, Cedricka Shanice
Griffin, Kevin Daniel
Grizzle, Timmy Eugene
Groves, Briggs Anne
Guardado, Jose Alexander
Guevara, Susan Lorraine
Haddan-White, Paula Jean
Haefele, Rebecca Ann
Harris, Lisa Jean

Davidson, Joshua Scott
Davis, Corrine Moye
Davis, Phillip Dean
Demps, Varhondia Nichole
Dodd, Jack Ernest
Downing, Christina Aileen
Dunn, Wendy Leann
DuQuette, James Foster
Eckhardt, Byron Keith
Elliott, Jeffery Drake
Ellis, Diane
Ellison, Carol Diane
Fann, Alvin
Farr, Blakeley Shane
Faulkner, Adam Alexander
Feaster, Sammy Antonio
Ferrell, Marcie Ann
James-Brown, Abena Syoini
Jennings, Tajuanna L.
Jones, Mathew L.
Jorsling, Tracy Annette
Juarez, Erika Alejandra
Kelley, David Lawrence
Kerber, Alicia Andrea
Key, Dwight Eric
Kimbrell, Barbara Elaine
Kimbrell, Candida Marie
Kimbrell, William Edward
King, Jeffery Lamar
Kingdom, Barbara Renee
Kinney, Robert Herman
Knight, Valerie
Kock, David Anthony
Kurzeja, Joslyn Patricia
Lachner, Robert A.
Lee, Janis Lynne
Lester, Timmie
Lewis, Trisha M.
Llanas, Christopher George

Harrison, Craig Leroy
Helm, Halekia Anthilia
Hendrix, Deana Laverne
Henslee, Randy Larry
Herbert, Eric D.
Hewell, Charles Dwight
Hicks, Allan Christopher
Highsmith, Sharon Connors
Hopkins, Kenikya Kumi
Hopwood, Cresencia
Howard, Randy Edward
Howell, Adraine Michele
Hulsey, Chad Jennings
Hunt, Bobby Edward
Hunter, David Lithonia
Ivey, Tim Charles
Jackson, Merika Joy
Moore, Ashley Michelle
Moore, Linda Ann
Morgan, John Charles
Moses, Eugene Alexander
Mosley, Roel Deneiro
Motes, Steven Michael
Mount, Michael Dennis
Mull, Lindsey Hope
Murphy, Kerri Estrella
Mustachio, Cynthia Leigh
Newberry, Mark Andrew
Nguyen, Aaron Ashley
Nix, Kenneth D.
Osborne, Justin David
Osborne, William Grady
Ownby, Jerry Wayne
Pacheco, Richard
Paduani, Joseph Patrick
Palmer, Jeffery Lanier
Palmer, Kirk Lee
Parker, Jonathan Matthew
Parrish, Nichlos Paul

Loggins, Ronald Davis
London, Jacob Bradley
Long, Andrew Benjamin
Loyd, Janet Audrey
Madera, Yasenia
Marcus, Jeffery Carlton
Martin, Anmarie Vargas
Martin, Sharon Wilson
Martin, Susan
Mason, Mark Joseph
Mason, Pamela Anne
Mayfield, Sammi Joy
Mayfield, Stephanie Elaine
McCloud, Dana Paul
McNeal, Christopher Thomas
Meads, Tyrone
Miller, Alice Leann
Robinson, Justin Thomas
Roche, Francis Thomas
Sanchez, David Noel
Savage, Michael Edward
Scruggs, Thomas Carlton
Seymour, Scottie Lamar
Sheriff, Phillip Andrew
Sherrill, Jeffrey Taylor
Simmons, Rondal, Michael
Simpson, Kamilla Elisa
Singleton, Terrelyn Sheree
Smith, Jacqueline Annette
Smith, Jourdan Alexander
Smith, Michele Lynn
Smith, Quinntara Bernae
Stephens, Joel Robert
Storey, Keenan Jermel
Stovall, Michele Renee
Stroud, Donette Audrey
Studer, Rodney Edward
Sturgill, Philip R.
Sullens, Marcia Alene

Parton, Britton William
Patterson, Jametta Louise
Patton, Wanda Jean
Palham, Matthew Gene
Peppers, Phil Dustin
Perry, Larry
Pharris, Mitchell Lee
Phillips, Jerry Wayne
Pickens, Stephanie Turner
Pittman, Edward Wayne
Rae, Brian David
Randolph, Lisa Twanna
Reaves, Donna Marie
Richie, Barry Lafarrell
Riggans, Georgette
Roberson, Stephen Jelin
Roberts, Anthony Wayne
Weaver, Danny Gordon
Wengert, Carrie Ann
Wester, Michael Allen
Wheeler, Judy Lynn
White, Donna Maria
Wigner, Candy Shannon
Wilbanks, Stephen John
Wilford, M. Delores
Williams, Angel Luis
Williams, David Parks

Sunderman, Jeffery Donald
Talley, Robert Walter
Teasley, Tyeward Jerome
Thomas, Cara Richelle
Thompson, Benjamin V.
Thrasher, Michele England
Tolbert, Mona Kay
Townsend, Timothy Jacob
Turk, John Randy
Turner, Travis McKinley
Udzinski, April Lynn
Underwood, Jonathan Scott
Wade, Judy Morgan
Walker, Marcus Antonio
Wallace, Janie Gray
Waters, Joyce Marie
Waters, Robert Lee
Williams, Torrick Eugene
Williamson, Bradley Roger
Williamson, Christopher Z.
Wilson, Bobby Joe
Wood, Rainey Nathan
Woods, Danny
Worrell, William Henry
Yarborough, Kenneth Lynn
Young, Brianco Shardae
Young, Christopher Eric

HALL COUNTY SHERIFFS DEPARTMENT - 2010

Uniform Patrol
Capt. Donnie Jarrard, Div. Cmdr.
1st Lt. Joe Carter

Arquette, Joseph Norman
Ayers, Joel Steven
Bagwell, John Neal
Bailes, Jason Brian

Egerton, Jason Douglas
Evans, Jason Wayne
Farmer, Christopher Allen
Fleming, Jeffrey Alan

Blihovde, Jeffrey Mark
Boggus, Joseph 'Tony' Anthony
Bradburn, David Sean
Brewer, Phyllis Jean
Brown, Chance Gregory
Brown, Marcus Scott
Burrell, Vickie Lynn
Cagle, Clifford James
Carey, Stephen Emory
Carter, Ralph Joel
Casper, Michael Todd
Choate, Heather B.
Clark, Phillip Wayne
Clore, Tyler Jeffrey
Cobb, David Marshall
Coker, Cassie Mechelle
Coleman, Dannette Iolanda
Coley, George W.
Comeaux, Conner Jeremy
Comparini, Ezio Eduardo
Dailey, Stuart Wesley
Dale, Christopher Daniel
Dale, Michael Shane
D'Anna, Stephen
Davidson, Timothy Allen
Davidson, Timothy Dale
Dawson, John Lester
Dobbins, Ronald Gilbert
Edwards III, Lewis James
Joy, Fred Eugene
Keinard, James Angerson
Kelley, Anthony Duane
Kiser, Bradley Christopher
Lane, Kenneth P.
Langford, Keith Wendell
Lauricella, Salvatore Paul
Lusk, Michael Paul
Manley, Johnny Nathan
McIntosh, Ian Winston

Forrester, William Douglas
Free, Michael Morris
Friedrich, Maria Thompson
Gazaway, Vic M.
Giaquinta, Charles R.
Gill, Ryan Adam
Gilleland, Corey Shawn
Ginn, Scotty Lee
Greenwell, Charles Francis
Grier, Shandra Nicole
Haban, Joseph Mitchell
Haight, Thomas J.
Haley, Susan Downs
Hall, Shadrick Aaron
Haney, Jacob Mitchell
Harris, Lester Gene
Harrod, James Dewayne
Hoffman, Robin Lee
Hooper, Jeffery Conley
Hummel, Jesse Byron
Hunter, Jason Edward Jr.
Hutchins, Stephen Scott
Hyde, Jr., Thomas Joseph
Ivey, Jay Darrell
Jackson, Jonathan Evan
Jackson, Russell Shane
Jackson, Shawn D.
Jones, Jack Nelson
Jones, Jesse "Bobby" Robert
Sanders, Nicholas Todd
Santiago, Rafael Guillermo
Sexton, Christopher Scott
Smith II, Robert Oscar
Smith, Ana Marisa
Smith, Kristi L.
Smith, Randall Gary
Smith, Shannon Hartwell
Snyder, Kevin Lee
Southers, Wilda Lee

McNair, Brian Keith
Mealor, Jimmy Chad
Mealor, Vicky Lynn
Mickels, Stephen Edward
Miller, Joshua David
Montelongo, Armando L.
Newton, James Willis
Nix, Ricky Edwin
Norman, Amanda Gail
Orme, Jeremy Davis
Parker, Cameron David
Parrish, Donald Evans
Pearson, Brian Keith
Pike II, Revell Wade
Pirkle, James Ronnie
Poteet III, Charles Curtis
Presgraves, Deron Shane
Prickett, Jeremy Grady
Provost, Ryan William
Rayner, Robert Keith
Reeves, Johnny Mattison
Reynolds, Scott Wesley
Roach, Jr., Earl Banks
Roach, Michael Christopher
Robinson, Chris William
Rose, Michael David
Rounds, Bradford Scott
Roush, Ronald Scott
Russell, Katherine E.

Stewart, Calvin Edward
Stewart, Hulon Kacy
Still, David Christopher
Sugarman, Scott Merrill
Sullens, Kevin Chad
Sullivan, David Jacob
Suttles, Chad Eric
Taylor, Jerry Mitchell
Tempel, Louie Christian
Thompson, William Dwain
Treadwell, Jr., David Myron
Venable, John Matthew
Wallace, Charles Garnett
Watson, Glenn Keith
Watson, Jr., Stanley Gary
Watterson, Robert L.
Watts, Rodney Jay
Welsh, Donna Lee
West, Ricky Lamar
Wiggley, Robert Walter
Williams, Bennie Don
Wilson, Thomas Lee

HALL COUNTY SHERIFF'S DEPARTMENT – 2010

PATROL DIVISION LEADERS

Cpt. Donnie Jarrard/Asst. 1/Lt. Joe Carter

A Watch - dayshift (12 hours)

Lt. Brad Rounds
St. Sgt. Steve Michels
Sgt. Mark Blihovde

B Watch - dayshift (12 hours)

Lt. Mitch Taylor
Sr. Sgt. Steve Carey
Sgt. Chris Tempel

C Watch – nightshift (12 hours)

Lt. Bryan Pearson
Sr. Sgt. Michael Lusk
Sgt. Ian McIntoch

D Watch – night shift (12 hours)

Lt. Neal Bagwell
Sr. Sgt. Jake Haney
Sgt. Keith Rayner

Traffic Unit
Sr. Sgt. Kelly Edwards
Sgt. David Sullivan

Officers gather at the precincts before each shift.

County is broken down into 15 zones – patrol unit in each zone.

County gets approximately 2,000 calls a month.

COLONEL JEFF STRICKLAND

CHIEF DEPUTY

*Setting an example is not the main means of
influencing others; it is the only means.*

Albert Einstein

For 28 years Col. Jeff Strickland has been setting the example while serving
as a protector and public servant to the citizens of Hall County.

Jeff knew as a young boy that he wanted to be a police officer. He attended Gainesville High School and graduated in 1983. Before graduation, Jeff completed an internship with the Sheriff's Department, and shortly after graduation, he was hired by the Department as a detention officer.

In 1984, Jeff graduated from the Northeast Georgia Police Academy. He started at the bottom and worked up through every rank to his present position as Chief Deputy. Having completed over 2,000 hours of advanced law enforcement training, he is a seasoned officer equipped with the skills and experience needed for his demanding yet rewarding position.

Jeff is a hands-on leader who has experienced almost every situation imaginable during his career. As a traffic motorcycle officer and supervisor, he has worked many traffic fatalities requiring detailed reconstruction of the accident. In addition, he assisted during the jail riot and fire in 1988 at the old Detention Center on Main Street. Col Strickland worked around the clock during the 1998 tornado in Clermont where there were thirteen fatalities. He worked for forty-five days protecting the Clermont residents and their property and assisting them in their recovery.

Further, when there is a serious crime or a drowning, he is always on the scene to assist his subordinate leaders. Also if the SWAT team is deployed, he is available to assist in the situation.

Col. Strickland is basically on duty 24 – 7. He accepts this responsibility with honor and is humbled for the opportunity to serve as Undersheriff of Hall County; he was promoted to Major in 2005 and Colonel in 2008 by Sheriff Steve Cronic. His achievements have come through loyal and dedicated work as a model law enforcement officer.

Second in command under Sheriff Cronic, Col Strickland oversees the three major divisions of the Sheriff's office: Police Services, Sheriff Services and Administrative Services divisions. This includes Uniform patrol, Criminal Investigation, Court Services, and the Hall County Jail. Col Strickland's goal is to provide quality service and protection to the citizens of Hall County in a professional and financially responsible manner.

Colonel Strickland has been recognized and honored numerous times during his career to include Officer of the Year in 1990. The Gainesville Elks Lodge selected him as the recipient of the 1990 and 2000 Public Safety Officer Finalist of the Year. The Hall County Board of Commissioners honored him with a Proclamation for Outstanding Service in 2001. He received the 1999 Respect for Law Award from the Gainesville Optimist

Club. He also received the Roy C. Moore Memorial Award for his service in 1990, and the Hall County Sheriff's Office awarded him with a Special Commendation for Outstanding Support and Dedication to the Sheriff's Office in 2002.

Col. Strickland serves on the Board of Directors of the Gateway Domestic Violence Shelter. He is a member of the Georgia and the National Sheriff's Associations, as well as the International Association of Chiefs of Police and the Fraternal Order of Police.

A lifelong resident of Hall County, Colonel Strickland and his wife, Linda, reside in South Hall County and attend Lakewood Baptist Church.

RETIRED COLONEL TONY CARTER

Tony Carter is a lifelong resident of Hall County. On June 30, 1972, at age twenty-three, he was hired by Sheriff Wilburn Reed, and joined the Hall County Sheriff's Department as a jailer. At the time, he did not know of the impact he would have on the department over the years.

When Tony was hired, he had an Associates degree from Gainesville Junior College – the only one in the department with any college at that time. Soon after he was employed, he attended the GA Police Academy. Later he attended Woodrow Wilson Law School in Atlanta for three years at night, earning a Juris Doctorate degree in 1980, and in 1994, he earned a BS degree in Criminal Justice/Public Administration from Brenau College. He served five years in the U S Army Reserves as a Company Clerk for the 802nd Ordinance Company in Gainesville.

After approximately nine months working in the jail, Sheriff Ed England selected him as a Detective in April, 1973. He worked all types of crimes – and worked homicides for about three years. He was then promoted to Detective Captain, and served as acting Chief of Detectives. In 1981, Sheriff Dick Mecum promoted Tony to Captain and he was assigned as Commander of the Hall County Detention Center.

Sheriff Dick Mecum had previously abolished the position of Chief Deputy, but in May, 1983, he promoted Tony to Major, and made him Chief Deputy of the Department. Major Carter was responsible for all the Division Captains - Commander of Investigations, Commander of Administration, Commander of Patrol Division, and Commander of the Detention Center.

Tony Carter served as Chief Deputy under three Sheriffs – Dick Mecum, Bob Vass and Steve Cronic - making him the longest serving Chief Deputy in the history of the department. He retired in October, 2004, with a total of 33 years; more than 21 as Chief Deputy. At his retirement, Sheriff Steve Cronic promoted him to Colonel.

Colonel Carter dedicated 33 years of his life as a protector and servant to the citizens of Hall County. As Chief Deputy, he made diligent efforts to ensure that the Department was successful throughout the years of his tenure. He was always actively involved in the community and was cooperative and helpful when called upon by citizens and fellow officers. Because of his genuine interest and support, Colonel Carter helped make Hall County a better place to live.

Serving under five different Sheriffs, Colonel Tony Carter is one of the pioneers who blazed the trail and laid a firm foundation on which the Hall County Sheriff's Department is built. He is also known as an excellent homicide investigator, working many high profile cases during his years of service.

Colonel Carter is a member of numerous police and civic organizations. Most of his 33 years of service was in a leadership position, and he attributes this to education, training and dedication to duty in law enforcement. Colonel Carter and Sheriff Mecum were the first certified divers at their level – Chief Deputy and Sheriff – they led by example.

In his position, Colonel Carter was always available to give advice if one was willing to listen. He is very thankful that no one died in the line of duty in the Department during his tenure.

Tony's father, Roy Carter, was an auto mechanic. He loved his job because he had a different car with a different problem to work on each day. According to Tony, he had the same outlook as his father– he liked something different to solve each day, and he found that in his position as Chief Deputy.

Colonel Carter and his wife of 36 years, Tanya, are members of Free Chapel Worship Center. They have a daughter, Chrissy Goss, and two granddaughters, Aleah and Ally Goss.

RETIRED MAJOR JAMES DOYLE ASH

Jim Ash was born in Walton County, Georgia to the late James R. M. Ash and Odessa Presley Ash. He moved to Hall County at an early age where he lived for the remainder of his life. He was a graduate of Gainesville High School. While attending Gainesville College, he worked in construction. Jim joined the Hall County Sheriff's Office as a Deputy in November of 1973.

During his law enforcement career, he worked in Patrol and Investigations, rising through the ranks to the position of Captain where he served as the Commander of the Jail for many years before retiring in 2003.

His expertise in construction and jail operations resulted in his being requested to return to the Sheriff's Office in 2004 to oversee the construction of the new Hall County Jail. It was completed ahead of schedule and under budget in 2007. During this time, he also served as the Major over Sheriff's Services, directing operations of the Jail, Warrants and Courthouse functions. He again retired from the Sheriff's Office in March of 2008.

Jim embraced his all too short retirement, traveling extensively with his wife, Chris, to such places as Canada, Prague, Germany, Ireland, Turkey, Italy and several other Mediterranean countries. He was preparing to visit Israel for the second time when he was diagnosed with cancer.

Retirement also gave him the time and opportunity to indulge in such activities as studying Spanish and taking classes in culinary arts and ballroom dancing. He enjoyed raising cattle and trout, riding his tractor, vegetable gardening and watching the birds and wildlife on his property.

Jim was a member and past President of the Gainesville Lions Club and a member of Stone Lodge 715 F & AM for nearly 34 years. He also belonged to the FBI National Academy Associates and the Peace Officers Association of Georgia. Jim especially enjoyed his weekly Bible study group and his Thursday night supper club meetings. He was a member of St. Gabriel's Episcopal Church, a church he loved and where he truly felt at home.

Jim Ash passed away at the young age of 57 on March 12, 2010. Officer Ash lived a short and productive life and will be remembered by all as one of the most efficient Jail Commanders in the history of the Sheriff's Department.

HALL COUNTY JAIL FACILITY ON BARBER ROAD

(JAIL DIV CMDR – CAPTAIN MARK BANDY)

Motorcade enroute to new jail

On November 13, 2007, Hall County Sheriff Steve Cronic and his Chief Deputy Col. Jeff Strickland were faced with the mission of moving 500 inmates from the old Detention Center on Main Street to the new facility on Barber Road, a distance of six miles. They needed to complete this move in three days time. About 100 inmates were moved the first day, another 200 the next day and the last 200 were moved the night of November 15, 2007. It was a massive undertaking which required months of planning.

The inmates ranged from non-violent to extremely violent, including some who were incarcerated for multiple murders. The Sheriff had plenty of manpower on hand. The show of force was impressive; heavily armed SWAT members and a pair of aggressive German Shepherds, in case anyone had the foolish idea to attempt an escape. The motorcades each day included an inmate bus with Sheriff's Department cars and motorcycles, with blue lights flashing, surrounding it. Also included was a SWAT van with a Georgia State Patrol helicopter above.

Therefore, on the night of November 15, 2007, the new Hall County jail, located on Barber Road, opened for business. Thanks go to Hall County Commissioners who spent several years planning the $54 million project. The new jail accommodates 1,026 inmates, and has a medical section where the inmates can receive federally mandated medical, dental and mental health treatment. It has served to reduce crowding for the inmates and its expansion has added jobs to the community.

The funds for the jail came from the Special Purpose Local Option Sales Tax (SPLOST), passed by voters of Hall County. An extraordinary security system – one with no blind spots – is a feature of the new building. This is a big improvement over the old three story reinforced concrete jail on South Bradford Street as well as the old Detention Center on Main Street.

Sheriff Steve Cronic encouraged retired former Hall County Detention Center Commander Jim Ash to return to duty to be liaison officer over the construction of the new jail. Returning as a Major, Ash had extensive experience in Construction as well as jail management – he was the best. Major Ash served on this assignment from 2004 until the completion of the jail in 2007. He was instrumental in seeing that the new jail came in ahead of schedule and about one million dollars under budget, and he went beyond the call of duty to come out of retirement to aid the Sheriff and the citizens of Hall County. Upon completion of the jail, he then retired a second time.

Through the leadership of Sheriff Steve Cronic and the expertise of Major Jim Ash, the new jail was completed as planned, and benefits every citizen of Hall County.

Inmates and SWAT team await move to new jail.
Colonel Jeff Strickland is coming through door.

SENIOR SERGEANT KILEY M. SARGENT

Sr. Sgt. Kiley M. Sargent began his law enforcement career in September, 1989, with the Hall County Sheriff's Department under the administration of Sheriff Richard V. Mecum. In 1990, he graduated from the 93rd Session of the Northeast Georgia Police Academy in Athens, Georgia. Since then some of his training has included Traffic Accident Reconstruction Certification along with Advanced Motor Officer Certification, as well as being certified as P.O.S.T. General and Specialized Instructor.

He moved through the ranks from a Peace Officer Trainee in the Hall County jail in 1989, to the Uniform Patrol Division in 1991. In

1995, Sargent moved to the Traffic Enforcement Unit and held positions of Deputy, Corporal to Sr. Sergeant within that Unit until he moved to Criminal Investigations in 2009. He currently serves as Sr. Sergeant in the Property Crimes Unit within the Criminal Investigations Division under the Command of Captain W.W. Tripp.

Sr. Sgt. Sargent serves as Back-Up Public Information Officer for the Sheriff's Office since 2004. He has written over 200 traffic safety articles published in the Gainesville Times that was printed weekly for four years (2002-2006).

He was also responsible for researching and writing the Governor's Challenge reports, which led to the recognition of the Hall County Sheriff's Office Traffic Enforcement Unit at the state level as well as nationally for their efforts in traffic safety in 2004, 2005, and 2007. The Governor's Challenge is a Governor's Office of Highway Safety incentive program designed to award outstanding achievements in highway safety enforcement and education. Georgia law enforcement agencies are judged on both the approach and effectiveness of their overall highway safety programs. Agencies are evaluated not just for enforcement initiatives, but for innovative problem solving in their communities, using public information activities, and creating departmental policies that support their traffic enforcement campaign efforts. The law enforcement agency with the highest overall evaluation will be presented with the "Governor's Cup." Because of this recognition, Hall County Sheriff's Office was awarded a new $50,000 Ford Expedition in 2004 and a $20,000 Harley Davidson Road King Police Motorcycle in 2007.

Kiley Sargent was born in Hall County and raised in the New Holland village. He and his wife and son are members of the First Baptist Church of Gainesville, and he is a member of Stone Lodge #715 F&A.M of New Holland and the Gainesville B.P.O.E.

SGT. JEFF SHOEMAKER

HALL COUNTY SHERIFF'S OFFICE
TRAINING DIVISION

Sgt. Jeff Shoemaker's Dad was a Lieutenant with the Whitfield County Sheriff's Department during his entire childhood, and he was Jeff's hero. He would sit around and listen to the stories and tales his father and the other officers would tell, and some of them were a little rich for a boy's imagination. Jeff grew up in and around the Sheriff's Department; and he was the Captain of their Junior Deputy program.

In 1991, Jeff joined the Whitfield County Sheriff's Department as a Jailer and remained there until 1993. That same year Jeff married Andrea, whom he had actually met in Dalton before she moved back to Gainesville.

Her Grandfather, Rudolph Clark (brother of Melvin Clark who was slain as a revenuer and former Hall County Sheriff), helped him get a job at the Hall County Sheriff's Office as a Jailer.

In 1995, Jeff left Hall County and went to work as a Policeman in Jefferson, Ga. There he was regretting his move and began to work back towards Gainesville. In 1996, he went to work with the Gainesville Police Department and spent most of his time as a motorcycle officer and accident investigator. He also served on the honor guard as a bagpiper.

In 2002, Jeff accepted a position with the Hall County Sheriff's Office as a Deputy Sheriff and felt like he was back at home. He worked on patrol and later transferred to the traffic unit where before long he was back on a motorcycle. He said this assignment was one of the best he has ever had. The motorcycle division participated in and won several police motorcycle rodeos. Jeff was promoted to Sergeant in 2008, and assigned to the training division. This has proven to be a very rewarding experience for Jeff and he says he feels like he's able to help make our Deputies safer. In 2009, he was assigned to the SWAT team and this proved to be very demanding and challenging. Jeff considers this to be one of the highlights of his career.

Jeff served as Master of Stone Lodge in 2001, 2005, and 2009. He says his greatest assets are his wife Andrea and their three children - Katie, Andrew, and Ashley.

Hall County Traffic Division, c 2003. (l to r): Rodney Watts, Stan Watson, Donnie Jarrard, Sgt. Kiley Sargent, Jeff Shoemaker.

*2004 – Gov Sonny Perdue presents keys to a Ford Expedition to
Sheriff Steve Cronic. The vehicle was awarded to the Hall County Sheriff's
Department as winner of the Governor's Cup, recognizing
the Georgia Sheriff's Department with the highest overall evaluation. Pictured
(l to r) Ft row: Hall County Rep. Stacy Reece, Rodney Watts, Sgt. (GSP) Clarence
Prince, Steve Cronic, Gov. Perdue, Col. Wayne Mock, Donna Welch, Kiley Sargent,
M. Nix. Back Row: Donnie Jarrard, Tammy Crawford, GSP Officer,
David Miller, Stan Watson, Jeff Strickland, Major Jim Ash, Jeff Shoemaker,
Mark Blihovde, GSP Officer, Kelley Edwards*

*Hall County Honor Guard
October 6, 2005*

Hall County Honor Guard Rifle Squad led by Cmdr. Bonner Burton. Pictured (l to r): Scott Ginn, Chris Dale, Thomas Hyde, Charles Wallace, Stephen Weaver, Bonner Burton (no rifle), Jonathan Jackson

SSGT BONNER BURTON

Bonner Burton comes from a military family. His father is a retired US Army Vietnam veteran, who now lives in Washington, GA. Bonner was born at Fort Gordon, GA, and because of his father's military service, the family lived in several different locations before Bonner graduated from high school in Newport News, Virginia. He has an Associates Degree in Criminal Justice from Georgia Military College in August, GA.

While a student at North Georgia College, he learned of an opening in the Hall County Sheriff's Department. On August 14, 1995, Bonner was hired by former Detention Center Commander, Capt. Jim Ash, as a detention officer in the Main Street location, and then attended the Athens Police Academy in 1996.

Bonner has held various positions over the years with the Detention Center, Uniform Patrol Division and Special Operations. He has also been School Resource Officer at West Hall High School. In addition, Bonner has been a member of the SWAT team for several years. The SWAT Commander is 1st Lt. Joe Carter, Asst. Cmdr. of the Patrol Division. The SWAT team consists of approx. 25 highly trained officers. According to SSGT Burton, the mission of the SWAT team is to save lives and to help those in need.

Bonner is the Commander of the Hall County Honor Guard consisting of approx. 30 members. He joined the Honor Guard in 1996, and in 1998 became Asst. Commander, then Commander in 2008.

The Honor Guard has participated in three national competitions, taking third place in the National FOP competition in Washington, DC in 2007. In addition, in 1999, the team spent a week training with the Old Guard, 3rd Infantry Regiment in Washington, DC. The Hall County Sheriff's Office Honor Guard is the ceremonial unit of the department, comprised of deputies from all four divisions of the department.

The Honor Guard participates in funeral services for fallen or retired law enforcement officers and military veterans (working through Fort McPherson, GA), parades, and other community events.

In addition to the Rifle Squad, Flag Detail and Mounted Detail, the Honor Guard includes two buglers and two bagpipers. Each Memorial Day, at the veterans section of Memorial Park Cemetery, the Honor Guard marches the entire twenty four hours of the holiday period as a tribute to the veterans of Hall County. The Honor Guard is made up of highly skilled Hall County deputies who volunteer and train for this duty. The Hall County Sheriff's Office Honor Guard is one of the most elite units in Georgia.

SSGT Bonner Burton is currently a Training Officer at the Willard Baxter Training Center in Gainesville, GA.

SWAT team members (l to r) Jonathan Jackson and Joe Groover

GUNMAN NEAR LULA ELEMENTARY SCHOOL

On the morning of August 11, 2008, Deputy Joseph Groover, Hall County SWAT/K-9 Officer, reported for work like any other day. Just as he was getting out of his patrol car, a call came over the radio regarding shots being fired in downtown Lula, and then an encounter between an off-duty officer and a man who had allegedly pointed a gun at him in downtown Lula. The gunman retreated toward Lula Elementary School and into the woods, and later secured a position inside his camping trailer. It was just about 9:00 am. For the safety of the students, Sheriff's officers asked school officials to place the elementary school under lockdown.

At this time, all available patrol units scrambled and quickly headed up I - 985 North, including Officer Groover along with his canine partner, Katie. Upon arrival at the scene, other officers had already set up a security perimeter for the command post. At the end of a short driveway, and in close proximity to Lula Elementary School, was a small motorhome in a heavily wooded area. At times, the officers could hear banging noises and movement inside the trailer, and surmised that the gunman was barricading the door and windows.

Due to the closeness to the school, the officers had to plan their actions very carefully. Negotiators, with the use of the PA system on their patrol car, tried for about an hour to convince the gunman to surrender, but it was to no avail. K – 9 Officer Charles Wallace was positioned in the woods behind the trailer in case an escape out the back was attempted. Later on, three snipers were positioned in the woods behind the camper.

One door was located on the right rear side of the camper as well as the two doors on either side of the cab. In addition to the windshield, which remained covered with a blue tarp, and the two side windows in the cab, there were two windows on either side of the motorhome. The camper was positioned so that the suspect had a clear view of the driveway from the window on the left. The camper was set up on higher ground with the sun shining directly into the eyes of the approaching SWAT team members.

The officers had a patrol car parked at an angle at the entrance of the driveway. After the negotiations failed, the initial plan of action was to approach the trailer in a four man stack formation in order to get close enough to fire a gas round through the window so that the suspect would be forced out into the open for apprehension. The four member SWAT team was made up as follows: Point Officer – Bonner Burton with protective shield, Officer Joe Groover, Officer Chris Tempel, and Officer Nix.

Behind the patrol car blocking the driveway, on opposite sides of the vehicle, were Officers Chris Farmer and West Mills providing cover for the team. Due to the location of the school and the thick vegetation surrounding the scene, the only approach for the team was up the driveway leading to the camper. In a tight stack formation, the team advanced up the driveway. When they were within 15 – 20 yards of the target vehicle, a gas round was fired according to plan – it missed the window and bounced off the side of the trailer. Immediately, the gunman opened fire with a .44 cal. pistol. The team could hear the bullets whizzing past their heads and see the smoke and fire coming from the window as each shot rang out.

While returning fire, the team maintained the tight stack and slowly withdrew backwards to a covered position. They needed to regroup with a different plan. From inside the trailer, there was complete silence from the gunman. SWAT members had been unable to get a 'throw phone' or any other means of communication inside the camper. At this point, the scene was so quiet team members could hear nothing but the sounds of nature around them – birds chirping and rustling the leaves. Everyone was listening intently for any sound coming from inside the camper. No one knew whether the gunman had been hit – or if he was just waiting for another approach by the team.

Therefore, the negotiations started again over the PA system, pleading with the gunman to surrender, but it was futile – there was no response at all from him. A decision was made for the SWAT team to make a second approach to attempt the same plan. During this hair raising advancement, they made it to within about 20 yards of the trailer, and fired another gas round through the screen window – and this time it hit the target. Once again, the gunman immediately opened fire on the team. It appeared he was firing from different positions out the same window. Once again, bullets were cutting through the air past the team members. And once again the SWAT team, while engaging the gunman, executed another backward withdrawal, keeping their tight stack formation.

They were within a few yards of reaching the covered position (a patrol car) when Officer Joe Groover was hit in his right forearm while returning fire with his weapon. The impact knocked him down, and produced immediate devastating pain. He was patting the ground, trying to find his weapon. Disoriented from the impact of the round, he was fighting the shock and pain. The .44 cal. round entered his right forearm, traveled up his arm and exited, then re-entered his upper arm, and he was bleeding profusely.

Officers Chris Farmer and West Mills bravely ran from their covered position out into the open, under fire, and dragged their teammate to a secure position on the other side of the road, leaving a trail of blood all the way across the road, but saving his life. Officer Groover was then carried to the carport of a house where a triage unit had been set up, and a fire department medical team was waiting. They began medical treatment immediately, and continued until a medical helicopter airlifted him to Grady Hospital in Atlanta.

Officer Jonathan (J. J.) Jackson arrived at the scene just as the officers were dragging a wounded and bleeding Joe Groover across the road. He quickly assessed the wound and was horrified to see the ground through the hole in Groover's arm.

After Groover was safely evacuated, the SWAT team started preparing for a third approach to the camper. It was discovered that the multi – smoke grenade launcher had become inoperable. Officer Jackson rushed to the SWAT truck to get a replacement launcher. Inside, he retrieved two single launchers with grenades, and quickly returned to the patrol vehicle at the driveway entrance.

On request, Jackson and another officer fired a volley of gas rounds at the site. Another SWAT group was organized for a third advancement to the trailer. This group was Point Officer Bonner Burton and Officers Jason Smith, West Mills, Brian Pearson and Chris Tempel. This team, in a tight stack, was able to make an undetected advance to the rear area of the camper. In the process the hooligan tool was lost and the only thing available to break in the rear door was a shovel. While attempting to breach the door, the suspect again started shooting through it. The officers had to seek individual cover. They advised that they were pinned down at the back door!

At this point, Officers Mike Myers, Jonathan Jackson, Brad Rounds and Mike Nix were able to maneuver along the wood line and came out at the front portion of the site. During all this, while performing his duties as a grenadier, Officer Jonathan Jackson met the suspect face to face at the front window where the suspect fired point blank at him – the smoke and flash momentarily obscured his vision but then he realized the round had missed him. Later when the suspect stopped shooting, the team was able to bend the corner of the trailer door enough to make entry and crawled inside.

Led by Officer Bonner Burton and followed by Jonathan Jackson and West Mills, the suspect along with his weapon was apprehended, and he was transported by ambulance for treatment — he expired shortly after arriving at Northeast Georgia Medical Center in Gainesville.

After the officers performed their after-action duties, they were released. After he went home and changed his clothes, Officer Jackson as well as other officers traveled to Grady to check on the condition of Officer Groover, who by this time had undergone major surgery on his arm.

Officer Groover maintained consciousness throughout the ordeal, even during the helicopter flight to Grady and during initial treatment there. He said that as the altitude of the helicopter increased, the level of pain increased dramatically. Although he was in a great deal of pain, he could not be given morphine due to his medical condition, and the emergency medical team did a wonderful job in keeping him stable so that he did not go into shock. He spent eleven days in the hospital, undergoing three surgeries, followed by two additional surgeries later on.

Hall County Sheriff's Department officers were with Deputy Groover 24 – 7 while he was in the hospital. Afterward, he had to learn to write and shoot with his left hand. The surgeon had to leave the bullet in his upper arm, saying it would do more harm than good to try to remove it. The good news is that he shoots left handed better than ever.

Officer Groover praises the other team members who were left at the scene to complete the mission of apprehending the gunman. All the officers named are heroes, and Hall County is fortunate to have this caliber of brave, dedicated officers.

Officer Joe Groover is a role model for present and future officers. He has set the standard high with his 'can do' attitude and willingness to serve mankind and the citizens of Hall County.

Officer Groover has been awarded the Medal of Valor and the Purple Heart. He credits his fellow officers for risking their lives for him — it was a team effort, he says. He was also chosen as the 2008 Hall County Officer of the Year. Further, his fellow officers were also recognized by the Hall County Sheriff's Department for their bravery on August 11, 2008.

Joe Groover is back on duty as a K9 Trainer, doing what he loves best — serving Hall County citizens. He began his law enforcement career in Savannah, GA. prior to joining the Hall County Sheriff's Department. When he came to Hall County, he brought his family (wife Kristie and four sons) and his K9, Nero, with him from Savannah — Nero is now retired, and living at home with Joe and his family.

NOTE: As a three tour combat veteran, my interview with Officers Joe Groover, Jonathan Jackson and Bonner Burton was most touching. According to Officer Bonner Burton, Officer Jonathan Jackson's heroic actions as a grenadier saved the SWAT team. We appreciate the heroic actions of the officers of the Hall County Sheriff's Department who responded on August 11, 2008, and kept Hall County citizens safe.

l to r: Injured SWAT team member Joe Groover and Officer Jay Ivey with K9 Katie

Hall County SWAT Team 2010 - Front row (l to r): Tim Grizzle, Sgt. Sean McCusker, Corey Gilleland, Sgt. Kelley Edwards, Glen Watson, Sgt. Mike Lusk, West

Mills. Back row: Lt. Mike Myers (Asst. Cmdr.), Sgt. Jason Smith, Sgt. Jake Haney, Stephen Wilbanks, Sgt. Chris Tempel, Sgt. Bonner Burton, Kacey Stewart, Cpl. Chris Farmer, Joe Groover, 1ˢᵗ Lt. Joe Carter (Cmdr.), Sgt. Stephen Mickels, Mark Thomason, Sgt. Jeff Shoemaker. Not pictured: Jonathan Jackson, Lt. Brian Pearson, Sgt. Don Scalia, Sgt. David Sullivan.

L to r: Officers Donna Welsh and Tammy Crawford in confiscated Mustang

Photo courtesy David & Ina Griffin
L to r: June 26, 2003 - Sheriffs Dick Mecum, Steve Cronic, Bob Vass, and Ed England. These dedicated law men are responsible for making Hall County the safe place we enjoy today.

SHERIFFS OF HALL COUNTY, GA (1818 – 2010)

Hall County was founded on December 15, 1818, and named after Dr. Lyman Hall, one of Georgia's three signers of the Declaration of Independence. The following are Sheriffs who have served the county since that time.

COMMISSION DATE	NAME	WHEN SUCCEEDED
March 19, 1819	Michael Dickson	
January 14, 1820	John McConnell	
January 24, 1822	Jacob Eberhart	
January 22, 1824	John McConnell, Sr.	
January 13, 1826	John Eberhart	
January 17, 1828	Aaron B. Hardin	
February 17, 1830	Jacob Eberhart	January 19, 1832
January 19, 1832	Abraham Chastain	January 18, 1834
January 18, 1834	Jacob Eberhart	January 13, 1836
January 13, 1836	James Floyd	August 23, 1837
August 23, 1837	Benjamin Porter	January 18, 1838
January 18, 1838	Benjamin Dunagan	
January 10, 1840	Jonathan J. Baugh	January 10, 1842
January 10, 1842	Benjamin Dunagan	
January 16, 1844	James D. Hardage	
February 5, 1844	Ambrose Kennedy	
January 15, 1846	Richard H. Waters	January 22, 1848
January 22, 1848	Ambrose Kennedy	
January 12, 1850	Richard H. Waters	January 10, 1852
January 10, 1852	Ambrose Kennedy	January 11, 1854
January 10, 1854	Col. H. Boyd	January 12, 1856
January 12, 1856	Alexander M. Evans	September 24, 1856
September 24, 1856	Claiborn Revel	January 14, 1858

January 14, 1858	Benjamin Bryan	January 13, 1860
1860	R. H. Waters	*See Note 1*
January 13, 1861	Richard H. Waters	
January 23, 1862	Ambrose Kennedy	February 16, 1864
February 16, 1864	R. H. Waters	January 22, 1866
January 22, 1866	W. H. Griffies	September 24, 1866
September 24, 1866	L. A. Simmons	
September 25, 1868	John Robison	
	John Pierce (Acting Sheriff)	*See Note 2*
1869	J. H. Hulsey	*See Note 3*

COMMISSION DATE	NAME	DATE SWORN IN
February 9, 1871	J. S. Latham	March 18, 1871
January 15, 1873	James L. Waters	February 13, 1873
January 11, 1875	James L. Waters	February 3, 1875
January 16, 1877	John L. Gaines	January 27, 1877
January 11, 1879	John L. Gaines	February 6, 1879
January 10, 1881	John L. Gaines	February 10, 1881
January 30, 1883	John L. Gaines	January 25, 1883
January 20, 1885	John L. Gaines	February 2, 1885
January 10, 1887	James F. Duckett	January 19, 1887
January 5, 1889	A. J. Mundy	January 9, 1889
January 12, 1891	A. J. Mundy	January 20, 1891
January 6, 1893	A. J. Mundy	January 26, 1893
January 9, 1895	A. J. Mundy	January 31, 1895
October 15, 1896	A. J. Mundy	November 14, 1896
October 19, 1898	A. J. Mundy	November 12, 1898
October 18, 1900	M. O. Gilmer	December 31, 1900
October 10, 1902	M. O. Gilmer	December 26, 1902
October 17, 1904	W. A. Crow, Sr.	December 15, 1904
November 1, 1906	W. A. Crow, Sr.	December 21, 1906
November 3, 1908	W. A. Crow, Sr.	December 4, 1908
November 5, 1910	W. A. Crow, Sr.	December 29, 1910
October 12, 1912	E. A. Spencer	October 15, 1912
November 30, 1914	E. A. Spencer	December 29, 1914
December 4, 1916	W. A. Crow, Sr.	December 9, 1916
December 9, 1920	W. A. Crow, Sr.	December 18, 1920
December 20, 1924	B. A. Rogers	December 16, 1924
December 20, 1928	W. A. Crow, Sr.	December 31, 1928

March 26, 1929	W. A. Crow, Jr. (Acting)	*See Note 4*
April 22, 1929	Irvin L. Lawson	April 23, 1929
December 15, 1932	Irvin L. Lawson	January 17, 1933
December 3, 1936	Arthur W. Bell	December 28, 1936
August 19, 1943	Melvin J. Clark (Acting)	*See Note 5*
September 30, 1943	William A. (Bill) Crow	October 4, 1943
November 20, 1944	William A. (Bill) Crow	December 14, 1944
December 20, 1948	Ferd Bryan	December 31, 1948
May 11, 1950	Mrs. Constance Bryan	*See Note 6*
June 21, 1950	C. W. (Cal) Wilson	June 22, 1950
December 10, 1952	C. W. (Cal) Wilson	December 20, 1952
December 10, 1956	C. W. (Cal) Wilson	December 22, 1956
December 20, 1960	E. L. (Ed) England	December 23, 1960
December 18, 1964	Wilburn L. Reed, Jr.	December 23, 1964
December 16, 1968	Wilburn L. Reed, Jr.	December 28, 1968
December 15, 1972	E. L. (Ed) England	December 28, 1972
December 15, 1976	E. L. (Ed) England	December 17, 1976
Terms (3)	Richard V. Mecum	1981 – 1992
Terms (2)	Robert G. Vass	1993 – 2000
Terms (3)	Steve Cronic	2001 - Present

The above data was confirmed by documents from the Executive Department – Georgia Archives/History Division

Commission Date: the date which appears on the Commission signed by the Governor

Notes:

1. Information located in Hall County Court House, Deed Book I, pp.256, 301, 323
2. Information located in Hall County Court House, Deed Book J, p. 178; "October 16, 1869 – John Pierce, Coroner, was Acting Sheriff."
3. Election information from files of Air-Line Eagle 1869, compiled by W. H. Craig.
4. W. A. Crow, Sr. died of a heart attack while in office. His son, W. A. Crow, Jr. was appointed Acting Sheriff until a special election could be held.
5. Arthur W. Bell died of a heart attack while in office. Melvin J. Clark was appointed Acting Sheriff by W. F. Wood, Ordinary, until September 22, 1943.
6. Ferd Bryan also suffered a heart attack while in office. His wife, Mrs. Constance Bryan, was appointed to act as Sheriff by Governor Talmadge until a successor could be elected and qualified.

GAINESVILLE COURTHOUSE
1895

*This Hall County Courthouse had been built in 1883 by J. M. B.
Winburn and was located on South Bradford Street.*

Destruction of the Hall County Court House, Hall County, Georgia historical photograph collection, Hall County Library System.
The remains of the Hall County Courthouse are in the upper left corner of the photograph.

Photo courtesy Judy Mecum
Hall County Courthouse c 1938, rebuilt after the 1936 tornado

ADDITION TO HALL COUNTY COURTHOUSE
DEDICATED IN 1978

Court Services Division c 2009, led by Capt. Chris Matthews, 9th from left

PART III

LAW ENFORCEMENT IN HALL COUNTY, GA 1818 – 2010

MISCELLANEOUS HISTORY OF HALL COUNTY AND IT'S LAW ENFORCEMENT

Early settlers pushed into Hall County from Franklin and Jackson Counties in the mid-1790's. The first settlement in Hall County was at Stonethrow, now known as Gillsville. The elections were held at the house of John McDuffie before a suitable courthouse was erected.

. . .

The first Superior Court for the County of Hall was held at the house of John McDuffie on Thursday the 19th day of August, 1819, the Honorable John M. Dooly presiding. The first True Bill was the State vs. Ellis Treadaway (assault and battery); the second True Bill was the State vs. Robert Fluker, James Morgan (murder).

From the Superior Court Records, Hall County Courthouse

. . .

Hall County was so named in honor of Dr. Lyman Hall on December 15, 1818. The county is 30 miles in length, 24 miles in breadth and has 430.9 square miles. When Hall County was eight years old (1825), there were 8,245 residents in the county.

. . .

The Presbyterians were the strongest religious denomination, dating back to 1825.

. . .

March 6, 1920 – Georgia, Hall County: Early sheriffs, such as Michael Dickson and John McConnell, had to swear that they had not been engaged in a duel directly of indirectly since the first day of January, 1819.

. . .

SHERIFF ORDERED TO HANG INDIAN
State Rights: The Hanging of George Tassel

In December, 1828, the Georgia Legislature passed a bill enacting that the Cherokee country should be put under the jurisdiction of the laws of Georgia. The Act was passed on the grounds that, as the Cherokee country was part and parcel of the State of Georgia, it should be governed by the laws of Georgia; but the real object was to move the Cherokees from the State. In order to give them plenty of time, the Act was not to go into effect until June 1, 1830. The Cherokees felt deeply outraged, and they determined at the first opportunity to test the validity of this Act before the Supreme Court of the United States.

An opportunity soon occurred. In the summer of 1830, a half-breed Cherokee by the name of George (nicknamed 'Corn') Tassel, was detained for the murder of a white land in the Cherokee country. He was arraigned before the Superior Court, then sitting in Hall County, and was duly tried, found guilty and sentenced to be hanged. His attorneys appealed the case to the United States Supreme Court, asking that the verdict be set aside on grounds that the Act of Legislature giving the State of Georgia jurisdiction over the Cherokee country was a violation of the Federal Constitution, and was therefore null and void.

The case of George Tassel versus the State of Georgia was duly entered on the Supreme Court docket.

Governor George R. Gilmer was officially notified of the action, and was instructed to appear before the court of Georgia as defendant in the case. But the governor replied with spirit that the United States Supreme Court lacked jurisdiction in the case, and that the State of Georgia would scorn to compromise itself by appearing before that tribunal as defendant under these circumstances. It was a foregone conclusion that the case would be decided against Georgia. To prevent this, Governor Gilmer resorted to the extraordinary measure of dispatching a special messenger to the Sheriff of Hall County, Jacob Eberhart, with instructions to hang George Tassel immediately, before the case could e reached on the Supreme Court docket.

The Sheriff obeyed the order promptly, so poor George Tassel was hanged while his case was pending in the United States Supreme Court.

- L. L. Knight in *Georgia's Landmarks, Memorials and Legends*, 1913

According to additional information obtained from www.aaanativearts. com, a website on famous Cherokees:

Tassel deserved to be tried in a Cherokee court, since the Cherokee Nation was sovereign. The Cherokee Nation won a stay of execution from the United States Supreme Court, but the State of Georgia ignored the stay and murdered him anyway. His legal case became the first Cherokee legal document to set precedence on behalf of Cherokee sovereignty. This case is still considered an important precedent for Indian sovereignty today.

. . .

The coroner is apparently the only person with the authority to arrest the Sheriff. The court ruled on a motion for contempt of court against the Sheriff of Hall County, Jacob Eberhart, for failure to pay a fifa to plaintiff's attorney and that the coroner commit him to jail until the fifa is paid. However, Sheriff Eberhart paid the fifa and wasn't arrested.

January Term of Inferior Court, 1842

. . .

Good Tidings from Sheriff – All the hands connected with this office desire to express their thanks to Sheriff J. H. Hulsey for his kindly remembrance in the apples presented on Tuesday. Our devil says he is a lettle the cleverest man he has seen for a long time.

The Eagle, September 23, 1870

. . .

MOONSHINERS SHOT

James A. Grant, born July 4, 1854, and Joseph Prater, born October 17, 1862, were assassinated by government men.

TRADITION: These two men had a still on the property located at Grant Ford Road (off Cool Springs Road) across the road from WOW Camp. Government men came and shot the men on the spot. The men

(Grant and Prater) are buried where they were killed. One headstone has both names:

Grant, James A. – assassinated . . July 4, 1854 – December 16, 1884

Prater, Joseph – assassinated. . October 17, 1862 – December 16, 1884

Tombstone Inscriptions of Hall County, GA by Sybil McRay

. . .

HALL COUNTY JAIL BURNED

On Sunday night last, the Jail in this place was totally destroyed by fire. It was a wooden building, and had been standing nearly, or quite, forty years, having been constructed originally in a strong and substantial manner.

It was set on fire by Jesse Suggs, a prisoner, who had been committed some time previously on a charge of larceny from the house. His statement is that, with a few matches and a candle, which he was permitted by the jailer to have, and a ladder used for descending into the dungeon, which he broke up, he started a fire, and was attempting to burn the wall around the grate on the east side of the house, so that he could remove the grate and make his escape. Before he had accomplished his object, the fire was communicated to the weatherboarding on the outside of the house, and had passed beyond his control. As soon as he discovered the situation, he began to cry lustily for help, which gave the alarm, but too late to subdue the fire.

The prisoner was rescued from his perilous situation, but barely escaped suffocation. Fortunately, rain had fallen on Sunday afternoon, which, together with the prompt action of our citizens, prevented further damage.
- from files of Air Line Eagle of 1869
J. E. Redwine, Publisher – February 12, 1869

The Superior Court for this county adjourned on Saturday afternoon, having been in session through the week. The most important case tried was the State vs. Jesse Suggs – Arson (burning the Jail). The jury returned a verdict of guilty, but recommended that the punishment be commuted, whereupon Judge Davis sentenced him to the penitentiary for life.
- Air Line Eagle, March 26, 1869

HAVE YOU SOME TO EXPORT?
Sheriff Hall County, Georgia

Sirs: I want a man-trailing blood-hound. If you can procure me such or refer me to the owner of such a dog, kindly advise me at once. State their age, training and ability of the dog and his price, etc. (signed) Very respectfully, R. P. Franklin

The above is a copy of a letter received by Sheriff Mundy this week. As is seen by the date line, it is from the home of Honorable W. J. Bryan, who was here this summer at the Chautauqua; and it is presumed he heard of the wonderful feats of Georgia blood hounds and directed one of his fellow citizens to get one as they are guaranteed never to fail in catching all kinds of criminals from petty thieves up to the Presidency - that he wants a blood hound to catch him and keep up with him that he may know "where he is at". As the Georgia dog law soon goes into effect, now is a good time to get rid of dogs, and the Nebraskan's letter opens up wonderful possibilities for exporting canines.
- Eagle, Lincoln, Nebraska, December 14, 1899

. . .

During the early 1900's, there were many duels. Many times, both individuals would be killed.

. . .

The jail in the early 1900's was found by the Hall County Grand Jury to be unsanitary and exhibited poor security.

. . .

A tornado struck in 1903, leveling most of the southern half of Gainesville. The structures were rebuilt, but in 1936, tornadoes destroyed the entire downtown area. A new downtown grew out of the rubble, bigger and more attractive than ever before. Sheriff M. O. Gilmer and Sheriff I. L. Lawson were in office during these periods.

. . .

Early Sheriffs were elected to two year terms, later becoming four years. During the early years, the Sheriff was known as the BIG LAW or THE HIGH SHERIFF.

. . .

Early law enforcement did not have uniforms and marked cars. As late as the 1950's, Sheriffs and deputies did not wear uniforms nor did they have insignia on their vehicles.

. . .

With the establishment of Lake Lanier, new bridges were constructed and the population of Hall County grew tremendously. The lake was respectfully named after Sidney Lanier, a famous Georgia poet, who had once praised Hall County in his poem, *The Song of the Chattahoochee.*

By the late 1960's, the population grew to 70,000 and in 1980, there were 74,405 people scattered throughout Hall County. Lake Lanier's 540 miles (871 kilometers) of scenic shoreline have attracted throngs of people causing this growth. This growth in population has caused a heavy load on our Sheriff's Department while patrolling the lake area.

. . .

NO HANGING
Unique Story of a Hall Countian, Grady Reynolds

Bud Brooks and Grady Reynolds were not executed yesterday. Bud Brooks' attorneys yesterday filed a bill of exceptions in his case and it goes to the Supreme Court. The grounds upon which the bill was filed are not known. Both men were found guilty of murdering M. C. Hunt of Belton, Jackson County, and were to have been hung at Jefferson yesterday.

- Georgia Cracker, September 25, 1897

REYNOLDS RESPITED AGAIN

Governor Atkinson has granted Grady Reynolds, the Jackson County murderer, another respite which ends December 3. It will be remembered that his present respite would have ended next Friday, and the Governor extended the time at the request of the Solicitor C. H. Brand and the relatives of Hunt, who do not want Reynolds hanged before Bud Brooks pays the penalty of death for the crime also. Brooks' case has gone to the Supreme Court and it is not known when it will come up for a hearing.

- Georgia Cracker, October 16, 1897

. . .

BOTH WILL HANG

Grady Reynolds will die on the scaffold at Jefferson, December 14. Bud Brooks will share a similar fate December 17. Jude Hutchins passed sentence on Brooks Tuesday. It is hardly probable that anything else will be done for the condemned men by their attorneys; in fact, nothing can be done but appeal for executive clemency, and if it were made, it would doubtless avail nothing. Both men were convicted of the murder of merchant Hunt, and the crime was one of the most atrocious in the criminal annals of the state. The people of Jackson County will welcome the day of the execution of the murderers.

- Georgia Cracker, December 4, 1897

. . .

NECKS BROKEN

Bud Brooks and Grady Reynolds paid the penalty of death on the gallows at Jefferson, yesterday for the murder of merchant M. C. Hunt. There was no further attempt to interfere with the law. The bodies of the men will be interred in the county.

- Georgia Cracker, December 18, 1897

According to an exchange, when the wife of Grady Reynolds, executed a few weeks since for murder, asked the condemned man if she and the children could come to the hanging, he replied in the negative. Whereupon she rejoined: "You are just like you allus wuz, Grady Reynolds. You ain't changed narry bit, you never did want me an' the little 'uns to see no pleasure!"

- Georgia Cracker, January 29, 1898

Steve Brinson, First National Bank, shared these articles from research he has conducted. He found the burial place of Reynolds off Joe Chandler Road (on East Hall Road). A resident of the area told Brinson her dad dug his grave — three times! There was a superstition about leaving an open grave. Reynolds, according to Brinson, was a resident of Hall County.

. . .

LEGAL HANGINGS IN GEORGIA

It is believed that the first person to be legally executed in Colonial Georgia was a white female, Alice Ryley, who immigrated to America, and then was hung for the murder of her master, Will Wise. The last legal hanging occurred on May 20, 1925, when two men were hung in Columbus, Georgia. It is thought that about 500 hangings were carried out in Georgia between 1725 and 1925, when the electric chair became the new means of execution in Georgia.

. . .

The trend of crimes in Hall County appears to be as follows: in the early 1950's, moonshine was the big activity; in the early 1960's, it was auto theft — with A. D. Allen the ringleader. In the late 1960's, the drug problem became prominent with the use of drugs still being the primary contributing factor to crimes in the 1980's, 1990's, and on past the turn of the century, with increases in crimes such as burglaries and armed robberies in order to support the drug habit.

. . .

Law Enforcement in Hall County 1818 – 1980, First Edition **by Willard J. Langdon**
can be found in the Hall County Library and libraries of surrounding Universities

. . .

In the heyday of moonshine prosecutions, those convicted of the crime were sent to Federal prison. There they were held in close proximity with the more hardened criminals. In the opinion of some former law enforcement officers, the moonshiners made acquaintances and connections throughout the United States that allowed criminal activity to accelerate. Moonshine went out and drugs came in and spread rapidly through these previously made networks. This is the reason, they say, that drug activity spread so quickly and is so difficult to combat.

. . .

During my research, I learned that Masonry was prevalent among law men from the early days to the present. Many of the Sheriffs and deputies have been Masons.

PART IV

LAW ENFORCEMENT IN HALL COUNTY, GA 1818 – 2010 GAINESVILLE POLICE DEPARTMENT, GAINESVILLE, GA

Courageous, Outstanding, Professional

Photo courtesy Hoyt Henry, Jr.

Chief Hoyt Henry and two patrol officers

HISTORICAL OVERVIEW – GAINESVILLE, GA POLICE DEPARTMENT

The duties of a Marshall were mentioned in records dated in **1823**. It was noted that in 1873, the Mayor and Council selected the Marshall and Deputy by ballot. Those who violated the city ordinances, after being charged by the Marshall, would be brought to court, and the Mayor could sentence the violator to short jail terms or to work on the city streets.

In the **1870's**, the Marshall had to enforce ordinances such as cattle and livestock roaming in the city streets, and owners were assessed fines. In May 1875, the editor of the Gainesville Eagle warned the Marshall that "you have to lay aside the police suit, or you will never get up close. The boys can see you too far."

In **1877**, the Marshall arrested a black man who had in his possession a number of gold pencils and was offering them for sale at a very low price. On Wednesday night at about 1:00 am, the arrestee set fire to the calaboose (jail), and very nearly suffocated himself along with the other prisoners.

The first known newspaper report of an escape from the calaboose occurred in 1877. The prisoner took a file, cut off the door hinges and escaped.

Also in 1877, Marshall John A. Morrison was brought before the city attorney with charges against him by the city mayor for inefficiency and failure to execute his duties.

The last known reference to a Marshall was in 1878. It is generally believed that the title of Marshall was changed in the late 1800's to Chief. Actual reference to the Chief of Police in the city charter laws was not made until 1922; however, at that time the Chief also was designated ex-officio Marshall.

In **1884**, the mayor of Gainesville was S. C. Dunlap. The city owned two mules, a harness, a wagon and a cart. Total for feeding and upkeep of the mules for 1884 was $145.67.

At 4:00pm on Thursday, December 25, **1890**, Gainesville Police Chief William James Kittrell became the first Gainesville officer to be killed in the line of duty when he was shot while responding to a domestic incident at the local train station. A woman and her father were at or near the depot where the father was attempting to get his daughter out of town. The responding officers, Towery and the Chief, tried to stop them, and the father opened fire, striking Chief Kittrell in the spine. The other officer returned fire and killed the suspect. Chief Kittrell was only 35 years old, and left behind a wife, four daughters, and an unborn son. He is buried at Alta Vista Cemetery.

In **1892**, R. T. Bagwell was Chief of Police. His son, William D. Bagwell and grandson, William D. 'Bill' Bagwell, Jr. later became Gainesville Police Chiefs — three generations of Bagwell Police Chiefs in the City of Gainesville.

1903 – Chief Parks was Gainesville Chief of Police. In April of that year, Frank Redmond was shot by Chief Parks. Chief Parks was later exonerated by a coroner's jury.

Before there was such a thing as police radio in Gainesville, the police department had an unusual way of informing patrolmen of calls. There was a switch in the City Hall that controlled the street lights. If a call came in, the switch was turned off and the street lights blinked so that the policemen knew to return to City Hall and pick up the call. And before there were police cars, policemen either rode the street cars or walked. Street cars were once pulled by horses and switched to electric in 1903, the same year a tornado hit New Holland, inflicting severe damage and loss of life.

1936 – D. Jack Hopkins, Chief during the 1936 tornado.

On December 21, **1944**, work was started installing Gainesville's newest radio tower for station WHNX located in front of City Hall, a special frequency used by the Gainesville Police. Also in 1944, Hoyt Henry joined the Gainesville Police Department as a patrolman.

Early **1940s** – Chief Westbrooks with a twelve man department including Bill Bagwell, "Scrap" Whitmire, Frank Strickland, Bill Lipscomb, Rad Bonds, Charles Castleberry, Guy Cooper, Richardson, Patton, Bill Henderson and Carlin.

Late **1940s** - Guy Cooper worked as a patrolman for a number of years, and was promoted to Chief in the late 1940's. In **1947**, with about 15 men under his command, the department worked in three shifts of five men each, and had two patrol cars. One car patrolled the residential and business areas and ran 24 hours a day, while the other ran downtown at night. During the summer vacation months, young high school age students answered the telephone and operated the radio for the department. Cooper was Chief for several years. He continued working with the Department as a meter officer until his retirement in 1967. He then worked for the PWC for a while, and then was employed at First National Bank until his death in May, 1975, at age 72.

William D. 'Bill' Bagwell, Jr. became Chief in 1948 until 1952.

September 1, 1952 – Hoyt Henry became Gainesville Police Chief, and for a while, was the youngest police chief in the state at only 29 years old.

1956 – G. A. 'Red' Singleton and E. 'Cut' Parks were promoted by Chief Henry from patrolman to detective lieutenants, thereby beginning the first Detective Division of the Department. Officer Parks was praised by Gene Earls for teaching him detective work. Earls said that Parks was an excellent detective – the best.

1962 – Chief Hoyt Henry hired the first woman in the Gainesville Police Department, Annie Jo Harden, as a clerical worker for the Chief, later secretary for the detectives. In 1970, Ms. Harden was awarded the WDUN Community involvement award "for her dedication to efficiency and constant service to her city."

And in 1962, came the first Traffic Division, Canine Corps and School Crossing Guards.

1963 - Chief Henry hired the first black patrolmen ever in the history of Gainesville, Ernest Eugene (Gene) Earls and Royce Stephens. They were pioneers!

1964 – Chief Henry initiated the first in-service training and appointed Officer Harold Black as the first training officer. Officer Black won several awards and honors in the late 1960's and early 1970's. He was named the district representative for the Gainesville – Athens area in law enforcement television training, and was featured on the statewide Law Enforcement TV Training Project broadcast over Georgia Education Television. These programs were viewed by law enforcement officers throughout the state and were instrumental in saving the lives of Officers Gene Earls and Benny Allen in late 1967.

1971 – Chief Henry formed the first Juvenile Division, and the first black woman, Laura Giles, was hired as a juvenile officer.

Chief Henry retired as Chief in 1971, after being one of the most out-standing Chiefs in the history of the Department.

1971 – 1977 – G. A. 'Red' Singleton was Chief of the Gainesville Police Department. Chief Singleton hired the first female police officers, Judy Free and Patsy Simmons, and assigned them to the traffic division.

1972 – Officer Henry Davis, a four year veteran, was killed in the line of duty in a three car collision on Dawsonville Highway in September, 1972. Later, his badge #7 was retired.

1977 – July, 1985 – George Knapp was Gainesville Police Chief. Chief Knapp is currently employed in Court Services with the Hall County Sheriff's Department.

1985 – October, 1988 – Jerry Forrester was Gainesville Police Chief.

Note: Assistant City Manager Bill Lewis was acting Chief until a new police chief was selected.

1988 – 1998 – Fred Hayes was selected as Gainesville Police Chief.

June, 1998 – December 31, 2009 – Chief Frank Hooper was Chief of the Gainesville Police Department.

January 1, 2010 – Deputy Chief Jane Nichols was selected as Interim Police Chief, the first female Interim Police Chief for the City of Gainesville. On March 15, 2010, Interim Chief Nichols retired with 28 years of service.

March 17, 2010 – Chad White, Captain of Support Services Bureau, was selected as Interim Police Chief until the position of Chief could be filled.

May 10, 2010 – Lt. Brian P. Kelly was sworn in as Gainesville Police Chief by City Manager Kip Padgett.

Sources: Excerpts from the Gainesville Eagle, Gene Earls, Royce Stephens, Terry White, Judy Free, Harold Black, Chief Frank Hooper, and Hoyt Henry, Jr. (Buddy)

Note: I have attempted to be as accurate as possible while capturing this history.

Photo courtesy Frank Hooper
Gainesville Police Chief William James Kittrell

At 4:00pm on Thursday, December 25, 1890, Gainesville Police Chief William James Kittrell became the first Gainesville officer to be killed in the line of duty when he was shot while responding to a domestic incident at the local train station. A woman and her father were at or near the depot where the father was attempting to get his daughter out of town. The responding officers, Towery and the Chief, tried to stop them, and the father opened fire, striking Chief Kittrell in the spine. The other officer returned fire and killed the suspect. Chief Kittrell was only 35 years old, and left behind a wife, four daughters, and an unborn son. He is buried at Alta Vista Cemetery.

R. T. Bagwell, Gainesville Police Chief, Hall County, Georgia
historical photograph collection, Hall County Library System
R. T. Bagwell was Chief of the Gainesville Police Department in 1892. His son,
William D. Bagwell, and grandson, William D. "Bill" Bagwell,
Jr. – three generations - later became Gainesville Police Chiefs

*Gainesville Police Department, Hall County, Georgia historical
photograph collection, Hall County Library System.*
**The Gainesville Police Department in the early 1940s. Front row
(l to r): Bill Bagwell, Chief Westbrooks, 'Scrap' Whitmire. Back row: Frank
Strickland, Bill Lipscomb, Rad Bonds, Charles Castleberry, Guy Cooper, Richardson,
Patton, Bill Henderson, Carlin.**

CHIEF GUY COOPER

Photo courtesy Harold Black

H. Guy Cooper was a lifetime resident of Hall County and lived at 512 Osborne Street, Gainesville. He served a number of years as a patrol officer before being promoted to Chief of Police in the late 1940s. He held that position for several years, then returned as a police officer/ meter officer and retired in 1967. He worked for the PWC for a while. At the time of his death in May, 1975 at age 72, he was employed at First National Bank.

CHIEF WILLIAM 'BILL' BAGWELL

Photo courtesy Hoyt Henry, Jr.

William "Bill" Bagwell, a graduate of Gainesville High School, joined the Gainesville Police Department in 1942 as a patrolman. He was the first Gainesville patrolman to attend the FBI training school in Washington, DC, and was promoted to Chief shortly after his return in 1948. He was serving his fourth year as Chief and had received a LLB degree from Atlanta Law School when he resigned effective September 1, 1952.

Bill Bagwell's father, William Daniel Bagwell, Sr., served on the Gainesville police force for seventeen years, and was Chief at the time of his death in 1941. Bill's grandfather, Truman Bagwell, was also a member of the Gainesville force, serving twenty years and was Chief at the time of his death.

POLICE DESTROY BRADFORD STREET WHISKEY STILL IN BASEMENT OF HOUSE

In the late 1940s, Gainesville Police, led by Chief Bill Bagwell, captured a 35 – gallon capacity copper whiskey still and approx. 350 gallons of corn mash at 738 North Bradford Street, within eight blocks of the downtown square. Also found was nine gallons of illicit moonshine. The owner of the house had previously had electrical service cut off at the house in order to keep meter readers away.

Involved in the raid were Chief Bill Bagwell, Captain Hoyt Henry and Officer Frank Strickland. Fermenting corn mash, contained in six oak barrels and two large square wooden tanks was discovered in the basement of the house. The owner was arrested.

Chief Bagwell personally destroyed the still and furnace with an ax, and supervised destruction of the corn mash by the city sanitary department. Chief Bagwell said this was the eighth still destroyed inside the city limits in one week.

Photos courtesy Hoyt Henry, Jr.

Photo courtesy Hoyt Henry, Jr.
c 1949 - Front row (l to r): Joe Edge, Capt. Hoyt Henry,
J. L. Burel. Back row: James Harper, Clifford C. Strickland

CHIEF HOYT HERSCHEL HENRY

Photo courtesy Hoyt Henry, Jr.

Chief Hoyt Henry was a native and lifelong resident of Gainesville and Hall County. As a boy, he was raised on a farm in southern Hall County in the Mulberry River area. His father, W. H. Henry was a WWI veteran and a farmer.

Henry worked as a machinist helper at Chicopee Mill before joining the Army at age 19. There, as a squad leader for the Military Police, he learned his police skills. As a WWII veteran, he sustained a serious back injury, but he did not let this disability interfere with his doing a good job as a police officer. In November, 1944, Henry returned from military service to Gainesville where he accepted a job as a City policeman. He worked seven days a week, twelve hours a day earning a net pay of $85.91 per month after paying for half his uniform expense.

As a policeman, Henry knew how to be firm and still be courteous, which earned him respect from everyone on his beat. He had the natural ability to interact with others and knew how to defuse out of control situations. He was a hard worker and a model police officer, and he was promoted to Captain in 1948.

Hoyt Henry was selected Chief of the 12 officer Gainesville Police Department on September 1, 1952, and for a while, he was the youngest police chief in the state at only 29 years old.

During his tenure as chief, Henry's accomplishments proved he was forward thinking and ahead of his time. Within the Gainesville Police Department, he established the first Training Officer position, the first Detective Division, Traffic Division, K – 9 Corps (the first police dog was 'Hobo'), Juvenile Division, School Crossing Guards, and In-Service Training. The divisions are still being used today. He hired the first female clerical worker, the first two black patrol officers, and the first black Juvenile Officer, Laura Giles.

Chief Henry was a founding member of the Georgia Association of Chiefs of Police – and was rewarded with a life membership in 2006. He was recognized by all the local civic organizations and state law enforcement associations with scrap books full of certificates and letters of appreciation from throughout the United States, as well as from the citizens of Gainesville and Hall County. Chief Henry was a public servant, and was voted as the Goodwill Ambassador for the Gainesville Police Department and the City of Gainesville.

During the late 1960's when racial disturbance hit Gainesville, Chief Henry pulled his officers back to one point, walked by himself down the street into the crowd, and sat down on the grass to talk with those involved.

At Christmastime, after interviewing each prisoner, he would let them go home to spend Christmas Eve and Day with their families, with very few violators through the years. Chief Henry led by example and set the standards high for those to follow. He was one of the most highly regarded police chiefs in the southeastern United States.

In 1971, Chief Henry proudly retired with 26 years service – 19 years as Chief. During his time as Chief, he watched his department grow from a 12 man force to a 54 member team including four school crossing police-women. Among this team were eight black policemen and one black police-woman in the Juvenile Division.

On June 18, 1971, the Gainesville City Commission, in concurrence with the recommendation of the Gainesville Civil Service Board, named Chief Hoyt Henry Chief Emeritus.

Chief Henry continued his law enforcement career another 14 years as Chief of Police at Lake Lanier Islands; he started that Department, making it what it is today.

Chief Hoyt Henry passed away on February 29, 2008, at age 86, leaving behind his son, Hoyt H. Henry, Jr. (Buddy), a former GBI agent. A Mason (Gainesville Lodge #214), Chief Henry was buried at Alta Vista Cemetery with full police honors from the Gainesville Police Department and Hall County Sheriff's Department Honor Guards. The full ceremonial honors included a 21 gun salute and the playing of Taps. The Gainesville Fire Department extended its largest ladder truck displaying a large American flag over the gravesite.

Chief Henry continues to be a role model for others to follow, and is remembered for his dedicated service to his country, city and county.

NOTE: My interview with Hoyt H. Henry, Jr. (Buddy) about his Dad was a rewarding experience. Buddy Henry is a second generation law enforce-ment officer with 20+ years in the criminal justice system, 12 years as a GBI agent. He graduated from North Georgia College with a degree in Criminal Justice, and obtained four P.O.S.T. certifications before retiring with a medi-cal disability.

*Gainesville City Police, Hall County, Georgia historical
photograph collection, Hall County Library System*

*Chief Hoyt Henry, front center, Ed England is on
2nd row, 2nd from left, James
Harper on 2nd row, right end, and G. A. "Red" Singleton at top right*

Photo courtesy Terry White

Gainesville Police Department late 1950s –
Top row (l to r): A. "Mac"Vickery, H. Dale Sutton, Tom Pinson, Ray
Medlin, Roy Hooper, Richard Evans, Doyle Land, T. E. "Gip" Parks. 2ⁿᵈ Roy:
Harold G. Black, E. C. "Cut" Parks, Joe Edge, Chief Hoyt Henry (center), James
Harper, G. A. "Red" Singleton, H. Guy Cooper. 3ʳᵈ row: James C. Pierce, John
Burel, Frank Strickland, Rad Bonds, Clifford C. Strickland, Phillip Moore. Bottom
row: L. L. Bennett, Jack Lipscomb, Marvin Peek, Mrs. Annie Joe Harden,
Preston L. Grant, Leon Martin, Hugh Overby.

Photo courtesy Hoyt Henry, Jr.

Gainesville Police Department late 1950s – Top row (l to r): H. R. Overby, R. S. Medlin, C. C. Strickland, Capt. H. W. Nix, Roy H. Hooper, E. C. Parks, J. F. Bennett, Jr., R. C. Evans. 2nd row: L. L. Bennett, Jr., L. Martin. 3rd row: J. L Burel, Capt. J. V. Harper, Capt. J. J. Edge, Chief Hoyt H. Henry, Capt. R. L. Bonds, Capt. C. F. Strickland, M. H. Turk. Bottom row: T. E. Parks, J. Lipscomb, R. D. Buffington, G. A. Singleton, J. C. Pierce, A. M. Vickery, E. E. Bagwell, J. B. Phillips.

*Rad Bonds retirement – Hall County, Georgia historical
photograph collection, Hall County Library System.*

*August, 1965 – Capt. Rad Bonds turns in his gun to Chief Hoyt Henry
at Bond's retirement after 28 years, one month and 15 days of dedicated service.
Pictured (l to r): John Burel, Chief Hoyt Henry, Red Singleton, Rad Bonds, Cut
Parks, Mac Vickery and Frank Strickland*

RAD BONDS

Rad Bonds joined the Gainesville Police Department in June, 1937. The Department had only one patrol car, and Bonds was on the night shift seven days a week, making $99.00 per month. At the time of Bond's retirement in 1965, the Gainesville Police Department had six patrol cars, two scooters and two motorcycles.

Photo courtesy Hoyt Henry, Jr.
Chief Hoyt Henry, Miss America 1953 Neva Jane Langley
and GBI Agent Fred Culberson

Photo courtesy Hoyt Henry, Jr.

Chief Hoyt Henry, far right, in mid 1950s

RET. CMDR. HAROLD GRANT BLACK

A/K/A POPS

Harold G. Black is a native of Hall County, and he and his wife, Betty, have been married for 56 years. They have one son, Tony, and two grandchildren, Julia and Haley.

Harold graduated from Lyman Hall High School and attended the University of Georgia. He served four years in the United States Marine Corps, earning the rank of Staff Sergeant.

In March, 1956, Gainesville Police Chief Hoyt Henry hired the 28 year old as a police officer. His first job assignment was foot patrol writing parking tickets. According to Harold, on some days he would walk twenty plus miles by his meter.

For years, Black played Santa Claus at Christmas time — the fire truck would bring him into the Gainesville Square area and he would then visit the stores.

In 1964, President Lyndon Johnson visited Gainesville. Harold and fellow officer Tom Pinson were in the pilot car — the car closest to the President's vehicle. Officers involved in the planning for the President's visit were: Chief Hoyt Henry, Sparky Spence, John Burel, Tom Pinson and Harold Black.

Harold was the first Training Officer for the Gainesville Police Department and initiated the first in-service training. He won several awards and honors in the 1960's and 1970's, and was named the District Representative for the Gainesville — Athens area in Law Enforcement Television Training. As a police officer/actor, Harold was featured on the statewide Law Enforcement TV training project broadcast over Georgia Educational Television four times a week. The project was supported by a grant from the U.S. Justice Department's Office of Law Enforcement Assistance. In 1968, Harold was the first police officer in Georgia to receive an Associated Press Award for outstanding contributions to the field of broadcast journalism.

Harold wore many hats during his career — patrolman, Corporal, Sergeant, Captain and Commander. He retired November 30, 1988, with 32 years, 10 months and 10 days of dedicated service to the citizens of Gainesville and Hall County.

During his career, Harold served regularly as an instructor at the Regional Police Academy, and he has been awarded so many awards it's almost impossible to list them all. In 1967, Harold and Ron Attaway of the Hall County Sheriff's Department were the first officers to earn the Outstanding Officer award, which was presented by the American Legion. Harold also received this award again later in his career. He has been active in civic affairs, serving as President of the Civitan Club, and he has participated in the Peace Officer's Association of Georgia, Georgia Police Educators, American Legion, V.F.W., and is a member of Lakewood Baptist Church.

In 1970, Harold was awarded the Silver Badge Award for outstanding service to the community by Gainesville Mayor Joe Stargel and TV 5.

On December 15, 1972, Georgia Governor Jimmy Carter proclaimed it "Harold Black Day" in Georgia, and the Gainesville City Commission issued a similar proclamation declaring it "Harold Black Day" in Gainesville, offering him a key to the city.

In 1973, he was presented the Gold Badge Award by WAGA TV, honoring him as the most Outstanding Peace Officer for 1972. Harold has also earned the Bar Association Liberty Bell Award, and has been a Goodwill Ambassador for the Gainesville Police Department, serving three consecutive Police Chiefs.

Harold was known for and is proud of his spit-and-polish appearance and demeanor. He is perhaps the most visible of all the city's police officials. Harold is also known for his honesty, sincerity and respect for all. He is an exceptional person who has devoted his life to serving his country and community. Here's to your exciting career, Harold, and a job well done!

Discussing a Georgia law enforcement TV training film are, (l – r), Sergeant (now retired Capt.) Harold Black, Gainesville Police Dept., Professor Mark Player, University of GA, Officer Benny Allen, GPD, and John Truitt, training project coordinator. The use of television in training for safety, crime prevention and education was done as a means of deepening respect for the law by the understanding of why and how the law operates. Officer Harold Black made maximum use of this program as a training officer for the Gainesville Police Department during the late 1960's.

RET. SGT. BENNY ALLEN

(SGT. ALLEN IS PICTURED IN GROUP PHOTO OF GPD CRIMINAL INVESTIGATION DEPT.)

Benny Allen was twenty seven years old when he was hired by Chief Hoyt Henry and joined the Gainesville Police Department on September 2, 1967, after a recommendation from Officer Gene Earls. He was sworn in on a Saturday, and his first official police call was a woman with a gun chasing after another woman behind Pepper's Grocery. When Benny first started, he was assigned to patrol only in the south/east part of town.

Benny was drafted into the U. S. Army and served two years, with eleven months of that in Korea, and he attended Gainesville College and earned an Associates Degree in Criminal Justice.

During the interview, Benny spoke about the night he and Earls almost died while chasing two hubcap thieves. Benny was driving and didn't know the road was a dead end. They wrecked on a dead end street, striking a power pole and the transformer fell on their car. Benny credits Officer Earls with saving his life on December 15, 1967. Immediately after the crash Benny was about to exit the vehicle, but Earls stopped him. There was about 72,000 volts in the live wires which fell on top of the patrol car. It knocked out all the power in the area, including the power to the police station. Benny and Earls could talk to only one person – Officer Tom Pinson.

The power company didn't rush to cut the power at the scene because they thought the officers were dead. The fire department sprayed dry chemicals on the patrol car to keep it from igniting. That was a close call for both officers – other officers later caught the thieves.

In 1972, Benny was promoted to Sergeant over the Juvenile Division and stayed there ten years. Then he moved to the Detectives for ten more years. He retired in 1990 with twenty-four years of service. Later he worked as

Chief of Security at the hotel and golf club at Lake Lanier Islands, and then worked with Sears and other security jobs.

Benny Allen helped to blaze the trail for many other officers to follow. Thank you, Benny, for your years of dedicated service.

ERNEST EUGENE EARLS, SR.

Photo courtesy Ernest Eugene Earls, Sr.
Royce Stephens and Gene Earls

Ernest Eugene (Gene) Earls, the middle of eleven children, was born on October 3, 1933, in Lumpkin County (Dahlonega), GA. He later moved to Gainesville and took his first job at the Avion Restaurant, then went into the U S Air Force from 1951 – 1954. In 1963, Ernest, along with Royce Stephens, became the first black police officers hired by the Gainesville Police Department or Hall County. They were pioneers!

Gene worked a total of 37 years in law enforcement at different agencies – City of Gainesville, Hall County, Lanier Islands Authority, and Georgia Department of Corrections. Royce Stephens worked for four years with the City of Gainesville before leaving for a teaching position.

In 1965, Gene was the first black postal worker at the Gainesville Post Office. He worked two jobs — police officer and postal worker, and he was burning the candle at both ends in order to support his family. He later quit the Post Office.

In 1958, Gene married Catherine Buffington, and together they raised three children. Catherine was the first black female bookmobile librarian in Hall County. Gene and Catherine were married 47 years before Catherine died in 2005. According to Gene, Catherine was the one who kept him motivated and happy — they were a great team.

Gene needed Catherine most of all when he and Royce were crossing the blue lines' color line in 1963. He received threats from Dawson County bootleggers, false calls set up by fellow officers, and prejudice from both blacks and whites. He had to install bars over all his windows and doors to protect his family. At times, Gene wanted to quit, but Catherine kept him going.

Once, someone drove by and threw a Molotov cocktail and it set his house on fire. His daughter narrowly escaped injury. Today his house still has the bars over the windows.

Gene and Royce were assigned to patrol the south side, and they arrested all who broke the law, regardless of race. Later they were allowed to patrol the entire city. Both Gene and Royce say they were blessed to have been hired by Gainesville Chief of Police Hoyt Henry. Their mission was to do an extraordinary job and be thankful for the opportunity to serve. They focused their attention on their police duties. Later, those who had been disgruntled about their being hired came around. One Captain made it known that he did not want them on his shift; however, he later had a change of heart, and asked them to join him.

Both men praised Chief Henry and Judge C. Winfred Smith — without them, things would have been more difficult, they said. Gene said that Chief Henry was a military veteran and wanted to treat everyone the same.

Gene served twelve years with the Gainesville Police Department, rising to the rank of Sgt. Detective. He was also Officer of the Year in 1973.

Later, after Gene became a Hall County Deputy (hired by Sheriff Ed England), I was assigned to him as his riding partner. I had just retired from the Army with only a few weeks on the job as a deputy sheriff, and I was thankful for the opportunity to work with an experienced officer like Gene Earls. We rode together for approximately two years, and during this time he made this rookie into a well trained officer. Right off the bat, we agreed to stick together in all situations. His initial advice to me was that in order to enforce the law, you must know the law. If not, an officer would be afraid to do their job. Also, you better learn to think like a criminal in order to catch one. Lastly, always protect your pistol.

We didn't have a training officer in those days, so it was up to Gene to train me right. One day I asked Gene, "Why do people always jump on me instead of you when we respond to a disturbance?" Gene was polite; "Well, they have never seen you before, so they figure you must be new on the job – they're testing you." In other words: You're a rookie and you stand out like a sore thumb!

We had a good time working together – we soon learned to mesh like a well oiled machine. For example, subjects who are involved in a disturbance can tell immediately upon arrival of officers, if they are team players. If we were on a call on the south side or wherever, and Gene was on his soap box talking, I was always focused and paying attention to everything. When Gene would get tired of talking, I could tell it, and, like a tag team, I would step forward saying the same thing but in different words. We both wanted to go home to our families after each shift!

Gene later took a job with the Lanier Islands police, and then became a Corrections Officer for the State of Georgia where he retired. He was named to the Grady Young Foundation Hall of Fame in 2007. Royce Stephens' name is also on this distinguished list.

Gene Earls and Royce Stephens to this day are filled with joy for the opportunity to have served the citizens of Gainesville and Hall County. When I told Gene that he and Royce were pioneers, I caught a glimpse of tears in his eyes.

Thanks to Gene Earls and Royce Stephens for their service and for blazing the trail for others to follow. This story relates only a small part of what these men had to face each day, both on and off the job. It was a pleasure writing it!

NINETY GALLONS OF WHISKEY
(Officers Earls and Stephens)

It was 1964 or 1965, about seven o'clock in the evening around dusk when Gene Earls and Royce Stephens, Gainesville Police Officers, observed a suspicious vehicle while on patrol on Myrtle Street. The vehicle, an early '60's black, four door Chevrolet, was so low in back that the bumper was almost dragging the pavement. The front was reared up like a wild horse, the driver barely able to see over the hood.

The officers made a quick observation – either the car was in bad need of shocks and springs, or it was way overloaded with . . . something. Earls, driving north on Myrtle, flipped on the blue lights and made a rapid turn around. The suspect did not stop; instead he turned onto Fair Street, going toward the hospital near Fair Street hill. He got half way up Fair Street hill and bailed out of the car, leaving the vehicle in gear and running.

Royce Stephens was in top physical condition and had been a track star. He exited the patrol car at the same time as the suspect and they both disappeared in a foot race. Gene jumped out, too, but Gene had to give his full attention to the suspect's car, because it was rolling backward down the hill toward the patrol car! Being fast on his feet, too, he jumped into the suspect's car and slammed it into park – making an awful noise in the transmission, but the vehicle finally stopped about one foot from the grill of the patrol car!

Gene looked around and the back seat had been removed from the car. Cases of jarred whiskey were stacked in the rear seat area up to the top of the front seat, going all the way through to the trunk. Ninety gallons of whiskey were boxed in Mason jars. WOW!

By this time, Royce had chased the suspect down a hill and he fell face first into a stream. He was a middle aged, skinny, white male, with a mouth full of dirt from the stream! Gene and Royce were heroes for a while, but then came the bad news – a local bootlegger personally told both officers that the Dawsonville bootleggers had a $1500 - $2000 bounty on their heads, and to be careful. That was big money in those days! Also, some local police officers got the same information and warned them. Later, someone set Gene's house on fire with a Molotov cocktail, but the officers did not cave – they kept locking up criminals.

TWO LUCKY BIRDS
(Officers Earls and Allen)

It was a dark night on December 15, 1967, Gainesville Police Officers Gene Earls and Rookie Benny Allen were on routine patrol checking the hospital parking lot for any illegal activity.

Benny was driving and Earls was shining the spot light when they observed a vehicle, driver inside, suspiciously not moving and making no attempt to find a parking spot. With his spot light Earls observed another individual with four hub caps cradled in his arms, who ran and jumped into the waiting vehicle.

The thieves left the scene at a high rate of speed with Benny and Earls in hot pursuit. The getaway car was disregarding sirens and blue lights. The subjects left the hospital parking lot, turned onto Spring Street, then turned right on Prior Street, going through Brenau College campus at about 80 mph. Then the fleeing suspects turned right onto Candler Street – a dead end street.

Bad move for the fleeing car – also for Benny and Earls. It won't be long now! Earls was on the radio reporting the chase to the dispatcher on duty, Officer Terry White, while young Benny Allen was getting the in-service training of his life. Benny didn't cave – he had the pedal to the metal, right on the bumper of the fleeing thieves.

Gene looked up from talking on the radio and realized they had turned down a dead-end street. By now both vehicles were wide open. Gene started yelling "dead-end, dead-end". Moments later the suspects' car ran out of road and disappeared into the woods, demolishing their vehicle. The culprits bailed out and fled the scene. Simultaneously, our heroes' police car also ran out of road and centered a power pole which broke in half. The pole with high voltage transformer attached, fell and planted itself squarely in the center of the roof of the patrol car. Live wires were going in all directions, draped across the windshield and car like an octopus.

The transformer was putting out 72,000 volts; fire and sparks were flying everywhere. The wires were so hot, they would blow holes in the pavement when they touched it. Gene immediately took charge and made a decision to sit tight and not touch anything inside the car. He used the rubber tubing inside his uniform hat (used to maintain its shape) to wrap around the ignition key to turn off the patrol car. They sat on the edge of their seats leaning forward. They resisted the urge to open the doors and bail out. In addition, they were expecting the patrol car to ignite at any moment.

Earls said that he and Benny were crying and praying. In the middle of all this, he remembered that he had put all his kids' Christmas presents in the trunk of his personal car, and he had not told his wife where they were. He said he was thinking "how will she know where to find them?" Their entire life flashed before their eyes in a matter of seconds as they thought "This is it!"

While the transformer was resting on top of the patrol car, it recharged itself three different times, making a loud roaring sound – moaning and growling – each time. It finally burned itself out, but they didn't know it! They were trapped in the police car for about 45 minutes before the power company arrived and gave them the OK to exit the car. In the meantime, other law officers apprehended the two suspects when they came out of the woods behind Sherwood Plaza.

Earl's and Benny's supervisor would not let them go home after this incident. His experience told him that there was a high probability his officers may not come back to work if they were allowed to go home and think about what had just happened. They were immediately given another car and sent out to complete their shift. Their patrol car was a total loss – all this over four stolen hub caps.

This case has been used as instructional material in subsequent years, teaching other officers proper procedure in similar situations. Officer Harold Black, Gainesville Police Department's first training officer, had just completed a movie training course for officers in emergencies which also aided in the officers' survival that night.

Police have no way of knowing the end result of any given situation. They just have to do their jobs and let the chips fall where they may! They must react with split second decisions every day, not knowing what the outcome will be. They have to go with their training, and they keep on keeping on!

ARMED ROBBERS CAUGHT IN SIX MINUTES
(Officers Earls and Hughey)

In 1971, Gene Earls was selected by Chief Hoyt Henry to be in charge of the Gainesville Police Department's first Juvenile Division. In the fall of 1971, Earls and a rookie officer John Hughey were patrolling in their juvenile wagon. Only on the force for a few weeks, John had not even had a chance to go to Atlanta yet for his uniform. He was working in civilian clothes and carrying a .38 cal pistol.

Earls was out teaching the rookie the ropes when the police radio announced that Price Parks Grocery Store right off the square in downtown Gainesville had just been robbed by two white males, one wearing a black leather jacket. That was it – no other description of the perpetrators or their vehicle was given. Gene started running things through his head – based on the location, Dawsonville Highway would be a good escape route, so he turned onto Academy Street and headed toward The Gym of 36 and St. Paul United Methodist Church area. Cruising slowly past Harrison Tire Company, visually checking all vehicles for someone with a black leather jacket, he proceeded down Academy and stopped at the red light at Academy and Washington Street. A blue car with an Ohio license plate came through the intersection at a regular rate of speed. It contained two white males – and the passenger was wearing a black leather jacket! The car continued down Washington Street toward Gainesville High School.

Light bulbs went off in Earls' head – that vehicle was suspicious; he called for back up and fell in behind the car. After conditioning his mind, he turned on the blue lights on his juvenile wagon at the bottom of the hill near the high school. Things did not look right – his gut feelings were in full action. The suspects pulled over and stopped, calm and cool.

Over the PA, Earls told the suspects to put their hands out the windows, and they did as they were told. Officer Hughey covered the passenger side of the vehicle while Earls cautiously approached the driver's side with his hand on his gun (Gene is left handed). He could see that there was a brown paper bag in the middle of the console between the two men.

The driver appeared to be an educated man, and was a calm, cool, smooth talker. He was friendly and asked why they had been stopped. Earls told him there had just been an armed robbery and that he was just doing his job – nothing personal. The driver started laughing, "It's going to be embarrassing when I get back to Ohio and tell about being caught up in the middle of an armed robbery!"

Gene said the suspect was so calm that he almost let him go. But his instinct kept screaming that something was wrong with this situation. Earls said, "Could I ask you a question, Sir?" "Sure, go ahead", replied the driver. "What do you have in that bag?" The driver replied, "Oh, that's my dirty underwear."

Sounded good, but things still didn't add up. Earls said, "One more question before you can go", and the driver said, "Sure". "Will it be OK for me to check that paper bag with your underwear in it?" The driver told him to go ahead.

Earls, with one hand on his gun reached across the driver and tilted the bag with his finger. Through a small opening in the bag, he could see green paper money. Earls jumped back — and unconsciously said an expletive! Moments later the back up unit, David Merck, arrived and the suspects were handcuffed and put in David's patrol car. Earls drove the suspect's vehicle and Rookie John Hughey drove the juvenile wagon back to the station. '

When Gene got to the station, he found a loaded .25 cal automatic pistol underneath the driver's seat. Also, after checking further, they discovered that the vehicle was stolen. After questioning by the detectives, the suspects confessed, and the educated driver wrote a detailed statement, even covering the expletive Earls had used; Gene then remembered yelling "Oh, *#$*!" when he saw the money in the bag.

One of the suspects was a 20 year old from Florida, and the other was 24 from Cleveland, Ohio. They had been staying in a motel on Dawsonville Highway, and had test driven the car a day or two before from Gainesville Ford Company on Main Street. During the test drive, they had an extra key made before bringing the car back. Later, they came back and used the key to steal the car from the dealership, and then put the Ohio license plate on it.

Earls and Hughey recovered all the stolen money - $324.00 — plus the stolen vehicle. From the time the robbery occurred to the time of the arrest was only 6 minutes!

Later on, Gene was transferred to the Detective Division. Officer John Hughey left the department after a few years, and went to work with the Post Office, where he retired after a successful career.

Photo courtesy Harold Black
Harold Black, first training officer for Gainesville
Police Dept. and Chief G. A. "Red" Singleton

GAINESVILLE POLICE DEPARTMENT IN 1973

G.A. (RED) SINGLETON, CHIEF

Sgt. Benny Allen
Gary Anderson
Buck Ballenger
Elaine Barnes
Capt. Harold Black
Rudi Bromley
Capt. John Burel
Jimmy Cain
John Campbell
Harry Chapman
Doug Childers
Doris Corn
Sgt. Marion Darracott
Doug Davis
Jack Dodd
Steve Duke
Sgt. Ernest Earls
Jerry Evans
Russell Elrod
Sgt. Jerry Forrester
Sgt. P. L. Grant
Annie Jo Harden
Sgt. Roy Hooper
Jack Hulsey

Darrell Ivey
Jack Johnson
Jim Kiser
Sgt. Doyle Land
Sgt. Jack Lipscomb
Phillip Loggins
Melvin Long
Sgt. Ray Medlin
David Merck
Nick Moore
Sara Morton
Garland Murphy
Lowell McNeal
Ralph Newell
Don Parks
Robert Pelfrey
Capt. Cohen Pierce
Capt. Tom Pinson
Randall Scroggs
Harry Nelson Stanley
Curtis Stewart
Bill Taylor
Robert Werner
Terry White

A total of 49 employees

FIRST FEMALE OFFICERS

Photo courtesy Judy Free

*Judy Free, first female Gainesville Police Dept. patrol officer,
later had a successful career as a Hall County Deputy*

Judy Free and Patricia (Patsy) Simmons were hired by Gainesville Police Chief G. A. (Red) Singleton in January, 1974. They were the first female police officers in Gainesville or Hall County! Officer Free believes she started a few days before Officer Simmons by working a shorter notice at her previous employment.

They took their first step toward their law enforcement career by calling the Sheriff's office and inquiring about employment. Tom Whelchel answered the phone and didn't give a 'yes' or 'no' answer to Judy's question. However, he did say, "You can fill out an application." Judy and Patsy decided to go in person to the Gainesville Police Department and talk with the Chief. When Chief Singleton found out their wishes, he granted both the women an immediate interview. He was excited to see their enthusiasm and desire to serve. They were immediately hired and sent over to take the exam. Arrangements were made to get them uniforms and, in a matter of days, both were on the job — and they love it!

Chief Singleton sent them to Banner Uniform in Atlanta with instructions to not alter their uniforms once they were issued by Banner. He wanted to be sure their skirts fell below their knees. However, the ladies out maneuvered the chief — they had Banner to raise the skirts' hemline at the store before they issued them. Chief Singleton didn't have a clue!

Officers Free and Simmons were both assigned to the traffic division under the supervision of Sgt. P. L. Grant. Their duties included working wrecks, directing traffic, working school crossings — the same duties as their male counterparts. They were favorably accepted in the department and by the public. As far as they were concerned, they were not there for show but to do a job — serving the citizens of Gainesville. They did get a few second looks and wolf whistles but it was all harmless and in fun. One wise guy even ran into the police station yelling, "Help! There's a woman outside with a gun!" He was referring to the policewomen.

The Police Department was not prejudiced and they gave the new female officers more than a chance. Judy Free was a former payroll clerk and always had the most respect for law enforcement. When asked what enticed her to join the blue line, she said that she was bored and wanted a more exciting job. She said, "Going into law enforcement had nothing to do with women's liberation." Judy just believed that a woman should be paid the same as a man doing the same job.

Judy had the highest respect for Chief Singleton for giving her the opportunity to serve. She later became acquainted with some of the county officers and decided to make a lateral transfer to Hall County Sheriff's Department. Chief Singleton and Sheriff England had a working agreement not to hire the other department's employees. So Judy had a career meeting with Chief Singleton, who supported her request, and he made it known to Sheriff England that he approved of Judy moving to Hall County.

LT. E. C. 'CUT' PARKS

(CUT PARKS' PHOTO CAN BE FOUND IN MOST OF THE GROUP PHOTOS HEREIN)

E. C. "Cut" Parks started his career with the Gainesville Police Department in March, 1948, under Chief Bill Bagwell. He spent the first seven years riding seven days a week with G. A. Singleton, and for the next three years, they worked six days a week with one day off per week.

In February of 1965, Cut Parks and G. A. Singleton were promoted from Patrol to Detective Lieutenants in the newly created Detective Department, and worked different shifts.

Cut Parks was highly trained, attending numerous schools. He worked under three Chiefs: Bill Bagwell, Hoyt Henry and G. A. Singleton.

Detective Cut Parks was known for making people laugh, as well as for being a seasoned detective. He retired in 1973 with 25 years of dedicated service to the City of Gainesville.

CAPTAIN ROY FRANKLIN HOOPER, SR.

Capt. Roy Hooper married his wife, Lorene, on July 2, 1949, in Hall County, GA. Roy and Lorene had one son, Roy Franklin Hooper, Jr. Roy served in the Gainesville Police Department from August 18, 1952 to November 1, 1977 – 25 years and 3 months.

Hired by Chief Hoyt Henry, Capt. Hooper was a member of the old school of police officers, working his way through the ranks, to the rank of Captain. He served with dignity until his retirement in 1977, and passed away on December 14, 2001.

RET. LT. TERRY WHITE

Terry White chronicles decades of history of the Gainesville Police Department:

Here are the things I remember going through and being told about the Gainesville Police Department in no particular order.   I will include dates or near dates as best I can.

My individual history in law enforcement:

- I began as a summer temporary dispatcher on July 6, 1966, at the age of 15. Hoyt Henry was the chief who hired me.
- To put this in perspective, this was two weeks after the Miranda decision had been handed down by the United States Supreme Court. The old timers were still cursing about having to tell violators they "had the right to remain silent."
- I turned 16 the next day and took my driving test in a 1964 Dodge police car. I passed.
- The department consisted of the three shifts, traffic division, and detectives division. Each shift and traffic division had a Captain in charge and a Sergeant as the line level supervisor. The Detectives Division consisted of two Lieutenants and one Sergeant. Lt. G. A. "Red" Singleton worked days, Sgt. Tom Pinson worked afternoons and evenings, and Lt. E.C. "Cut" Parks worked nights.
- During the fifties and sixties, Chief Henry would hire a high school boy to work as dispatcher so the Desk Sergeant could be moved out onto patrol to fill in for officers who were on vacation. All officers in the department were required to take their vacations during the summer months. Others who did this job (summer dispatcher) before me included C. Winfred Smith who went on to become a state court judge and several others who became doctors and lawyers.
- The three shift Captains were Capt. Joe Edge, Capt. Frank Strickland, and Capt. John Burel. The traffic Captain was Capt. James Harper. The traffic Sergeant was Sgt. T.E. "Gip" Parks, the three shift Sergeants were Sgt. C.C. Strickland, Sgt. James C. Pierce, and Sgt. "Mac" Vickery. There was also a Desk Sergeant and that was Sgt. Harold Black. As best I can recall, all the other officers in the department at this time were patrolmen. The chief also had a secretary, Mrs. Annie Jo Harden.
- When I started as a dispatcher, Capt. Rad Bonds had recently retired and John Burel had been promoted to Captain. Officer Jim Kiser was the newest officer in the department.
- The police department during this time was housed in the west wing of City Hall. The jail was in the basement of City Hall with the exception of two holding cells which were also part of the west wing. The men's room on the west wing hallway had an old mirror that advertised the Wallis Sand Company (which later became Wallis Asphalt on Industrial Boulevard) and listed two phone

numbers, both of which were only three digits. I'm not sure if that mirror is still there, but it was last time I looked.

- I took this job again during the summers of 1967 and 1968. When I returned in 1967, Miss Doris Jones (later Mrs. Doris Corn) had been hired as a secretary to the detectives. She later became the chief's secretary and was still in that position when I retired from the department in 1991. But I'm getting ahead of myself…

- After graduating high school in May of 1969, I again worked that summer as a dispatcher. When summer ended, Chief Henry kept me on as a temporary dispatcher until December of that year when he appointed me Deputy City Marshall. I did that job until April of 1971 when I went into uniform and was assigned to one of the three shifts. I was still considered a temporary employee because I was only 20 years old and at that time a male employee had to be 21 years of age to be hired under civil service (females only had to be 18). I went under civil service in July of that year when I turned 21. Since I was a sworn, armed officer as Deputy Marshall, it is my belief that I was one of the youngest sworn officers in the state since Atlanta Police Department was hiring officers at the youngest age of which I'm aware, 20 years old. This changed in later years when court rulings and law changes dropped the age to 18 for males and females, and some officers were hired in Gainesville at that age.

- I attended basic training at the Georgia Police Academy which was the only place you could take the mandated basic course at that time. The nine regional academies in use during most of my career came along at later times. I went through basic in November and December of 1971 (basic was only 3 weeks long at the time).

- I was promoted to Sergeant in June of 1976 at the age of 25. It is my belief that I was the youngest sergeant in the history of the department at that time, it may have changed later.

- I was promoted to Lieutenant in 1983 at the age of 33 when Gary Anderson and I became the first uniformed lieutenants in the history of the department. At the time we were promoted, Gary was an administrative sergeant and I was the sergeant in charge of Crime Prevention and Training. Uniformed lieutenants on the three shifts were added later on and I believe are now the shift commanders in the department (replacing Captains in that role).

- From 1979 until 1984, I was the Crime Prevention and Training Officer for the department. During this time, I served as an adjunct faculty member of the Northeast Georgia Police Academy in Athens, Ga., part of the University of Georgia. In this role, I taught Patrol and Observation, Crime Prevention, Report Writing, Traffic Law, Firearms Qualifications, and Defensive and Pursuit Driving.

- In 1984, I attended and graduated from the 136th Session of the F.B. I. National Academy. This had been a goal of mine from the beginning of my career and I still am active in the National Academy Associates chapter.

- I retired from the Gainesville Police Department on November 30, 1991. At the time, I was a uniformed shift Lieutenant and had been since finishing the National Academy. In February of 1992, I moved to Nashville, Tennessee.

- In the fall of 1992, I began work at Belmont University, a four year liberal arts university in downtown Nashville that is the second largest private university in Tennessee and best known for it Music Business Program. (The largest private university in Tennessee is Vanderbilt which is about 2 blocks away from Belmont). Graduates of Belmont University include Sarah Cannon (better known as Minnie Pearl), Trisha Yearwood, Lee Ann Womack, Brad Paisley, and Josh Turner. These are all well established country music artists.

- My first work at Belmont was as a shuttle bus driver, two days each week. After the director learned I was a retired police officer, she began talking me into working security "just on weekend mornings." I did that for about a year before marrying my wife, Josephine, at which time I transferred into a full time position as a patrol officer. I quickly became the Administrative Supervisor, then Director in 1997. I currently serve in that position, though we later adopted a police department type rank structure, so my title now is Chief of Campus Security.

- The Office of Campus Security at Belmont consists of 26 officers and 8 student workers and has two divisions, operations and administration. Each division is managed by a Major and we also have four Captains and three Sergeants in our department as well as a security systems technician. We utilize vehicle patrol, bicycle patrol, and foot patrol in order to secure about 6000 students/faculty/staff. I feel I've come full circle since Belmont Security is about the same size Gainesville Police Department was when I started my career there.

- During my time as a police officer, I have ridden motorcycles both on duty and as personal recreation. As an officer, I rode Harley-Davidson and Kawasaki bikes. I have put over 250,000 miles on personal bikes, mostly Honda Gold Wings. I have ridden in all 48 contiguous states at least twice and am a member of the Blue Knights, the Law Enforcement Motorcycle Club. I currently serve as the chaplain for the local chapter of the Blue Knights, Chapter Tennessee V. I am also a member of the Gold Wing Road Riders Association since 1990. I was a charter member of the Middle Tennessee Precision Drill Team which won three international championships and several other awards from its inception in 1992 until 2003 when we decided to disband while "on top".
- One of the highlights of my time at Belmont was in 2008 when we hosted the second of the three national presidential debates, the town hall debate. I worked with the United States Secret Service for over a year preparing for security for the two candidates, Senator John McCain and Senator Barrack Obama. This debate was held in the Curb Event Center at Belmont on October 7, 2008.
- At this time, I have over 43 years in law enforcement as a career. I intend to stay at Belmont for another 5 years or so until I retire to go camping and fishing.

Other notations and memories of the Gainesville Police Department.

- When I started in law enforcement, virtually all officers carried revolvers. Now, most officers carry semi-automatic side arms. We had no utility type uniform, only the class A uniform. If we wore long sleeved shirts, we had to wear a tie. If we wore short sleeves, we wore no tie. In the beginning, it was up to the individual officer which he wore, but we later went to a specific date to change from long to short or short to long.
- When I started in Gainesville, all uniformed officers wore white shirts and we had no departmental patch, U. S. flag, or anything else sewn on the sleeves. We designed the patch currently used in about 1972, but then it was only on the left sleeve, nothing on the right sleeve. At some point later, about 1978, we added the departmental patch to the right sleeve. By then, we had gone to the dark blue uniform shirts, around 1977.
- Most of my career, the cap was considered a very important part of the uniform. The first two chiefs I worked for insisted that officers

have their caps on at any time they were outside the patrol car or building, especially if they were on a call or coming into contact with the public in any way. Failure to wear your cap usually resulted in disciplinary action. This was in a time when the only cap we had was the eight point official police cap, not fatigue type or baseball type caps that are relatively comfortable.

- When I began, the city only furnished shirts, pants, caps, badges, and waist length "Eisenhower" style jackets. The individual furnished everything else including weapons, leather goods, shoes or boots, socks, ties, and nameplates. Today's officer is furnished everything he or she needs to do the job and wears except underwear.

- I remember hearing stories of the times before the police department had two way radios in all cars. It is my belief that two-way radios came about around 1956. When I started ten years later, some of the cars still had the original radios in them. These had metal hand held microphones which were very heavy and would hurt if you dropped them on your toe. They hurt worse if there was ever an electrical short created in the microphone, it would severely shock the individual holding it.

- Before two-way radios, it is my understanding that there was a "master switch" at the department that controlled all the street lights in town. If the dispatcher got a call after dark, he would "flash" the street lights so the officers out on patrol would know he had a call waiting. They would stop at a "police call box phone" and call in or drive by city hall, whichever was easier and took less time. I'm not sure how this was handled in the daytime.

- When I started, the police cars cost about $2200. each and had only a heater as optional equipment. The two-way radio was added by the department, but none of the cars had AM radio (much less FM), power steering, air conditioning, any other power equipment or anything else that we take for granted today. To help keep cool, each June we would buy the weave seat cushions available at that time and put one in each car, but these would be worn out in a couple of months, usually by our guns wearing against them. None of the cars had "cages" in them.

- When I started, all patrol officers worked as two man teams. The only time we had a "one man car" was if we had an odd number of officers on duty that day and then the highest ranking supervisor (Captain or Sergeant) usually rode by themselves. This changed in

1974 when we went to all one man cars except for one double unit to answer the more violent calls or if someone was in training.

- When we worked day shift, at least two officers would take parking ticket books and go walk foot patrol in the area of the Square. This was more to be of assistance and to act as information givers than to actually write that many parking tickets. This practice worked very well for the first few years of my career and ended around 1975 or 1976.

- During this "foot patrol" on the square, the officers had no cell phones or even radios, we were completely without contact and on our own. The only means of contact we had was if we went into a shop or store and asked to use their telephone to call in. We often made arrests for whatever offense (usually public drunk) and walked the arrested person to city hall to lock them up by ourselves. Though this would be unheard of now, we never thought about this being unusual or dangerous, it was just the way things were done back then.

- When I started, I worked with the first two African American officers ever hired at the department: Officer Ernest (Gene) Earls and Officer Royce Stephens. The first female officers assigned to patrol did not come about until several years later, when I was a shift Patrol Officer.

- I was working when Officer Earls and Officer Benny Allen were involved in a serious accident while chasing a violator on Prior Street, then onto Candler Street where they crashed into a utility pole at the dead end of the street. Power lines came crashing down on the police car and the officers were stranded inside until the power could be turned off. During this time, the car engine ran hot and the officers had to turn the ignition off by using a rubber grommet from one of their uniform caps and wrapping it around the key so they would not be electrocuted. They were able to exit the vehicle safely about an hour or so after the crash first happened. If I remember correctly, the suspect(s) they were chasing were apprehended by other officers during this time.

- I was working in September of 1972 when a five day long racial riot took place. This riot was of such magnitude that it made national news. Most of the officers worked over 90 hours during the five day period. This was during a time in America when racial riots were not uncommon.

- I was also working later that month when the only Gainesville Police officer killed in the line of duty during my career was killed. An auto accident on Dawsonville Highway near the city limits took the life of Officer Henry T. Davis at the age of 27 years. His funeral was one of the saddest times I can remember for the department as a whole.

- In my time at Gainesville P. D., I worked for five different police chiefs: Chief Hoyt Henry, Chief G.A. "Red" Singleton, Chief George Knapp, Chief Jerry Forrester, and Chief Fred Hayes. From each one, I learned management skills I still use today (or make it a point not to use, as the case may be).

- When I began as a patrol officer, starting pay for Gainesville police officers was $407.00 monthly gross, or about $4884 annually. Part time jobs paid $3.00 per hour, and usually consisted of directing traffic or working security for wrestling matches.

- When I first started policing, there was very little radio traffic on the police radio. We did not call in traffic stops or other contacts with citizens, things that are routinely done today. The department only had two hand held radios, both very big and bulky and heavy enough to require a shoulder strap to help support the weight. Because of this, officers rarely took these radios out to use, they just stayed in the gun locker in the dispatch center. Today all officers are routinely issued hand held radios that easily fit on the duty belt and weigh only ounces.

- When I began, no officers wore bullet resistant vests simply because they were not yet available and wouldn't be for most of my time in Gainesville.

Thanks go to Terry White for his first hand recollections of the Gainesville Police Department over the years. He was also very helpful during the writing of the first edition. I located him in Nashville, TN, (Belmont University) where he moved after his retirement from the Department. I have left his remembrances just as he wrote them because they paint such a great picture of days gone by.

Photo courtesy Harold Black

Gainesville Police Department – December, 1982
First Row (L to r): Capt. Ray Medlin, Capt. Jerry Forrester, Chief George Knapp
(Center), Maj. Harold Black, Capt. Bill Taylor. 2ⁿᵈ Row: Ofc. Jerri Boykin,
Paula Robinson, Sgt. Jimmy Lee Latimer, Sgt. Nick Moore, Sgt. Terry White,
Sgt. Therion Boyd, Linda Gibbs Collier. 3ʳᵈ row: Det. David Frazier, Det. Jerry
Evans, Det. Ricky Rich, Det. Benny Allen, Det. Garland Murphy, Det. Jack Dodd,
Det. Curtis Stewart, Det. Marion Darracott. 4ᵗʰ row: ? Allen, ? , Russell Elrod,
Jane Nichols, Frank Hooper, Lowell McNeal, John Campbell, Steve Cronic,
John Brooke, Harry Chapman, Jeff Wimpy, Lane Acrey, Chuck Smith. 5ᵗʰ row:
Lynn Darby, Ron Cosgrove, Ronnie Edge, Richard Wiley, Donnie Lyle, Marty Lee,
Mark Kersh, Don Lloyd, Danny Owen, John Strickland, Bennett Patrick,
Melody Strange. NOTE: Some officers are not pictured.

RETIRED CAPTAIN BILL TAYLOR

(PICTURED FAR RIGHT FRONT IN 1982 GPD GROUP PHOTO)

Bill Taylor was born in South Georgia and, while he was in his teens, his family moved to Buford where his dad was Chief of Police. A third generation police officer, Bill joined the Atlanta Police Department at the age of twenty as one of the youngest patrolman in Georgia. In Atlanta he learned his technical police skills, was certified and received extensive training in vehicle investigation.

While an Atlanta Policeman, he joined the Army National Guard as a Military Policeman and served for six years. After a couple of years with the Atlanta Department, he took a break from law enforcement.

Then in March, 1967, Bill was interviewed by Gainesville Police Chief Hoyt Henry and hired the same day. Initially, he worked as a City Marshall, and then transferred to the traffic division. Because of his certification, he became a motorcycle officer (he had been riding motorcycles since he was fourteen years old) and was assigned the same Harley Davidson that Officer Dale Sutton had ridden – with a kick start! Bill rode as a motorcycle cop for fifteen years in all kinds of weather, through all kinds of conditions. His call sign was Unit #4, and the motorcycle made it easier to get to accident scenes.

Then he became Assistant Training Officer under Officer Harold Black. He trained the 25 officer riot squad – out of this came a five member SWAT team that he also headed. He was Traffic Training Director for three years and was promoted to Sergeant.

While off duty in 1972, Officer Taylor came upon a traffic accident minutes after it happened on Dawsonville Highway involving his best friend,

Officer Henry Davis. Davis was killed in the accident in the line of duty. Bill came to the aid of his fellow officer and rode in the ambulance with him to Northeast Georgia Medical Center. Both Bill and Henry Davis lived in the Sardis community and were fishing buddies. They were great friends and had many things in common. Officer Henry Davis was highly respected by all the members of the Gainesville Police Department, and they were deeply saddened with his loss. Even after all this time, it was touching to see the sensitive manner in which Bill spoke of his friend during our interview.

Officer Taylor attended the FBI Academy in Quantico, VA in 1982; in those days only about 10% of police officers were sent to the academy. During his FBI training, he won the Fitness Challenge Award and qualified with the highest score for the pistol (Master) Award. He was then promoted to Captain and went on the road as a Patrol Shift Captain.

Captain Taylor also designed and supervised the first Honor Guard and five member SWAT team, and trained jointly with the Hall County Sheriff's Department. Capt Taylor was Director of Technical Service for two years, and he was in charge of the indoor firing range for ten years. All officers were required to qualify monthly and the Department as a whole had an average qualifying score of 98.4%(the highest average in the state), making all officers experts with their weapons. The firing range could also be set as a night course with blue lights flashing, making it appear as realistic as possible. During his career, Captain Taylor has won sixteen shooting trophies.

Later Capt. Taylor was Public Information Officer for the Department, retiring in that position. He then worked for the State of Georgia for three years, teaching field sobriety classes — he has taught more than 2000 classes.

Capt. Taylor's law enforcement career encompassed thirty years of service. His wife Harriett also retired with a successful career with the Department of Public Safety — they are now enjoying their retirement. Capt Taylor has over 500,000 miles on a motorcycle — and he's still riding. He is known by all as the Gainesville Police Department's motorcycle cop! A big salute goes to Bill and Harriet Taylor for their dedicated service.

(Photo Courtesy Milton Martin Toyota & The Times)
GPD Administrative Division – 1986

Ft Row – (l to r) Ollie McGabee, Lt Gary Anderson, Chief Jerry Forrester, Capt Harold Black. 2nd Row – Jan Huyck, Patti McCrary, Lynne Randolph, Doris Corn, Darlene Bartlett, Paula Robinson, Iena Sewell. Bk Row – Ron Cosgrove, Richard Gecoma, Frank Hooper, Melvin Long, Mike Cape, Joey Carter, Donnie Lyle.

(Photo Courtesy Milton Martin Toyota & The Times)

GPD Criminal Investigation Department

Ft Row (l to r) – Sgt Benny Allen, Lt Jack Dodd, Capt Marion Darracott, Sgt David Frazier, Sgt David Merck. Bk Row – Ricky Rich, Garland Murpby, Annie Jo Harden, Robert Gable, Nick Moore, Russell Elrod, Richard Wiley.

(Photo Courtesy Milton Martin Toyota & The Times)

GPD Operations Division Uniform Watch

Ft Row (l to r) – Kirk Williamson, Lowell McNeal, Capt Therion Boyd, Lt John Campbell. 2nd Row – Chuck Smith, Alan Schindley, William Thompson, John Cuda. Bk Row – Gary Daniel, Jeffrey Kemp, Wayne Seymour, Bobby Standridge.

(Photo Courtesy Milton Martin Toyota & The Times)

GPD Operations Division Uniform Watch 1 Ft Row (l to r) –
Layne Acrey, Junior Clore, Sgt Jeff Wimpy, David Rhodes, Danny Peck.
Bk Row – Bryan Strickland, Benny Patrick, Darren
Glenn, Steve Hemphill, Ron Sharpley.

(Photo Courtesy Milton Martin Toyota & The Times)

GPD Operations Division Uniform Watch 2

*Ft Row (l to r) – Randy Hoagland, Lt Terry White, Capt Bill Taylor,
Todd Ross, Chris Robinson. Bk Row – Mike Dale, Joel Tapp, Ed Hollis,
Lee West, Marty Lee, Jane Nichols.*

SCHOOL RESOURCE OFFICER BRIAN CLARK

SRO Brian Clark was born in Fulton County, GA, and his family moved to Habersham County when he was about five. He graduated from Habersham Central High School in 1989, and jointed the U. S. Air Force in January, 1990, serving four years before being honorably discharged in 1994. Brian served two tours in Iraq; the first during Desert Storm. His first duty station was for eighteen months in Turkey, and then Altus Air Force Base in Oklahoma.

After Brian's military service, he joined the Alto State Prison as a prison guard and stayed there for two years. He also worked for Hall County P.W.C. for four years as a CDL driver before being hired by Gainesville Police Chief Frank Hooper in 2002 as a patrol officer.

Brian attended the Athens Police Academy and served as a patrol officer for two years before he was promoted to Corporal – Training Officer/patrol duty for approximately two more years, then about two years as a Crime Scene Investigator (CSI).

In April, 2008, Officer Clark became School Resource Officer (SRO) for Gainesville Middle School as well as New Holland, Enota and Fair Street Elementary Schools.

Officer Clark has eight years as a Gainesville Police Officer and enjoys his job as a School Resource Officer.

Thank you, Officer Brian Clark, for your dedicated service to your country and to the citizens of Gainesville and the City School System.

SCHOOL RESOURCE OFFICER CHRIS COY

SRO Chris Coy is originally from Lansing, Michigan. He served in the U. S. Army as a Military Policeman from 1983 – 1986, before moving to Georgia. He worked approximately one year with the City of Oakwood Police Department under Chief Dan Ford. On September 13, 1990, he was hired by Gainesville Police Chief Fred Hayes as a patrol officer.

With over nineteen years of service to the city of Gainesville and the school system, Officer Coy has been a School Resource Officer since 1997. He has worked at Gainesville Middle School and is presently working at Wood's Mill Academy.

SCHOOL RESOURCE OFFICER CHARLES NEWMAN

Originally from Connecticut, SRO Charles Newman is a nineteen plus year veteran of the Gainesville Police Department, and works at Gainesville High School. He began his law enforcement career in Lumpkin County in 1988, and then was hired by Gainesville Police Chief Fred Hayes in 1991. He has worked in the jail, on patrol, and as a motorcycle traffic and accident reconstruction officer before becoming a School Resource Officer in 1994.

CHIEF ROY FRANKLIN HOOPER, JR.

Chief Frank Hooper joined the Gainesville Police Department in January, 1978, as a patrol officer. He is a second generation Gainesville Police officer, serving after his father, Captain Roy F. Hooper, Sr. (deceased), retired from the department in 1977 after 25 years.

Chief Hooper was born in Gainesville and is a lifelong resident of Hall County. He is a 1975 graduate of North Hall High School, and a 1978 graduate of the 32nd session of the Northeast Georgia Police Academy. Since employment with the City of Gainesville, Chief Hooper has completed P.O.S.T. advanced law enforcement training in supervision and management. He is a currently certified Police Instructor with a specialty in firearms.

During his tenure with the Gainesville Police Department, Chief Hooper has advanced through the ranks and has served as Patrol Officer, Sergeant, Lieutenant, and Chief of Police. The Department is recognized by the Commission on Accreditation for Law Enforcement Agencies (CALEA) as a Flagship Agency. Chief Hooper served as program director of the Police Department's successful CALEA accreditation effort in 1993, and successful State Certification effort in 1997. He has served as the Commander of the Criminal Investigations and Administration Divisions of the Police Department. He has also served as an Assessor for CALEA and the Georgia Law Enforcement Certification Program.

The American Legion Post #7 recognized Chief Hooper as Police Rookie of the Year in 1978. In 1993, he was recognized by the Gainesville Elks Lodge as Police Officer of the Year. Rotary International's Gainesville Club presented Chief Hooper with the 2007 Lee Arrendale Award in June, 2007, and in July, 2007, the Georgia Association of Chiefs of Police presented him with the prestigious Outstanding Police Chief of the Year award. The Gainesville Elks Lodge honored him with the 2007/2008 Public Safety Officer of the Year award in March, 2008.

Chief Hooper is an active member of the International and Georgia Associations of Chiefs of Police. He is a past Chairman of the Hall County Multi-Agency Narcotics Control Board, and he currently serves as a board member of the Domestic Violence Task Force, the Edmondson-Telford Center for Children, the Gateway Shelter for Battered Women and the Hall County Commission for Children and Families. He also serves on the Criminal Justice Advisory Board of Lanier Technical College, the Advisory Board of the Northeast Georgia Police Academy, the Georgia Supreme Court/Chief Justice mental Health Study Committee, and the Georgia Emergency Management All Hazards Council for Area I. He is the Georgia Association of Chiefs of Police District Representative for Region 9, and serves as the chairman of the Georgia Association of Chiefs of Police District Representatives. In addition, he serves on the Georgia Association of Chiefs of Police Executive Board and is co-chairman of the Georgia Law Enforcement Certification Program.

Chief Hooper has been married to the former Teresa Lynn Mote for 34 years. They have two adult sons, a daughter in law, and two granddaughters. He is a member of Montgomery Memorial Baptist Church in Gainesville.

The Chief has had a successful 32 year career while devoting his life to serving the citizens of Gainesville/Hall County, GA. He was selected Police Chief in June, 1998, by then City Manager Carlyle Cox, who recommended Hooper be appointed chief by the City Council. Chief Hooper served for twelve years. During his tenure as Chief, he accomplished all his visions and molded the Gainesville Police Department into one of the most elite departments in Georgia, a Flagship Agency – only 10% of accredited agencies qualify for this title. This was achieved by hard work, experience, leadership, devotion to duty and caring for people. During his career, Chief Hooper has been instrumental in training many young men and women to become police officers. He is ranked with the top Chiefs in the nation. His career revolved around caring for his department and serving the citizens of Gainesville. Among the items displayed in his office was a plaque referring to the way he led his department – Matthew 20:27 - *And whosoever will be chief among you, let him be your servant.*

Chief Frank Hooper has set the standard high, leaving some big shoes to be filled. He retired on December 31, 2009, with gratitude and respect from Gainesville and Hall County. Chief Hooper is a role model for those to follow, and we salute him for a job well done.

Sheriff Steve Cronic and Chief Frank Hooper.
In 2007, Sheriff Steve Cronic was named Sheriff of the Year for the state of Georgia. Also, in July, 2007, the Georgia Association of Chiefs of Police presented the prestigious Outstanding Police Chief of the Year award to Chief Frank Hooper. This is the first time that two law enforcement leaders in the same city have won such awards in the same year. Photo taken at Chief Hooper's retirement reception on December 18, 2009.

Chief Frank Hooper and the retirement board showing his accomplishments as a police officer. Pictures of Chief Hooper's father and badge are shown in bottom right corner.

Willard Langdon, Alex Taylor, Sheriff Steve Cronic, and Charles Baker, Hall County Clerk of Court, at retirement reception for Chief Frank Hooper.

INTERIM CHIEF JANE NICHOLS

Jane Nichols became Interim Gainesville Police Chief on January 1, 2010. She had always had a liking for law enforcement, so in the early part of 1982, she applied for a job with the Gainesville Police Department. She was interviewed by then-Chief George Knapp and reported for duty the next day, February 22, 1982.

The day after graduating from the police academy in the summer of 1982, Jane worked her first traffic fatality on Green Street. She focused on accident investigations and reconstruction and became the city's first, and only, female motorcycle officer. In 1988, she was promoted to detective with primary responsibility for the investigations of sex crimes and homicides. Promoted to Sergeant in 1992, Lieutenant in 1995, Captain in 1998, and Deputy Chief in 2007, Jane says she was blessed throughout her career to be at the right place at the right time for promotions and job appointments.

Interim Chief Nichols worked her way up through the ranks but has never forgotten where she came from. In her own words, she's just "a Gainesville Police officer with rank." She is a professional who enjoys being a servant and protector to her fellow officers and the public. She retired on March 17, 2010, after 28 years service.

INTERIM CHIEF CHAD WHITE

Chad White was raised in South Hall County and graduated from Johnson High School in 1986. A fifth generation Hall Countian, Chad and his family now live in the North Hall area.

After graduation, Chad applied for a job in law enforcement at both the Hall County Sheriff's Department and the Gainesville Police Department. He was hired in 1987, at age 19 by Captain Billy Barnes as a jailer in the Hall County jail. He worked with Hall County from 1987 until 1989, and then re-applied with the Gainesville Police Department.

He was hired by Gainesville Police Chief Fred Hayes (basically a transfer from county to city law enforcement), and again began working in the (city) jail. He then transferred to the Patrol Division.

Officer White attended the Athens Police Academy in 1990, and in 1995, he attended the first class (GPSTC) in Police Cyclist Training in Forsyth, GA. He was one of six officers — now there are approximately fifteen bicycle patrol officers. The Community Police Program works in three housing projects and city wide. In 1998, Chad was promoted to Sergeant of the Community Police Program. This program has proven to be very effective, and has developed a better relationship between citizens and police. The main focus of the program is to remove the vehicle window, placing the officer back in touch with the public, similar to the foot patrol of the 50's and 60's, but allows more mobility.

In 2000, Chad transferred as a Sergeant in the Patrol Division, supervising eight patrol officers. In 2003, he was promoted to Lieutenant as a Shift Commander in the Patrol Division. In 2004, Lt. White moved to the Criminal Investigation Division to include Gang and Drug Task Force.

In 2007, Lt. White was promoted to Captain of Support Services Bureau which included three divisions — Training, Support Services and Criminal Investigation.

On March 17, 2010, Captain Chad White was selected as Interim Police Chief for the city of Gainesville until a new Chief of Police could be appointed. Captain White accepted the position and feels it was an honor to be chosen. Interim Chief White is 42 years old and has been with the Department for twenty years. He and his wife, Rhonda, have two children, and attend Calvary Cross Church in north Hall County.

Interim Chief White is a highly skilled seasoned officer who stepped up when the Department needed him. His willingness to serve should be commended.

CHIEF BRIAN P. KELLY

Gainesville Police Chief Brian Kelly was born in Fulton County, Georgia, and was raised in Spalding County, Warner Robins – Cairo, GA. Chief Kelly is a second generation police officer. His father, James Kelly, was Chief of Police in two southwest Georgia towns, retiring as Police Chief of Cairo, GA.

Chief Kelly's education includes an Associate degree in Wildlife Management at Abraham Baldwin Agricultural College, a Bachelor's degree in Criminal Justice at the University of Georgia in 2000, completion of the FBI National Academy in Quantico, VA in 2004, completion of the Georgia Law Enforcement Command College in 2009, and a Master's degree in Public Administration at Columbus State University in 2009, making him one of the most highly educated police chiefs in the history of the Gainesville Police Department.

Chief Brian Kelly began his law enforcement career at the University of Georgia Department Of Public Safety in 1994, rising to the rank of Corporal. He began college studies in Wildlife Management, but changed to Criminal Justice after transferring to UGA.

In 1996, Brian was hired by Gainesville Police Chief Fred Hayes and joined the Department as a patrolman. Chief Frank Hooper promoted him to Sergeant in 1998, and in 2003, he was promoted again to Lieutenant. He applied for the position of Chief when Chief Hooper retired on December 31, 2009.

On May 10, 2010, Lieutenant Brian P. Kelly, age 37 and a fourteen year veteran of the Department, was sworn in at the Georgia Mountain Center as the new Police Chief for the City of Gainesville, by City Manager Kip Padgett. The department has 100 officers and 13 civilian support staff for a total of 113 employees. Chief Kelly was selected for the job over a field of more than seventy applicants. He has been a patrol officer, a field training officer, a Sergeant assigned to the community policing program, Uniform Patrol Division, a Watch Commander in the Uniform Patrol Division, a Commander of Criminal Investigations, a public spokesman for the Department, and head of the Division that includes traffic services and special events.

Chief Kelly is a model police officer who has met his ultimate goal through dedicated hard work and leading by example. He is a proactive leader who believes in involving the community.

Looking forward to moving into the new police headquarters on Queen City Parkway tentatively set for the fall of 2010, Chief Kelly is a big proponent of community policing, and he wants to be able to challenge the public to engage and assist in those areas. He is looking forward to a long tenure as Chief of Police, working with the community to continue to improve the quality of life in Gainesville.

As Chief Kelly said in his acceptance speech, "I am invested in this community and department, and I am looking forward to us all working together to make Gainesville and Hall County one of the safest communities in which to work and live."

Chief Kelly has been married to his wife, Lyn, for fourteen years and they live in North Hall with their eight year old daughter.

GAINESVILLE POLICE DEPARTMENT - 2010

ADMINISTRATION

Brian P. Kelly – Chief of Police
Angie Standridge, Administrative Assistant

OFFICE OF DEPUTY CHIEF

Sgt. Johnny Ray, Accreditation Manager
Investigator David Miller, Internal Affairs
Lynne Randolph, Senior Account Clerk

SUPPORT SERVICES BUREAU

Capt. Chad White, Support Services Bureau
Mark Ezuka, Senior Secretary

Support Services Bureau Sgt/Quartermaster

Sgt. Stan Kimbrell

Records
Judy Weaver, Records Manager
Melanie Campbell, Records Clerk
Vanessa Gresham, Records Clerk
Tyra Millwood, Records Clerk
Sandy Key, Records Clerk

Community Service Associates
Cindy Quaife-Young
Mari Andersen

Warrant Officers
Ofc. Scott Davenport
Ofc. Stacy Roberts

Data Terminal Operators
Cynetia Banks, Terminal Agency Coordinator
Gail Law
Lequeda Scott

Training Division

Lt. Ken Canup, Training Director
Sgt. Michael Martin, Training Sergeant
Cpl. Jeff Bull, Range Master/Armorer Corporal

School Resource Officer
Ofc. Chris Coy
Ofc. Charles Newman
Ofc. Brian Clark

Criminal Investigations Division

Lt. Carol Martin
Sgt. Shawn Welsh, General Investigations
Sgt. Kevin Gaddis, Special Investigations
Diana Perez, Senior Secretary
Investigator Melissa Begley
Investigator Margaret Dawson
Investigator Billy Day
Investigator McCray Filiatreau
Investigator Gordon Hendry
Investigator Bryan Majors
Investigator Tift Mattox
Investigator Dan Schrader

Property & Evidence
Ofc. Gina Sherman
Annthonese Hughey

Multi-Agency Narcotics Unit
Investigator Keith McCoy
Investigator Chris Letson, K9 (Seda)

Gang Task Force
Investigator Joe Amerling
Investigator Andy Smith

OPERATIONS BUREAU

Capt. Paul Sherman, Operations Bureau

Uniform Patrol Division

A-Watch
Lt. Keith Lingerfelt
Sgt. Chad Ford
Cpl. Daniel Meeks, FTO
Ofc. Samuel Allen
Ofc. Jeremy Edge, K9 (Quenn)
Ofc. Erik Ellis
Ofc. Melinda Gardner, DV
Ofc. Richard Lloyd
Ofc. Justin Martin, Accident
Ofc. Danny McClellon
Ofc. Larry Sanford

B-Watch
Lt. Gary Entrekin
Sgt. Jonathan Ottaway
S-Cpl. Jason King
Cpl. Jesse Ray, FTO
Ofc. Daniel Adames
Ofc. Chris Campbell

Ofc. Joel Carter
Ofc. Zane Champion
Ofc. William Lee
Ofc. Stephen Mitchell
Ofc. Kelly Olson

C-Watch
Lt. Nina Harkins
Sgt. Jay Parrish, Range
S-Cpl. Chris Jones
Cpl. Doug Whiddon, FTO
Ofc. Phillip Cofield
Ofc. Benjamin Green
Ofc. Stephen Johnson
Ofc. Eric Leid
Ofc. Brett Peck
Ofc. Ed Roach
Ofc. Jonathan Williams, K9 (Anja)

D-Watch
Lt. John Robertson, Range
Sgt. Dean Staples
S-Cpl. Brad Raper
Cpl. Moises Vargas, FTO, DV
Ofc. Josh Adams, K9 (Vigo)
Ofc. Nicole Bailes
Ofc. Travis Barnette
Ofc. Glenn Ewing, CSU
Ofc. Michael Johnson, Accident
Ofc. Tommy McElroy
Ofc. John Sisk
Ofc. Sarah Wilson

Specialized Services Division

Community Policing Government Housing
Sgt. Jim Von Essen

West Precinct (Melrose Apartments)
Ofc. Brandon Harkins
Ofc. Kevin Holbrook

East Precinct (Harrison Square)
Ofc. Drew Reed

South Precinct (Atlanta Street)
Ofc. Chad Lovell
Ofc. Montana Thrasher

Park Ranger
Ofc. Mike Huckaby, Park Ranger

Community Policing Business/Police Traffic Services Unit
Sgt. Dale Cash

Aggressive Criminal Enforcement Unit
Ofc. Josh Shiflett, ACE

Police Traffic Services Unit
Ofc. Dallas Bright
Ofc. Stephen Lumpkin
Ofc. Griggs Wall
Ofc. James Redmon

Crime Prevention/Community Relations Officer
Ofc. Joe Britte

Officers:
Ofc. Casey Chastain
Ofc. Brandon Bowen
Ofc. Barry Edwards
Ofc. Christopher James
Ofc. Jason East
Ofc. Jason Pierce
Ofc. Brandy Oliver

WHAT WE CAN DO TO HELP

Our law enforcement officers alone cannot defeat crime. All of us have a duty to help combat this chronic disease. The first thing we can do is respect our law enforcement officers; there is a dismal lack of respect for them by some. As adults we can change this by setting examples for our children.

A law enforcement officer takes an oath to uphold the laws, and many officers are killed or wounded each year fulfilling their oaths of office. With our help and support, the officers can perform their duties in a more efficient and safe manner – after all, the officers are the ones who give us our security and enable us to live a more pleasant life. Every year, over two million homes are violated by burglars – one every fifteen seconds!

We can help by placing dead bolt locks on our doors and securing our windows – some insurance companies even offer discounts for implementing these and other security measures. Watch out for that spare key that we hid – criminals have spare keys, too, and they know where to look, so be careful. Use timers that turn lights on and off in different parts of the home at different intervals, and keep a radio or TV on when you're gone. A dog or home security system is helpful, too. The first place burglars look is the bedroom, underwear drawer, under the mattress and on closet shelves. Keep all bushes trimmed so that all windows and doors are visible from the street.

Make a point to get to know your neighbors, and start a neighborhood watch. Have them to pick up your mail and newspapers while you're away, and then volunteer to pick up theirs. You should know who lives in your neighborhood – be alert to people who do not live there. Be a nosy neighbor!

Always turn on the house alarm, even if away for only a few minutes – they are watching! The more activity burglars see, the less likely they are to target your house. Burglars spend only about fifteen minutes or less in each house as a rule.

Don't leave items in plain view in your vehicle, and always lock it. Never leave your keys in the ignition. Have your keys out and ready before getting to your vehicle. Be aware of who is around you, especially at night.

In my experience as a police officer and state probation officer, I learned that some professional criminals go to work five days a week from 9 to 5, riding around neighborhoods and shopping malls pulling reconnaissance, looking for opportunities to commit crimes. While you are at work, they are 'at work', trying to take your hard earned valuables.

Keep jewelry you rarely wear in a safe deposit box, and hide other valuables in places where burglars don't think to look – and don't hide all your valuables in one place.

Be careful of scams, con artists and flim-flam operations. We should all know that no one is going to give us anything for free – especially if that person is a stranger. Women should protect their purses like a police officer protects his weapon. If we all would think about how difficult the jobs of our police officers are, and become a team player with them, our neighborhoods and county would be safer and their jobs would be easier. We might even keep from becoming victims ourselves!

Yes, we can help!

Willard J. Langdon during research in the office of the Hall County Probate Court in the late 1970s. Judge Lloyd F. Smith was Probate Judge and he gave Langdon the authority to work at will. Some people thought he had a second job in the office, and would even ask him questions! Judge Smith opened each day with a group prayer with his employees. Willard participated in the prayer sessions and it left a lasting impression on him.

Made in the USA
Charleston, SC
18 September 2010